THE SAINTS
of
WHISTLE GROVE

Also by Katie Schuermann

FICTION

+ *House of Living Stones*
+ *The Choir Immortal*
+ *The Harvest Raise*

NONFICTION

+ *He Remembers the Barren*
+ *He Restores My Soul*
+ *Pew Sisters*

KATIE SCHUERMANN

THE Saints OF Whistle Grove

A NOVEL

KLORIA PUBLISHING + CASPER, WYOMING

+ *Soli Deo Gloria* +

This is a work of fiction. Names, characters, businesses, places, and events are either products of the author's imagination or are used in a fictitious manner. Any resemblance to actual persons, living or dead, or actual events or places is coincidental.

Kloria Publishing LLC
Casper, Wyoming
877-755-6742 • kloria.com

LCCN 2023948920
ISBN 978-1-933737-60-7 (Paperback)
ISBN 978-1-933737-61-4 (e-book)

Printed in the United States of America
1 3 5 7 9 10 8 6 4 2

For all the saints,
those coming out of the great tribulation
and those still walking through it

All thy works shall praise thee, O LORD;
and thy saints shall bless thee.
They shall speak of the glory of thy kingdom,
and talk of thy power;
To make known to the sons of men his mighty acts,
and the glorious majesty of his kingdom.
Thy kingdom is an everlasting kingdom,
and thy dominion endureth throughout all generations.
—Psalm 145:10–13, KJV

Editor's Note

It is commonly accepted that the geographic places where people live have a direct and profound influence on them. Their art, culture, cuisine, and even language are shaped by the land that surrounds them. But what is not always so quickly recognized is the effect that people have on places. I am not speaking so much about the obvious effects of humans on land, as seen in the form of industry, housing developments, cultivation, and the like. I am speaking of the subtler, less tangible ways that we mortals influence the places we inhabit. A house that is lived in, where love grows and thrives, will be different than an abandoned house that has not known laughter for years. Yes, there will be tangible differences between these two, but there will also be differences that we can never quite put to words.

This should not be a complete surprise to those of us who believe that the Lord has created mankind in His own image. When He gave the mandate and blessing to Adam and Eve to fill the earth and subdue it, He certainly meant that we are to take the raw elements of creation and bring them to their proper ends through industry, culture, and art. But just as our Lord changes things by His presence alone, it should not be so strange for us to think that we who are made in His image also affect things by our own presence, even if in subtle ways that cannot be measured or weighed. Our joy is completed when others are there to share it. Our sufferings are transformed when a friend sits with us, even when it is in silence.

What you hold in your hands is an exploration of this reciprocal influence that people and places have on each other as interconnected pieces of God's creation. The joys, sorrows, divisions, reconciliations, lives, and deaths of the people living in this corner of creation will have a profound effect on the grove that God has entrusted to them. This grove, for its part, will echo and rhyme these experiences from one generation to the next.

The story of this place and its people is not told chronologically. For those of us used to linear storytelling, that can be a different reading experience. But what Katie Schuermann is doing is setting you free to explore the grove to see the ways that all these creations of God influence each other in life, death, loss, and love. She is inviting you to hear the ringing of bells and see the blooming of perennials not only in one season, but echoing and blossoming across the story of God's people in this place. Mrs. Schuermann is a very good guide, so keep your eyes open and don't be afraid to go back and walk through that barn again or sit under that tree for another hour.

It has often been noted that we are on the cusp of seismic change in our own cultural time and place. Congregations are beginning to look different throughout our nation. Communities are drastically changed from what they were a few short decades ago. Some congregations may need to close their doors. Some beloved towns and villages, even cities, may feel a creeping fear of decay. That is why stories like this one are important. We are reminded that a church—that *the* Church—is more than a present moment. The people of God have had their influence on the places we live, no matter how they appear in a single moment, according to the measure God has given them. And that will resonate and weave itself into our own loves and losses, lives and deaths. It will even be part of our own resurrection and the life of the world to come.

Rev. Tony Oliphant
Redeemer Lutheran Church, Elmhurst, Illinois
Feast of St. Michael and All Angels, A.D. 2023

Foreword

All over America congregations are dying. Methodist, Baptist, Catholic — all kinds. Usually this is because of demographic reasons: young people move out and old people just move on. For each of these congregations, there's a story. Real people prayed and worshipped there; they were baptized and married there; and often as not they shared meals, played, and gossiped there — sometimes they argued and fought. And yes, they also died and were buried there.

The cemetery, like the sanctuary, is an essential part of the church, especially in country churches. This is where the story ends for its members. They get there by different routes, but they do arrive all the same. It's somewhat ironic then that when a church finally closes its doors, it's more likely to live on through its cemetery than any other way. Arrangements are made to take care of the dead, often legally imposed, even if buildings are repurposed or torn down. Thus the story of a dying church not only includes the cemetery, but concludes — or even continues — there as well.

Sometimes, historians try to tell these stories. They do so on the basis of evidence — documents, artifacts, and perhaps interviews with old members. Imagination plays only a limited role. Historians may make an educated guess now and again, but that's about it.

But people are more than documents, artifacts, and interviews. And people are the most important part of a church. If we really want the story of a church, we need storytellers, not historians, to give us the people. That's where Katie Schuermann comes in. She is a first-class storyteller, and in this book she gives us the story of a church in Whistle Grove, Illinois with its doors now closed (except to the occasional vagrant) after 150 years. Both the church and the community are products of Mrs. Schuermann's imagination, but the people we meet are very real, just like those we find in churches today. Their names might be a little different (originally, they were all Germans), they come from various time periods, and, with a couple of notable exceptions, all of them now reside in the church graveyard. But their fears and their failings, their hopes and their dreams, their loves and their hates will all sound familiar to anyone who reads this book. They are all very human.

Central to the story Mrs. Schuermann tells is the relationship of her characters to their church, their fellow members, and their pastor. From time to time, church doctrine and practice come up. But this is not a sermon disguised as a novel. It's about people who hold the name Christian and what their faith means to them in their living and dying.

Thornton Wilder's wonderful play, *Our Town*, concludes in a cemetery and with the audience in tears. A good novel about a cemetery can do something similar; and Mrs. Schuermann's certainly does. So keep the Kleenex handy. But her approach is different than Wilder's. For him, the cemetery is the end of the play and the end of life. That's where everyone goes and stays put. Mrs. Schuermann, however, calls the residents of her country graveyard "saints." That does not mean they are always "saintly." Far from it. Some are better than others, but none is perfect. Their imperfections are part of what makes the story realistic—and interesting. But the title she gives them is itself an affirmation of their own expectation that their final resting place in the cemetery is not, after all, final. They *are* saints through faith in Christ Jesus. While their church may be dead, in Him their story never really comes to an end.

Rev. Dr. Cameron A. MacKenzie
The Forrest E. and Frances H. Ellis Professor of Historical Theology
Concordia Theological Seminary, Fort Wayne

Contents

The Grove

The Church

The School

The Cemetery

Appendices

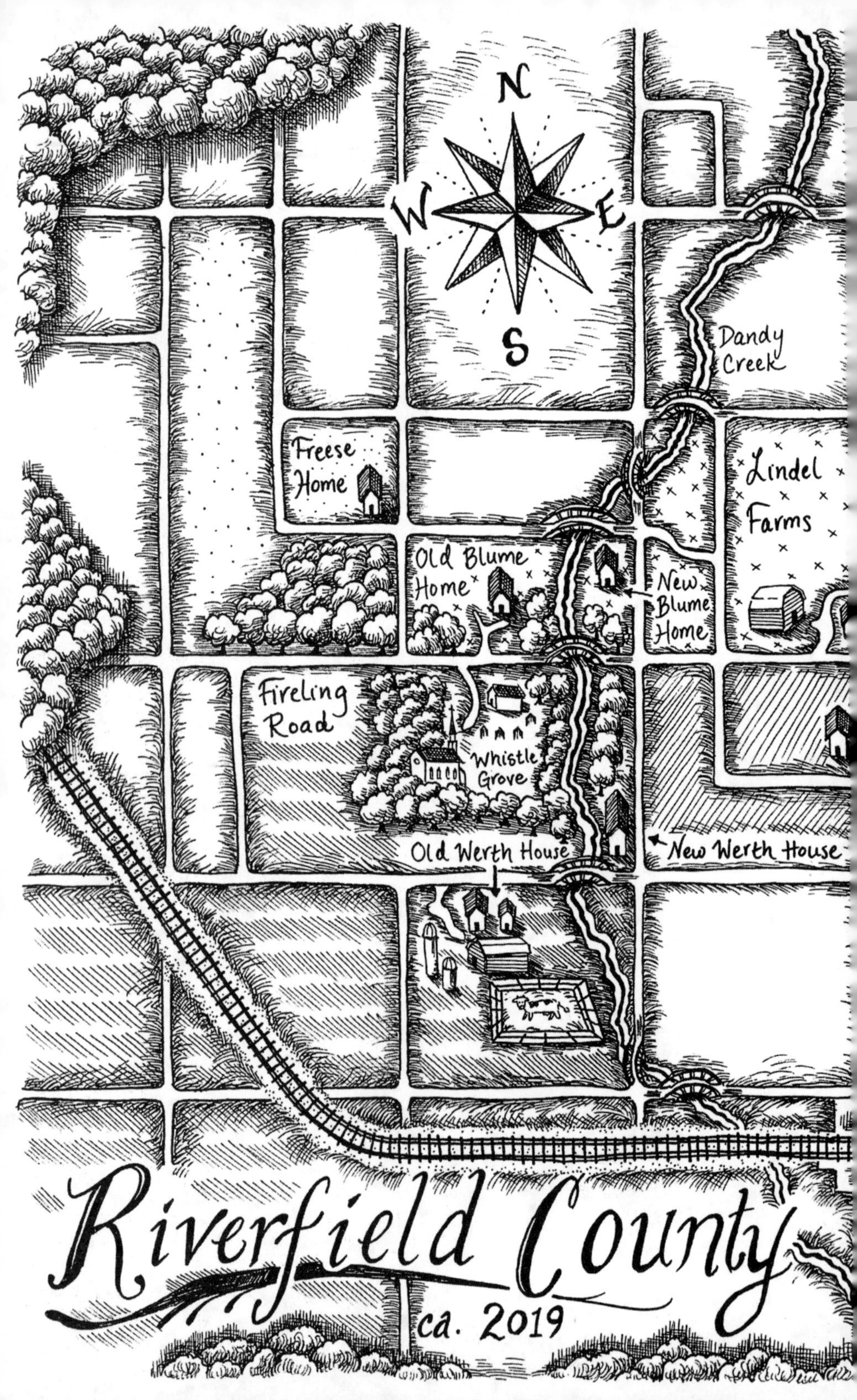
N
W
E
S
Dandy Creek
Freese Home
Lindel Farms
Old Blume Home
New Blume Home
Fireling Road
Whistle Grove
Old Werth House
New Werth House
Riverfield County
ca. 2019

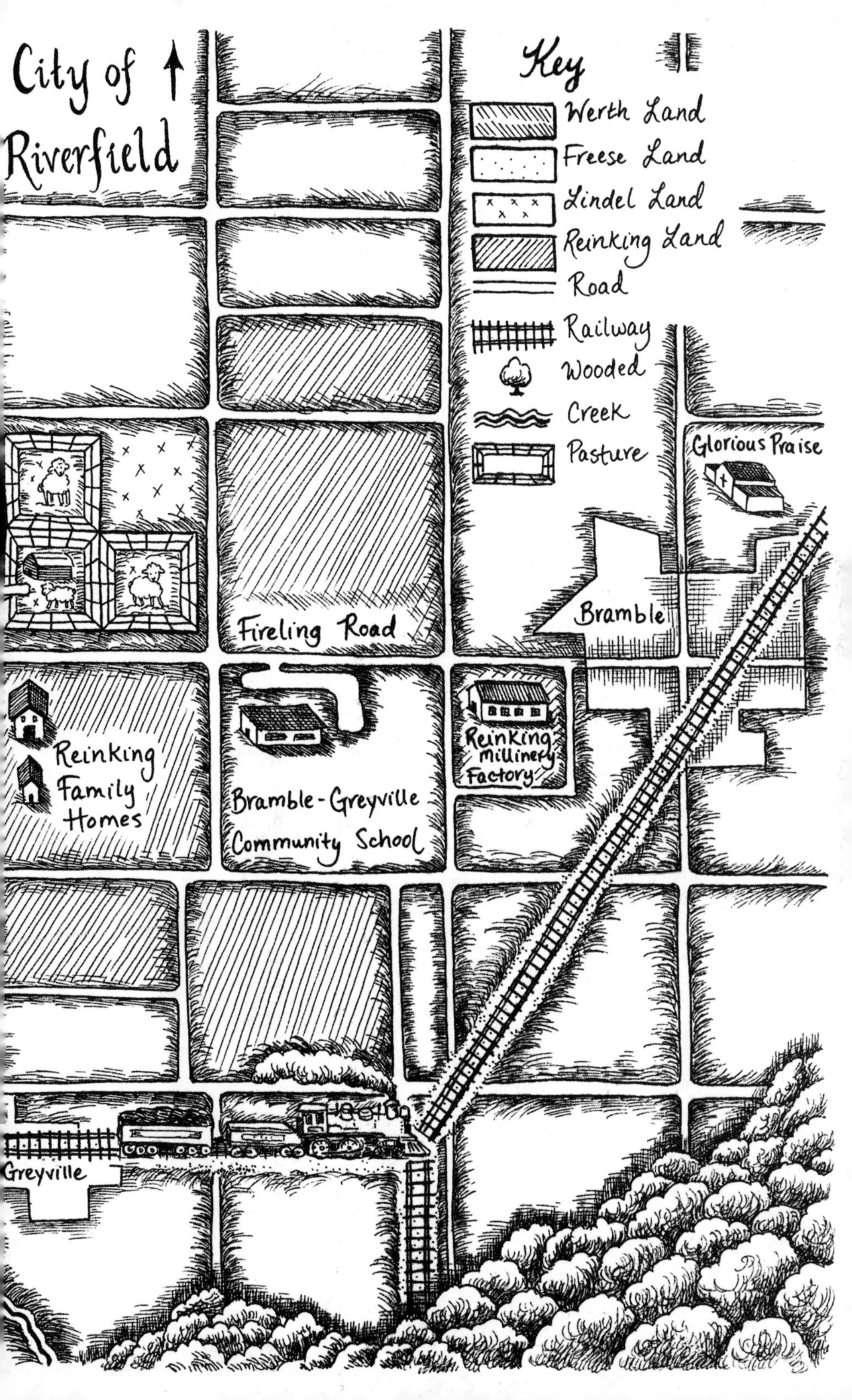
City of Riverfield
Key
Werth Land
Freese Land
Lindel Land
Reinking Land
Road
Railway
Wooded
Creek
Pasture
Glorious Praise
Bramble
Fireling Road
Reinking Millinery Factory
Reinking Family Homes
Bramble-Greyville Community School
Greyville

The Grove

Chapter One

Saint Miriam

✢ 2018 ✢

Five miles west of town, just beyond Lindel Farms and across the Dandy Creek bridge, crowds a motley grove of pawpaws, cottonwoods, silver maples, and sycamores. Their naked, intertwining branches comb the knots out of an unruly November wind, and the resulting flirty whistle tempts a line of stately pines, properly dressed against such indecencies, to turn and take a peek from across the grove. Concealed beneath the cavorting canopy is a quiet dirt lane whose quick end meets the crumbling front stoop of a white clapboard church. Few tires test their quality against the lane's petrified potholes anymore, but a solemn bell is tolling from the church's steeple, calling a procession of Buicks, Oldsmobiles, and four-wheel drives from all across the county to this frayed back pocket of the earth.

The line of cars is fifteen fenders deep, five more than the short lane can support, so the shiny black sedan transporting the officiating Rev. Edmund G. Oglethorpe makes a rogue right turn at the stoop, bouncing over frosted turf, half-buried paving stones, and ancient tree roots to forge a new trail around the backside of the church property. Thirteen cars obediently follow the good reverend's lead except for one silver rental currently waylaid in a Thrifty Fuel parking lot. Sally Grisbone, who lost both the funeral procession and her cellular reception back at the Greyville Switch, is hotter than a steam engine.

"Whistle Grove Cemetery?"

"Yes, ma'am."

"Where is it?"

"Nearby, ma'am. Not five miles from here."

Dull pencils get to the point faster than this attendant.

"Where *exactly* is it?" Sally hovers a black Jimmy Choo above the gas pedal and stares with unblinking contempt as the languid man lights a match—dangerously close to the tinder of her temper—and pulls a long drag from his cigarette.

"Well, ma'am." He exhales a puff of smoke. "You'll want to turn right outta this here parking lot. Then," another drag, "at the edge of town," another puff, "when you see a green house with white shutters—not the blue house with red shutters, mind you—" she feels her leg hair growing longer with every word, "point your engine west for near five miles till you cross a crick and come to a Jersey tied to a clothesline. That's when you'll—"

"See a sign?"

"No, ma'am. You'll see a cow."

Sally, cursing trains, mobile service plans, and men with the name "Larry" sewn to service station shirts, turns left at the green house with the white shutters and begins looking for a wretched cow. She passes much that she doesn't see—field after field of solid dirt, farmhouses surrounded by neighborhoods of outbuildings, a flock of sheep shearing a pasture to its scalp, Mr. Lindel's arthritic barn twisting around a 150-year-old central post — before crossing the aforementioned creek. And there, on the far-right side of the one-lane bridge, at the end of a wintered garden is — "You've got to be kidding me." — Larry's proverbial cow tethered to a sagging clothesline. To the left of the road, a dirt lane angles off through some trees, and the line of cars parked bumper-to-bumper is as good as any sign. She brakes hard, swings the silver rental into the ditch, throws the gear into park, tightens the sash on her black wool overcoat, and violates the ground repeatedly with her three-inch heels.

Fifty steps and she emerges from the wooded lane onto a gently sloping clearing. An old church sits atop the underwhelming summit, and while she is an atheist, she is not an imbecile. She nods a polite, respectful greeting to the steepled monument to human futility before turning her full attention to the business at hand. Here, finally, is Whistle Grove Cemetery, and there — under a blue tent pitched over an open hole in the ground on the far corner of the lot — is Aunt Miriam.

Sally picks her way through a sea of gravestones, some more grave than others, and approaches a cluster of bowed heads. Every person appears to be praying, so she takes advantage of the moment to sweep her eyes around the scene in swift assessment. Five hundred graves, perhaps? A thousand? She wrinkles her nose. Junkyards and dumps are not enough, apparently. People must also litter the land with themselves.

Of course, her maternal grandparents and great-grands are buried here, and soon, Aunt Miriam. But her mother, who was raised near Whistle Grove, refused to be buried here. "I'd rather die!" she had said, which was pretty funny at the time, but in the not-so-funny end, Mother was cremated. Her ashes, under very specific orders given from a hospital bed two days before entering hospice care, were thrown into the waves crashing against her beloved Rockland Breakwater. Mother was sensible that way. Aunt Miriam was the sentimental one.

"'Bless this grave . . .'"

Oh, yes. Sally sighs into a pose of projected reverence and commits to affecting the local culture.

"'. . . that the body of our sister may sleep here in peace until You awaken her to glory, when she will see You face to face and know the splendor of the eternal God . . .'"

Splendor. Now there is a word sorely neglected in modern conversation. These old liturgies, however bunk, do have a certain romance to them, and their rhythms feel familiar, as though they have forever been marking man's march through time. That's what makes fairytales appealing, she supposes. They sound older than they really are. She must find the time to read through the Christian funeral rite when she gets back home—Mother left a hymnal somewhere, didn't she?—if only to give literary context to Western civilization. And Aunt Miriam.

"Amen." The small congregation lifts its head as one.

"'We now commit the body of our sister Miriam to the ground.'" The vested reverend pours dirt onto the casket in the sign of a cross. "'Earth to earth, ashes to ashes, dust to dust, in the sure and certain hope of the resurrection to eternal life through our Lord Jesus Christ, who will change our lowly bodies so that they will be like His glorious body, by the power that enables Him to subdue all things to Himself.'"

More prayers, a hymn, a few corporate amens, and a blessing. The congregation disperses in silence, and three women step forward to remove roses from the spray atop the casket. The last woman, silver-haired, walks a stem over to Sally.

"For you."

"For what?" She is not in the habit of stealing flowers from the dead.

"To keep. In memory of your aunt."

"Oh. Yes. Thank you." Sally takes the rose and sniffs sharply, a strange and sudden sting burning her eyes. She waits for the uncomfortable sensation, as well as the stranger, to pass before acknowledging the old reverend now standing before her. He is shorter than her, and his black stole reaches almost to his shoes.

"How does that woman know who I am?"

The reverend's smile draws aside his wrinkled cheeks like curtains. "Lila Daniels rents the old farmhouse on your family's land. You are Marta's daughter from Maine, yes?" Then, by way of explanation, "You have the Werth nose."

"Sally Grisbone." She reaches out a gloved hand, and he shakes it.

"Miriam talked of you and your many talents quite often, Ms. Grisbone."

One of her talents is commandeering conversations. "Father, I'd like to see Aunt Miriam lowered into the ground, if I may?"

"Yes, yes. Of course. Verl?" He motions to a pair of rubber boots peeking out from behind the back flap of the tent. "Call Clark over, would you, please? It's time to put Miriam to rest."

Verl beckons to a man sitting in a tool truck parked against the trees, and Clark, presumably, pulls on a pair of worn leather gloves as he lumbers heavily over the dormant lawn to the tent. With capable hands, he removes two shafts suspending the casket over the grave and then, engaging some kind of hydraulic mechanism, lowers the cable-supported casket into the vault. Sally stands at the hole's edge, surprised at just how deep six feet look from the top down.

"A shovel did all of this?"

"No, ma'am," Verl answers, pointing to a rather grand storage shed near the dirt lane. "A mini excavator."

"Verl is our groundsman," the reverend confirms. Sally knows this is just a nice way of saying gravedigger.

They all watch as Clark, silent and steady, removes the cables, hand-cranks the vault lid over Aunt Miriam, and loads the unemployed rig into the bed of his truck. Man and machine are gone within minutes, and Verl, just as quickly, excuses himself to retrieve the excavator. Sally is left to ponder the dead with only the old reverend and a rather robust tufted titmouse whistling from a nearby cottonwood.

So many graves. Like pockmarks on the face of the earth.

"Was Aunt Miriam embalmed?"

"I believe so."

Gruesome business. She wrinkles her Werth nose and pushes her cause—another one of her many talents. "Embalming has Egyptian roots, yes?"

"That is my understanding."

"And Aunt Miriam was okay with this?"

"I don't remember her mentioning any aversion to the Egyptians."

She ignores the man's twitching lips and focuses on the matter at foot. "It just seems a bit duplicitous."

"Embalming the dead?"

"Christians adopting pagan practices into their sacred rituals."

"Ah," his smile is audible in the monosyllable. "Well, most funeral homes leave that bit of history out of their brochures these days."

"But why have their bodies pumped full of chemicals and preservatives if they believe this Jesus is going to — how did you say it? — change their 'lowly bodies' to be like His?"

"Why, indeed?" The reverend remains unruffled, but the titmouse blusters and shrills from his high perch. "I suppose it has something to do with the inconvenient smell of the dead."

She feels oddly checked by the little man's easy candor.

"You are concerned that Miriam is turning her carbon footprint into a tattoo, I think," he allows. "But perhaps your aunt found the idea of having her remains burned up in flames like some Hindu or heathen tribe a bit too dissenting for her Christian conscience."

He is referring to her mother's cremation, certainly, but it is a stretch to call Mother a Christian by any standard, even one held by a reverend in the know.

"You said 'ashes to ashes' over Aunt Miriam earlier. Why does it matter how the dead finally get to such a state?"

"Ha! You make a point, Ms. Grisbone."

A familiar refrain.

"But what if," he continues, almost as if he enjoys the feel of making a point himself, "people are missing out on something important in their mad dash to cross every finish line? What if, in all of our enterprising, we're losing the true bounty in failing to be patient? We have lost the art of waiting in this world, I think. Even in death."

A sudden gust of wind tears through the nearby cottonwood, unsettling both the titmouse and her hair. She grabs at the collar of her coat, drawing it closer around her neck. She is free to leave, she knows, but something about her business here feels unfinished. Cold and disgruntled, she gestures a glove toward the church. "Why are we out here instead of in there? Surely, Aunt Miriam wanted a proper funeral in the church."

"The church is closed."

"It can't be opened?"

"The congregation disbanded two years ago. A board actively maintains the cemetery, but the church is closed."

She has never heard of such a thing. "I don't understand."

"The economy is depressed in this area. Most everyone has moved out by now, and of those who choose to stay—well," he gestures to the closed vault, "they are a dying breed. And the few who are well enough to have a say in the matter choose to devote the church's remaining funds to the ongoing care of this cemetery."

"They think the dead are more important than the living?"

"They believe the dead are alive in Christ, and so they care for them still."

The Christian mindset is an endless maze, and she gets lost in the shrubs every time. "So these people have no church anymore? Aunt Miriam had no church in her final days?" Of course, she cares nothing for such things herself, but she knows this church meant everything to her nostalgic aunt.

"The few families who remain in the area have joined the church in town, and your Aunt Miriam was settled in assisted living long before the matter was put to a vote. Please, Ms. Grisbone," she feels her nose wrinkling involuntarily again, "do not be troubled. I cared for your aunt to the end."

The uncomfortable stinging returns, and she blinks fiercely. "You're out of a job, then."

"I am retired, yes. Though the occasional committal or pulpit supply brings my clerical out of the drawer."

"And the empty building? It just sits there?"

"She rests from her labors." The reverend turns an affectionate eye toward the weary structure. "I like to think of her as a monument to God's faithfulness to His people."

Sally backward-sniffs at the irony.

"Verl opens the vestibule to ring the bell for interments, but beyond that, no one uses the church anymore. Though we did have some trouble with a crowd driving over from Macatowa last summer." He wastes no time answering her raised eyebrows. "Some ruffians graffitied the north wall of the church, just under the windows."

Of course they did.

The reverend's shoulders begin to bounce with a chortle that sounds like marbles spilling onto linoleum. "Their intent was evil, no doubt, but Ms. Grisbone," more marbles bounce across a kitchen floor, "vengeance is the Lord's."

No one can resist touching shiny marbles. "So what happened?"

"Well, the unfortunate artist surely intended to write 'Satan' across the exterior wall, but his phonetics must have been underdeveloped in life. For instead, he sprayed 'Satin' in large cursive red letters the entire length of the church. It was marvelous. Even the Lord laughed, I'm sure. Your Aunt Miriam and the Lindels rallied funds to repaint the exterior, though the front doors remain locked. But even tombs need tending."

Against her will, Sally is fascinated by this little man, his bag of marbles, and his bizarre garden of tombstones. "I have a hard time believing only the outside of the church gets vandalized."

"Well, I do think a wandering itinerant hops off the Greyville line now and then and sleeps in a back pew, but that happened even when the congregation was active. I admit," he leans closer, lowering his voice, "I leave a key above the doorframe."

The man is either daft or blinded by goodwill.

"The local youth don't take advantage of that key?"

He shrugs. "What do youth care for keys to old churches these days when they already hold a digitized window to the world in their baby-hands? But even if they do know about the key, they don't abuse it. Most are too short to reach it. If not of stature, then of wits. Besides, the church is called a sanctuary for a reason, Ms. Grisbone. Who are we to shut out those in need?"

"I would think that word gets around, even in a place as remote as this. Beggars have networks, you know."

"'*Wir sind alle Bettler.*'"

"What?"

"'We are all beggars,'" the reverend translates. "Those words were found scrawled on a piece of paper on the body of the sainted Dr. Martin Luther on his deathbed."

"I didn't know he spoke German."

The little man's mouth stalls open for a confused second before lifting in a comprehending smile and arranging the wrinkles on his forehead in a perfect, colorless rainbow. "Ah, not Martin Luther King, my dear. Martin Luther. The reformer."

"Oh."

"Luther meant, I believe, that whatever our station is in life, we're all beggars in need of God's help."

She looks at her watch. This sermon is already too long.

"What do you beg from God, Ms. Grisbone?"

Definitely too long. "Nothing."

"I beg Him for everything."

"You should beg him for a congregation."

"But He has already provided me one." He waves toward the nearby gravestones.

"You preach to the dead?"

"No, Christ does that. But I do plant them in the ground."

"For what purpose?"

"To be harvested, of course. On the Last Day. Christ shall return in His glory and call my congregation from the ground. They shall see God with their own eyes and live with Him forever. He will change their 'lowly bodies so that they will be like His glorious body.'" His eyes glisten. "Have you ever seen such a bumper crop?"

Sally is weary of the cold, and the elderly man's antiquated world-view is growing tiresome, as well. "Cemeteries are a waste of space."

"Then what shall we do with your remains, my dear?"

"I intend to be cremated. Scatter my remains over the sea."

"Are you but fish food?"

"Are these people but fertilizer?" She doesn't like the sound of her own voice. It's too charged, too telling. She checks her excitement. "I'm just saying, leave the ground to care for the living. Save the dirt for something useful. This is middle America, after all. The richest farmland in all the world, right? Plant corn, not people. Reopen the church doors, and get some warm bodies in those pews." Is she really giving a pep talk to a minister? Why is she lingering in the cold with this peculiar man? "Evangelize or whatever it is you do to make a congregation."

"I cannot make a congregation. God builds His church. He calls to faith whom He calls."

"With a marketing strategy like that, no wonder your church is dead." She has gone too far this time, and she hastily redirects, "Who owns the land, anyway?"

"Why, Ms. Grisbone. I suspect you do. At least in part."

"What?"

His bushy silver eyebrows furrow for the first time, and she suspects it is out of some kind of misplaced paternal concern. "Your family gifted this plot of land to the church when it was founded with the one stipulation that a Werth always sit on the church cemetery board. Your Aunt Miriam bore that responsibility of late, but now that Christ has called her to Himself, I am certain the board hopes you will pick up the family mantle."

"But I live in Maine."

"The board meets only quarterly."

Is she to babysit a cemetery for the rest of her life? "You did not hear me, Father. I live in Maine."

The reverend remains silent, thoughtful. In truth, his silence irritates Sally more than his preaching. For reasons she cannot understand, she wants to know what the man is thinking, but her captive interest feels embarrassingly like a weakness. When he finally does speak, each word is weighted with import. "The board holds the deed to the church and cemetery, but your Aunt Miriam owns the surrounding acreage west of Dandy Creek and south of the Fireling Road all the way to the Riverfield County line. You are her only living relative, Ms. Grisbone. Surely you expect to inherit the land."

"Well, of course. That's why I'm here. The will is being read this afternoon."

"I should exhort you, then: You also inherit the care of its dead."

Ludicrous, presumptuous little man.

"And what if I refuse?"

"Then, at the least, the boat of good order will be rocked. At the most, you will lose a charge that is precious to you, though you do not yet recognize it as such."

Sally turns to leave.

"My dear," his tone is sympathetic, which irritates her, "I know you are somewhat poking fun at my profession when you speak of evangelizing this area and reopening the church. Come, now, Ms. Grisbone. We are alike, you and me. Neither of us suffers fools. But you must see that your interest, whether sincere or in jest, comes honestly. 'What do you have that you did not receive?' Werths are written into more than just the constitution of this church and cemetery. This land holds your history, your very family. I do not think you can dismiss it so easily as you think."

She dismisses the daft man easily enough, and as she makes her way back to the silver rental, she can't help but think, as any good Mainer would, that the old church is a lighthouse, and the gravestones are its harbored ships. The tree line curving around the cemetery is a breakwater that keeps this rotting bay from any possible wave of enlightenment, and she — no matter what that old man says — is a boat destined to sail out of this port for good.

Chapter Two

Saint Frances

+ 1951 +

Miriam's hands are in the kitchen sink, but her mind is in Clayton County. A Yankee soldier just set flame to the kitchen of the O'Hara family plantation, and she, spying from behind the expansive trunk of an old cedar guarding the front lane, sees a telltale wisp of smoke escaping through the open front door. Union soldiers have already set fire to the family's cotton stores. What will Scarlett do if her beloved Tara is also burned to the ground?

Miriam eyes the closed book resting on the counter. Her reading session with Mrs. Daniels had been cut short that morning. Just two more pages and she would know—"Miriam Augusta, if you ruin that book with your soapy hands, I will take the library fine out of your egg money."

She draws her hand back to the sink. Mother is in the pantry, but she can see through walls.

"When you finish up the dishes, help Marta hang the wash."

Marta is already out at the clothesline, an apron hugging her perfect waist, a ribbon tying back her perfect hair, and shiny shoes protecting her perfect feet. Miriam follows her younger sister's progress through the open kitchen window, wiggling her bare toes against the linoleum in anticipation of the feel of the soft June grass.

"What is that book, anyway?" Mother strides into the kitchen, setting two mason jars of cold-packed meat on the table. She reaches for the brown-and-gold volume, flipping open the cover to read from the inside flap. Miriam's heart beats feathered wings against her ribcage.

"*Gone with the Wind*. A 'stirring drama,'" Mother reads aloud, eyeing her cooly over the book, "about a 'spoiled, selfish' young woman?" She snaps the cover shut and walks it over to the basket sitting on the floor beside the back door. "Really, Miriam?"

She feels her cheeks flush. Mrs. Daniels had requested this story specifically, but Mother doesn't need to know that. "It's historical, Mother. It's about the Civil War and Reconstruction in the South and General Sherman's — "

"It's fiction."

"Actually, it's — "

"Still fiction. You know our deal."

Two nonfiction reads for every novel this summer.

"But I," she fights for a justification her mother will respect, "just finished reading *The Smalcald Articles* last night."

"Daughter of mine, do not even — "

A knock on the front door interrupts their debate. Mother holds up a finger, silently communicating that this conversation is merely paused, not over. Miriam bites her lower lip and uses her left shoulder to push her mass of black curls away from her sweaty cheek. Her hair is always so hot, but she refuses to tie it back. Marta once explained with a certainty not to be doubted that her raven hair is her only beautiful feature. Ever since, she dares not tie it where no one can see it. But the book. She must know what happens to Tara. If she can just scan the next few pages before Mother—

"It's here!" Viola Lindel's cry cuts through the entire house. Mother's reply takes on the familiar melody of hospitality, but no actual words make it as far back as the kitchen sink. Miriam hand-pumps fresh water over her soapy hands and reaches for a towel, mourning all the O'Haras have lost: the outbuildings, the fences, the livestock, the trees, the harvest. They can't lose the house, too.

"It's here, Ruthie. In Whistle Grove. Polio. The Daniels' baby was just hospitalized."

Miriam is violently yanked north of the Mason-Dixon line. What was that about Baby Frances?

"I don't know. That's all Drucilla told me. Look, I have to go. Art doesn't know, yet. I have to find him in the fields before he runs into Mark's men. That man'll greet the devil himself if he comes along with a friendly wave. Stay inside, Ruthie. Keep the girls in the house. God knows what the Daniels children have touched in these parts."

Mother returns, her mouth pursed. She is squeezing her hands together in that strange way of hers whenever she feels she has lost control of a situation. "Marta!" she calls out the window. "Come in here, Baby. Bring the wash with you. Come, now. Inside at once!"

Marta promptly enters with a half-empty basket at her hip.

"Girls," Mother draws them into her fold, one arm around each of them. "Frances Daniels is in the hospital. She's been diagnosed with polio. I don't know anything more, but I'm going to drive over to the old house to see what they need. You both are to stay inside until I come back. Do you understand?"

Marta nods obediently. Miriam's tongue is dry as a cotton bale.

"This is serious. You are to stay inside, and no matter who comes by, you do not answer the door for anyone. Am I clear?"

Again, Marta nods.

Mother is already moving, picking up the basket near the door and discarding the book onto a bench, grabbing the remaining bread from the box and wrapping it in a clean towel.

"Miriam, some milk."

She moves toward the icebox.

"No, the fresh milk."

She redirects for the pasteurizer on the counter and removes Belinda's most recent offering from that morning, still warm, pouring it into a clean jar.

"Marta, fill a bucket with a box of soap and some rags and whatever else you think might come in handy from the closet."

"Yes, Mother." Her sister never requires further instruction.

Mother disappears into the pantry and returns with onions, garlic, and two jars of pickles, arranging the produce along with the milk and the cold-packed meat in the basket. She tops it off with the loaf of bread.

"I'll be home as soon as I can."

Mother is gone with the basket and bucket before Miriam can wet her lips. Her flighty heart keeps dive-bombing her bare toes. Her hands are shaking. She hides them from Marta in the soapy, now cold, sink water.

"How do you get polio?" Marta asks.

She can think only of her shaking hands and everything she has touched in the kitchen: the pasteurizer, the sink pump, the lunch dishes—

"Miriam?"

—the latch on the window, the compost bucket, the book. The book! Mother touched the book after her. She turns wildly in search of the abomination, but Marta reaches out a hand toward her shoulder.

"Don't!" She jumps back, inadvertently flinging soapy water from her dishrag onto her sister's spotless apron.

"What's wrong?"

"Don't touch me, Marta. Just give me a minute." She closes her eyes, trying to gather her thoughts. What else has she touched? She snags up the miserable book, hugging it to her chest and wiping down the bench with her rag. She wipes down the hand pump, as well, and the window latch and everything else near the sink.

"Miriam, you're frightening me."

Frances had fussed that morning, so much so that Mrs. Daniels had grown distracted from the story. Miriam had been forced to stop reading several times so that Mrs. Daniels could check on her youngest daughter. The frequent interruptions had been annoying, and when Mrs. Daniels came back to the kitchen with Frances in her arms, saying, "She keeps fallin' down in her crib," Miriam mistook genuine illness for motherly overconcern. She had taken the fussy girl in her arms and walked her back upstairs herself, even changing Frances' diaper for good measure in hopes the girl would fall asleep and finally leave them to their story in peace.

"I was at the old house this morning."

Marta's perfect lips purse just like Mother's. "What? When?"

"When you and Mother ran into town."

"Why would you go there by yourself?"

There is nothing shameful in reading aloud to Mrs. Daniels, Miriam knows, but she never talks about her summer hobby at home. Mother is already critically disposed toward the wife of their farmhand, and if she should discover that Cherry Daniels never learned to read—well, Miriam admires the kind, deferential woman too much to sic the hound of Mother's high expectations on her vulnerabilities.

"I was reading to the children."

Marta takes a step backwards. "How does polio spread?"

"I don't know."

The sound of perfect Marta's whimper terrifies her more than polio itself.

"Go to your room, Marta. I'll go to mine. We'll be okay."

Assurances are like compliments, Miriam suddenly realizes. They need not always be true for the hearer's sake.

+ + +

The sun is low to the ground when Mother returns. Miriam hears the hand pump in the kitchen being worked, and she knows Mother will bathe before anything else. She could write a letter, but then Mother would have to touch the pages. So she opens her door and stands at the top of the stairs.

"Mother." Her voice is quiet, but so is the house.

"Not now," comes the tired response from the stove. "I need to wash."

"Please, I must speak with you. It's important—No, don't come any closer." She looks down upon the familiar posture of exasperation. She swallows more cotton. "I am sorry, Mother. I put you and Marta in danger."

"What are you talking about?"

"I was over at the old house this morning."

The gentle tick-tock of the hall clock explodes like bombs in her ears.

"Did you — "

"I held Frances. I put her to bed."

An involuntarily hum escapes Mother's throat. It is a sound worse than Marta's whimper.

"I sent Marta to her room as soon as I realized." More assurances. She is a thirteen-year-old emissary of she knows not what. "I scrubbed the kitchen. I burned the towel. I'm sorry, Mother. I'm so sorry."

She turns away from the stairs and locks her bedroom door behind her.

+ + +

Marta is moved to Aunt Fauna's within the hour, and Miriam remains in her room.

"Open the door, Miriam."

"No." This is the first time she remembers ever daring to say that word to Mother.

"Please, Miri." This is the first time she remembers Mother ever condescending to plead.

"It's okay. I can take care of myself."

"I know you can, but I'm your mother. I'm not going anywhere."

"I might have polio."

"We don't know that."

"What if I get sick? What if I get you sick?"

Mother's silence posits a few terrifying questions of its own.

"I'm not leaving, Miri."

"But I held Frances."

"And now," Mother's fragile tone shatters like glass against the locked door, "I would like to hold you."

A surprising thrill stabs at her heart, stinging on impact, before a soothing, warm happiness surges through her veins. Mother will not leave her. Sobbing, she unlocks the door and buries her one beautiful feature in the outstretched arms.

She is trying to be brave like Father, but she would rather not die alone.

+ + +

"Matthew Daniels is tilling the fields for his father today," Mother explains over a steaming cup of ginger-clove tea. They have been drinking it for three days straight, both of them. "For immunity," Mother recites every time she pours from the pot. It smells better than it tastes.

"Is Mr. Daniels staying at the hospital with Frances?"

"No one is allowed to stay with Frances."

Miriam's stomach turns at the thought of that sweet girl lying in a hospital bed away from her parents, her home, and everything she knows.

"For how long?"

"God only knows." Mother never says anything more regarding Frances, but Pastor Engel stopped by yesterday morning and Mother's lips have been perpetually pursed ever since. She suspects that God may not be the only one in the know about these things.

"It is our turn for supper tonight. I am thinking beef and noodles will be nice."

Mother and the women of the church are taking turns cooking meals and leaving them on the front porch of the old house every evening. No one dares go inside. Even mercy is subject to quarantine.

"Are the other children all right?"

"As far as I know."

"How did Frances get it anyway?"

Mother shakes her head. "The only thing Cherry can figure is that maybe Mark was exposed to it when he picked up feed in Syre. There is a case reported from over there."

"You can get polio from animal feed?"

"No, you can get it from the people who sell it. Drink some more tea."

Miriam nods dutifully and raises her cup, though the smell of cloves is making her head ache.

"I'm not sure what to do about the beans, though," Mother chats as she pours. "Mark can't leave Cherry, and young LJ should stay in, as well. I can't ask Matthew to do it while he's already busy with the tiller, and Art is — "

But Mother is interrupted by the crash of Miriam's teacup hitting the table.

+ + +

The work of suffering is waiting, Miriam soon learns, for a strange sort of relief sets in upon the arrival of physical pain. Now, at least, there is a purpose to the whiling of her hours, an actual goal to her enduring, and her vigil of dread can anticipate a blessed end rather than a miserable beginning. But the terrible spasms in her right arm may also qualify as suffering.

The nurse feeds her aspirin regularly for the fever and the pain, but there is nothing for the nausea. She tries to sleep, but the ache in her head and neck sometimes outperforms the pain in her arm.

The sun sets and rises, she supposes, though she cannot tell. The light in the hospital is eternal, casting no shadows, projecting no passage of time. Someone is always checking her, feeding her, washing her, changing her, stretching her. A man with a white buttoned shirt and big hands lifts her out of the bed and lowers her into the water. It is always too hot, but no one takes her out. She calls for Mother, but only the man comes.

"She is not here."

But then, one day, Mother is there, and Pastor Engel is waiting in the car. They drive her home and tuck her into her bed. The sun is still moving after all, for a tall stack of books on her windowsill casts a long shadow across the foot of her bed. She reaches for the top book, but her arm is rubber and knocks the stack to the floor.

Mother catches her empty hand. Kissing the palm, "We'll work on getting back your strength tomorrow, but for now . . ." She sits in a chair by the window and cheerfully re-stacks the books, one by one, settling with a familiar hardcover on her lap. It is brown and gold. "I thought we would read a bit of fiction."

Mother reads aloud, and Miriam weeps over all that she and Scarlett have lost.

+ + +

The hot baths continue at home.

"Take the soap, Miriam."

"I'm trying." She even purses her lips like Mother for good measure.

"Close your hand."

"I am," but her fingers hang limp in the water.

Both of them cry.

✢ ✢ ✢

Always, Mother is there, reading and watching and praying. Sometimes, Aunt Fauna appears, bringing meals on trays. Eventually Marta is there, too. She smiles politely at Miriam from the open doorway, but her sister never crosses the bedroom threshold. She walks past the doorway with her fingers folded perfectly at her waist, never touching anything and certainly never looking at Miriam's arm resting atop the covers. One evening, Miriam overhears her sister spraying the iron tub with vinegar water before drawing a bath.

"She has always been scrupulous," Mother dismisses.

Pastor Engel is there on Sunday afternoons. He brings Mother and Miriam the Supper, laying the consecrated bread on their tongues.

"'Take, eat; this is the true body of our Lord and Savior Jesus Christ, given into death for your sins.'"

He holds the cup to Miriam's lips. "'Take, drink; this is the true blood of our Lord and Savior Jesus Christ, shed for the remission of your sins,'" and she is pleased that he does not shrink from handling the cup of blessing after her partaking.

When Mother steps out of the room, Miriam whispers, "Is God angry with me?"

"If He were," Pastor enfolds her lame hand in both of his own, "would I be here?"

Her throat is sore with shame. She can barely speak. "Then, why?"

"Why what?"

She cannot hold back the sob. "Why me?"

"Because polio infects people with flesh and blood and bones. You happen to have flesh and blood and bones, Miriam. Polio infected you."

He makes it sound so simple, so ordinary.

"God is not punishing me?"

He places a hand on her head. It is warm with authority. "'There is therefore now no condemnation to them which are in Christ Jesus.' You are baptized into Christ, Miriam. The Lord does not punish you. No, He is 'nigh unto them that are of a broken heart; and saveth such as be of a contrite spirit.' The Lord is near you. He is saving you."

+ + +

Cherry Daniels is sitting by her bed when Miriam rouses the next afternoon.

"I— " is all Miriam can muster before her eyes, once again, take up a watery psalm of lament on behalf of her quivering lips.

Mrs. Daniels bows her head and apologizes to Miriam for her suffering. Mother, standing nearby, hears the apology with a lined forehead and pursed lips, staring in silent accusation at Miriam's exposed arm. But Miriam reaches out her good left hand to the humble woman and offers an apology of her own.

For Frances sleeps in the ground, while she lies awake on her bed.

After Mother shows Mrs. Daniels to the front door, Miriam catches Marta lingering outside her bedroom door. Her sister's perfect hands are folded, as usual, but her eyes, for the first time, are resting on Miriam's limp hand.

"You shouldn't have gone to the old house without permission."

Accusations are not like assurances, Miriam learns. They are intended to hurt the hearer, not help.

+ + +

The chicken salad has hard-cooked eggs.

"Mrs. Blume made it," Mother explains. "She baked the bread, as well."

Miriam sits at the kitchen table, resting her right forearm on a slice of bread while trying to spread the chicken salad with a knife held in her left hand.

"Here," Marta sighs, grabbing the knife to finish the task herself. Miriam is too embarrassed to protest, but Mother immediately retrieves the knife and restores it to Miriam's left hand.

"Patience, Marta," is all Mother says.

The soup from last week had lima beans. The pork roast from the week before was stewed with collards. These are not Mother's ways.

"The church women are making meals," she realizes aloud.

"Only the Blumes," Marta answers.

No one else? She thinks on Mother's harvesting food from her own stores within minutes of hearing the word polio. And there is a pot of stock simmering on the stove even now. Mother is making food for the Daniels family still.

"People are scared," Mother reads her mind.

Is Mother not scared?

"Oskar Blume brought today's basket." Marta, still a child, smiles like a woman.

Miriam remembers Mother going to the old house that terrifying afternoon. What she did there, Miriam never asked, but Mother rushed to help the Daniels family in their need.

"He came all the way to the porch," Marta continues.

Mother is scared, but she helps anyway.

"He even knocked on the door before leaving it."

Her bird-heart alights on an idea and sings: Fear does not have the final word with Mother.

"He cut the grass before he left, too."

Her song swells: Mother cares. Mother persists.

"I wanted to walk him to the end of the lane, but Mother refused." Marta frowns at Miriam's listless arm.

She pulls a second slice of bread on top of the open sandwich. She squeezes the knife and, pressing repeatedly, makes a rough, angled cut from the top right corner to the bottom left. The plate tips under the uneven pressure only twice. She rests the knife on the table and sets a triumphant triangle onto her sister's plate.

She is scared, but fear does not have the final word with her.

She cares. She persists.

She is Ruthie Werth's daughter.

+ + +

There are better hobbies than playing the piano, but on Tuesday afternoons when Marta stays after school for music lessons with Miss Green, Miriam cannot recall a single one. She hides her envy behind her curtain of black curls, now hanging almost to her waist, and bites her bottom lip for good measure.

The sunlight beyond the school door is speckled with the chaff of harvest, and she crosses gravel, asphalt, and drainage ditches in the moistureless mist to the crispy golden-green of the Lindel pasture. Simultaneously stepping over and ducking under the rails of a splintered wooden fence, she straightens to the familiar smell of baked sod. She dutifully keeps her shoes to the dirt-packed tire tracks, but her left hand escapes to brush against the bending purple plumes of foxtail lining the tracks. They are not ivory keys, but they do make a whispery music all their own in the late September wind.

"No sister today?"

The question is booming and bodiless. Miriam spins around to find a young man ambling along the tire tracks from behind. He is shorter than most other men, but his stolid gait and genial smile are tall in appeal. Everyone likes Oskar Blume, but no one more than her sister Marta.

"She has a piano lesson."

"I always preferred singing, myself."

Miriam wonders if this comment is meant for her benefit. No clouds are tolerated on Oskar's horizon, that much she knows.

The man falls in step alongside her. "I'm scouting the fence line for Mr. Lindel. He's considering going electric."

"Isn't that expensive?"

"Not in labor. Wood fences can be cheap for a man with forests, but it takes days out of the year for him to mend them. Electric saves a bank of time."

Miriam finds it interesting whenever a man farms for some father other than his own, but Oskar's hired work comes out of necessity, she knows. Mr. Blume doesn't own any land for his grown son to farm.

"What do you do while Marta plays the piano?"

She smarts. "I walk home."

"Have you ever tried painting or sketching?"

It is almost as if he has been talking with Mother. "My hand gets tired after school."

"Doesn't everybody's?"

"Not everybody has to learn how to write with their opposite hand."

"Not everybody has a mind such as you."

A gust of hot autumn wind blows through the pasture, unsettling her heavy hair and throwing it about. Oskar is walking too close to avoid the assault, but he seems anything but bothered. He merely pauses and closes his eyes against the tangling tresses, combing them away from his face with his fingers. For a still moment, he appears to hold them in his big hands before returning them to her own shoulder.

"Don't feel sorry for yourself," he resumes, setting one boot in front of the other.

"I don't." She is already embarrassed by her brazen hair, but this assertion of his leaves her feeling shamefully exposed.

"Well, don't start. You are more than your hand."

She turns on him. The man is six years her senior and three inches her better, but she towers over him in grit and resolve. "I'll race you to the tree line." His eyes are so brown, and when they are turned on her like this, she has trouble keeping her breath. "Loser carries my satchel home." It sounds juvenile, even to her.

"No," he counters, "loser joins the church choir."

She frowns. "You already sing in the church choir."

She may drown in the brown of his eyes.

"I have no intention of losing," he smiles.

It isn't until she is running toward the trees that she realizes she has no intention of winning.

He carries her satchel home anyway.

Chapter Three

Saint Lowell

+ 1934 +

"Love is loyalty," Papa always says, and so Lowell stays in Whistle Grove. Mama leaves, but he stays, even when the barn falls on little Beth. Even when the Lindel fire blows sparks onto their summer wheat. Even when the creek floods and washes away the new Fordson. Even when the bank forecloses on the farm and sells all of Papa's assets at auction. Even when Eastern offers Lowell a baseball scholarship and a chance at life beyond Riverfield County.

"There's nothin' worth learnin' that the land cain't teach you, son."

Never mind that no land is left in the family to teach him anything.

But Lowell stays in Whistle Grove, because Lowell loves Papa. He loves Priscilla. He loves his girls Mildred and Edna, and he loves Lowell, Jr. He doesn't love his job at the Reinking Millinery Factory, but God promises to work all things — even belts, bows, and brooches — for good.

Only once in his life is Lowell truly tempted to leave the county in which he was born. On that day, he holds a pamphlet in the front pocket of his bibs, close to his heart.

"Eugene Rademaker," he starts, his voice hoarse with nerves, "wants to sponsor him."

"What?"

He is talking to Priscilla after the children are in bed. He notices that his wife's eyes are rimmed with lines, and she is not yet a decade past her teens. The birth was hard on her. It was hard on everyone.

"Mr. Rademaker, the man who oversees my shift," he explains. He licks his dry lips. "The Mason, you know, from Bramble?"

Priscilla's eyes lift from the shirt she is mending in her lap. She understands, now, and her hope turns toward him like a sunflower toward the rising sun.

"He's offerin' to sponsor him, Cilla."

He hands his wife the pamphlet. She reads it faster than he can read her.

"Three pictures?" She shakes her head. "An' train fare? We cain't afford none of this."

That's why he knocks on the smokehouse out back and asks Papa.

"Train fare? You leavin'?"

"Not me, Papa. Junior."

Papa gestures toward the wide world contained within his four walls. "What's that boy need that he cain't get here?"

Lowell hands him the pamphlet.

Papa reads slower than Priscilla, but he understands it all the same. "No. Blumes don't take no charity, and cert'nly not from any heathen." He waves the pamphlet in the air and threatens before shutting the door, "I'm sure Pastor'll have a word to say 'bout this, if'n the good Lord don't strike us down first."

Pastor Engel does have a word, but it's not one Papa expects.

"Yes."

"Yes?" Lowell repeats.

"Take up Rademaker on his offer to help."

Lowell can't yet release his thoughts to joy. It would hurt too much to call them back. "Even though he's a Mason?"

"Christians aren't the only good citizens in the world." Pastor hands him a small package wrapped in brown paper. "And here. This should cover the train fare and the photographs."

+ + +

Priscilla cries when she stands Junior in front of the camera. The small boy is naked but for a towel about his hips, and there is no hiding his little legs that bow unnaturally outward like two rainbows on end.

Three photographs total are required, each of them full-length — one view from the front, one from the side, and one from the back — but the photographer is respectful and kind through it all.

"You're doing a good thing," he assures over the bowl of his pipe. "My sister was born with the rickets. She walks now, but I often wonder what her life would be like . . . if . . . you know?"

But love is loyalty, and Papa feels betrayed.

"Family takes care of family," he grumps, shutting himself in the smokehouse and refusing Priscilla's dinner.

Lowell is torn between the expectations of his father and the needs of his son, but when the day to board the train finally comes, he reassures himself, "Maybe love is leaving. Just this once."

Priscilla and the girls are standing on the platform while he and Junior chug away. His wife's shoulders are convulsing with what he knows are sobs of regret. Dear Cilla. Times are hard everywhere, and food is scarce on every table, but he hadn't realized his bride was going without for all of those months. While he was at the factory, selfless Cilla had fed their hungry daughters instead of herself, and none of them knew that the baby inside of her was suffering.

He holds Junior up to the window for the comfort of his diminishing wife.

+ + +

A typed letter arrives in the mail the following week.

To The Parents:

Parents or guardians will be permitted to visit their children in Shriners' Hospital from 2 P.M. to 3 P.M. Sundays only. Our doctors deem it wise to allow only the two visitors on one day. Children are very susceptible to undue excitement from too frequent and too numerous visitors.

They are also susceptible to digestive disorders from overeating and improper eating. No food or candy should be brought to the children at any time. Only new books, new toys or games will be accepted for them.

Yours very truly,
Zelma Bertram
Superintendent

Lowell shakes his head at his beseeching wife.

"You know we cain't, Cill. It's too far." And too expensive. He hates the emptiness both in his pockets and in his heart. "We cain't visit Junior, but we can visit the throne of heaven on his behalf."

+ + +

The first personal word comes in the form of a handwritten postcard, postmarked the fourth of August. The script is sloppy but readable, written in haste, most likely. There must be so many children.

Dear Sir,
Lowell was operated upon Thursday, and is doing nicely.
Shriners Hospital

"That's all?" Priscilla asks, but she stores the card in her apron pocket and pulls it out to reread whenever she thinks he is not looking. The card is addressed to him, but he lets her keep this paper link to their son. He got to ride with Junior on the train, after all.

Eight more postcards arrive within the month.

Dear Sir,
Lowell was so interested in his tray tonight, and wanted to help feed hisself. So he surely is feeling better.
Sincerely,
Shriners Hospital

Dear Sir,
Lowell smiles so much now. I guess he knows us better and is more happy.
Shriners Hospital

Dear Sir,
Lowell is doing nicely.
Shriners Hospital

Dear Sir,
Now that Lowell is in the front sun parlor he has such a nice time watching the cars pass.
Shriners Hospital

Dear Sir,
Lowell loves to talk hisself to sleep. We will think the ward is all quiet and Lowell will be making noises and half talking.
Shriners Hospital

Priscilla cries all through supper after this one. In the dark, he holds her in bed while she mourns.

"His first words, Low. We're missin' 'em."

Dear Sir,
Lowell and I had a nice little talk this morning. He is as friendly as can be now.
Shriners Hospital

Dear Sir,
Lowell is eating supper now and of course mealtime is happy time here.
Shriners Hospital

Dear Sir,
Lowell has been singing while the victrola was playing.
Shriners Hospital

Love is loyalty, and Lowell must hear his namesake sing lest his heart break in two. There is no money in the house for beef let alone trains, so early the next morning, before the sun rises on the Sabbath, he hitches a ride on the back of a coal car headed for Union Station, one of Mildred's picture books tucked in his front bib pocket.

When he returns that evening, he is covered in soot from head to toe. He replaces the picture book, unused, in the girls' basket. He can barely get the words out for his disappointment.

"They wouldn't let me in."

A letter of explanation, postmarked from the previous Friday and apparently lost in the mail for three days, arrives the very next morning.

To The Parents:

Due to the epidemic in St. Louis County of encephalitis, our City Health Officer and Pediatrician have decided that it will be best to close the Hospital to visitors for the time being.

Just as soon as we feel that it is safe to again admit visitors, we shall let you know.

Yours truly,

Zelma Bertram
Superintendent

When frost paints the smokehouse roof white, the surgeon himself sends a letter.

Dear Mr. Blume:

The bowing deformity of Lowell's lower legs was corrected today and he is doing very nicely.

You will receive three cards regarding his condition for three successive days following today's operation.

Yours very truly,
F. H. Kavanaugh
Chief Surgeon

Thankfully, that hurried, anonymous hand generously pens more than just three cards in the days and weeks ahead.

Dear Sir,
Lowell is resting comfortably today.
Shriners Hospital

Dear Sir,
Lowell has learned he can stand in his plasters in his bed. So he gets around his bed in a hurry now.
Shriners Hospital

Dear Sir,
Lowell thot we were passing him without a tray, but his was the next one. Then he started to smile. I was in the hall watching it, thot it was real sweet.
Shriners Hospital

Dear Sir,
Lowell is able to sit up in his plasters now and has a nice time playing with a little train.
Shriners Hospital

Dear Sir,
Lowell is sitting in the little swing just now, swinging nicely too.
Shriners Hospital

Dear Sir,
Lowell is out on the porch, even though it is the day before Thanksgiving.
Shriners Hospital

Dear Sir,
Lowell has some new shoes and is learning to walk.
Shriners Hospital

Their son's first steps.

There are no tears from Priscilla after this postcard, just a stabilizing inhale of breath. Her tender mother-hide has leathered in the sun of suffering these months. She is surviving the separation, but Lowell fears, at what cost?

The letter they have been waiting for arrives just after the first snowfall.

Dear Mr. Blume,

Your son, Lowell O. Blume, is now ready to be discharged from the hospital. Kindly arrange to have him leave here on Dec. 15 between the

```
hours of  12:00   and  2:00 P.M . It is of the
greatest importance that such arrangements be
made for the bed now occupied by him is urgently
needed for another patient. Kindly advise us that
the child will be called for on the date named
for discharge.
     We are able to obtain railroad charity fares
from St. Louis to any point OUTSIDE the State of
Missouri for the patient and one attendant. If
you wish to take advantage of this, do not buy a
round trip ticket. Charity fare means one-half
train fare.
                                  Yours truly,
                                      Zelma Bertram
                                      Superintendent
```

Junior has been gone for over four months when Lowell finally brings him home. The boy no longer prefers his mother.

"Syd!" Junior cries. "I wan' Syd!"

"Who's Syd?" Priscilla asks, hugging her son close even as he fusses and pushes against her arms.

"I s'pect that's who cared for him in the hospital," is all he says, but he thinks of that hurried, anonymous hand. Syd's hand, surely. His eyes water in jealous thanks.

Priscilla is still wrestling her son. "This is Mama, Junior. I'm yer mama."

That desperate tone. His wife is a branch — a mere twig — from which the hands of grief have been swinging. The slightest pull in the wrong direction, and she will break clean from the trunk. He would do anything to help her. Anything to make this transition easier.

"I was thinkin'."

She eyes him warily over their fussy son.

"'Junior' falls a bit flat on the tongue, don't you think?"

She frowns, bouncing the boy at her hip in an attempt to calm his protests. "I thought you liked sharin' a name with yer son."

"I do. It's just, well," love is loyalty, but loyalty to what is good for the other person. And his wife needs a fresh start. "He's a diff'rent person, now—No, I mean, he's the same person, but he's been through a lot. A lot that's good."

She might break, truly.

"I don't wanna change anything, Cill. I'm just sayin', what if'n we call him by his middle name, instead?"

He wants to add, "A new name for a new day," but thinks better of it.

Priscilla holds steady. She gazes at their son, measuring something none of them can see. As she calms, the boy calms. "Call him by his middle name?"

"Yes."

He holds his breath. Maybe it's a terrible idea. He's not even sure where it came from. He just wants his wife and his son to make it through this hour.

And maybe the next, Lord, he silently prays, *if that's not askin' too much.*

"Nothin' changes for him? We just call him by his middle name?" She adds in a whisper, "My brother's name?"

It is also the name of his father. Papa will approve. "Yes."

Mother and son gaze at each other, curious. She smiles. The boy smiles. She tickles his cheek, and the boy kicks his straight legs with obvious glee. At what, Lowell doesn't know, but he really doesn't care.

Those lines under his wife's eyes stretch into a laugh. Not all of her mother-hide is leather.

"Okay," she agrees, her eyes shining with something other than tears for once. It looks a lot like loyalty. "Welcome home, Oskar."

Chapter Four

Saint Alwin

✛ 1866 ✛

That star just winked.

Sarah sits up in the night air, searching in the dark for someone to tell, but no one is near to follow her finger's eager pointing to its sparkly end. Every youth old enough to find moonlight romantic is standing in between the orange of a bonfire and the black of the grove's wooded edge, throwing pinecones into the dancing flames. Every woman old enough to be tired at the end of a day is settled around Hermann Werth's hearth, casting hanks of wool from Vater's sheep onto needles and swapping stories for laughs. Every man old enough to tamp and smoke a pipe is sitting shoulder-to-shoulder on a makeshift circle of wooden crates and barrels in the barn. Sarah knows, because she puts an eye to the knothole at the base of the stall door to entice Felix, Ludwig Blume's weary old dog, out into the starry night.

So far, no one, Felix included, remembers stargazing Sarah, and that is fine with her. She is used to being forgotten. Or rather, she is reconciled to being unimportant. Nine-year-olds merit very little notice in a family overrun with double-digits, let alone in a gathering of neighbors with important matters to discuss. But just one more birthday and she will finally join the ranks of her older siblings and begin that mysterious apprenticeship in the secret art of ignoring others. In the meantime, a winking star is vying for her sole attention, and she remains young enough to be of a mind to give it. She lies back on the grass, a blue meadow rolling beneath her and a black one above her, the former dotted with specks of clover, the latter with flecks of light. That star, so big and bright, twinkles in perfect time to the merry music of Lesta Reinking's lone fiddle chirruping a *Schottische* across the grove.

The barn door opens. Ludwig Blume's boots stride toward the house, and Felix's gray snout sniffs a trail straight to Sarah.

"Old boy," she greets, scratching behind a furry ear with one hand and cupping her free palm over his warm, wet snout. She loves the dog, but she doesn't love his soggy tickles on her face. "Are they done?"

The Werth cabin answers for the dog. Women, laughter, and light stream out of its front door, and Ludwig whistles a sharp herald to cease all activity near the bonfire. Lesta's fiddle promptly silences and everyone old enough to matter follows the light of that star to the barn. Sarah follows anyway.

The barn smells of everything that keeps animals alive, but an alien atmosphere of human anticipation renders the inhabiting beasts oddly silent. Trousered knees shift and straighten without a word to make room for the women on the seats. Husbands young enough to stand unassisted reposition themselves behind their wives, and youths cluster according to clan around their parents. Hermann Werth, who never got around to marrying, plants himself beside his younger brother Friedrich's family. Old Johann Blume married young, but his wife died in childbirth long before Sarah was born. He stands near the door with his hat between his hands and Ludwig, his only son, at his side.

She is too short to see from behind the circle and too tall to sit on Vater's knee, so she settles comfortably on the dirt floor next to Felix at Ludwig's feet. The world smells better down here anyway. Mutti, directly across the circle, makes a subtle motion with her hand. Sarah understands immediately, blushing and pulling a wilted crown of clover out of her braids.

A sharp cry breaks the quiet. Baby Hans, the only child in Whistle Grove younger than herself, wails in disappointment to be shifted from his mother's left breast to her right, and a few empathetic cows bellow noisily in the dark. This is as good a start as any.

"We have come to an agreement," Herr Blume begins, his forehead serious, his shoulders straight, his eyes shining like that big star. He is a quiet man, but when he speaks, everyone listens. Even Baby Hans and the concerned cows hush to hear what the man has to say.

"We will call a pastor to minister to us here in Whistle Grove."

Three women touch hankies to their eyes. Several wives reach for their husbands' hands, and Lesta steals a longing glance at Ludwig Blume. There will be weddings here now, or at least some of them hope.

Baby Hans finally succeeds in latching onto his mother and suckles vigorously. Sarah stares in earnest at the fleshy, blue-veined point of contact. She will do this someday. She will feed a baby with herself. Her breath catches in happy expectation. There will be baptisms here, too.

"We have divided the pastor's earnings thusly. The Werths—er, Hermann?" Herr Blume prompts.

Sarah thinks Hermann Werth is the handsomest man in the circle, but unfortunately, his good looks spoil the moment he talks.

"Friedrich and I give this land. The grove, everything inside the tree line."

It's his voice. It is too high-pitched for a man with so much muscle. Herr Werth built the barn in which they are now gathering with his own strong hands, but Sarah can sneeze deeper than the man can speak. It makes her uncomfortable, the sound of his voice.

"My cabin'll serve as the parsonage. If everyone thinks it good enough."

Heads nod appreciatively. Sarah bites her lip until it smarts. She is dying to ask where Herr Werth will live when the pastor and his family take his home, but Vater will not tolerate her speaking aloud at such a time as this.

Friedrich Werth's booming bass takes over. "We can use this barn and our homes for gathering at first, but we hope to build a church as well as a school for the children — "

"And a cemetery," Alma Werth adds.

Friedrich rests a hand on his wife's shoulder, and Sarah remembers a story of a boy — Alwin? — who got sick on the boat on the way over to America. He died and is buried somewhere in this grove, or so she heard. Her breath catches, again, this time on the way out. There will be funerals here, as well.

Herr Blume nods at Doktor Conrad Freese.

"Noberta and I," the bespectacled man reaches for his wife's hand, "thank God for the opportunity to provide the lumber to build the church and school."

More hankies are lifted to wet faces. Sarah knows that the Freeses have no children, but they have been blessed with many trees on their land.

"My sons and I will raise and butcher the livestock needed to feed the pastor and his family from year to year."

This from Vater! Sarah's face burns with elation. The Lord is the Good Shepherd, she knows, but to be a Lindel who shepherds sheep to feed the pastor's family? Her heart may burst with such a joyful purpose. She suddenly wishes she were small enough to be sitting on Vater's knee, so she could kiss his cheek.

"The good Lord has blessed us greatly."

This crackly voice earns a respectful nod from every head. Herr Blume is the unspoken leader of this gathering, but Kermit Reinking is the eldest in the community. And as far as Sarah can tell, he is the holiest. No one else has hair as white nor eyes as kind. And his hands shake when he lifts them. Such proof of life expended must count for something important.

"We will donate land to be farmed for the pastor's wages," he says.

There are eight Reinkings in the barn, and every one of them grows taller as their patriarch speaks on their behalf.

Only one family in the barn has yet to give their accounting, and for that, Herr Blume looks to his only son.

"Vater and I will farm the land the Reinkings donate," Ludwig says, patting Felix's head, "and we will keep the pastor's woodpile and coal box stocked."

Sarah wants him to look at Lesta, but the man doesn't. Ludwig Blume rarely looks at anyone.

Five families, Sarah counts. The Lindels, the Reinkings, the Blumes, the Werths, and the Freeses. Herr Reinking settled here first at the invitation of a rich uncle in need of assistance with his textiles business, followed by Vater and the Blumes. Vater's emigration was sponsored by his three older brothers, but the Blumes left everything they had in Saxony to flee Rationalism in their state. The Werths and the Freeses came a few years after, but all of them, in their own time, left family and property and occupations to cross the ocean and settle this new, wild land. Now they all live together as a family, bonded by the nearness of their fences, the sweat of their brows, and the common language of their youth. They plant, harvest, pasture, butcher, build, sew, cook, toil, and dance, all together. And soon—with the help of a pastor—they will break bread together in a real church.

"All that is left," Herr Blume continues, "is to decide upon a name."

This piques Sarah's interest. She is never without ideas.

"Holy Trinity," Sylvia Reinking asserts straightaway, "after my home church."

Herr Blume holds up his hand, lest every woman decide to speak out of order. "We will not be naming our church after anyone's congregation from the homeland. The men have agreed."

"Yes," Herr Reinking nods his hoary support, turning those old eyes toward his son's wife. "It is fitting that a new church in a new land have its own name."

Sarah understands all that the men do not say: they cannot possibly satisfy everyone in this matter, so they will satisfy no one.

The gathering persists in its pious pondering, wives turning to their husbands in whispered conference. Sarah raises her hand excitedly, but a sharp furrow of Mutti's brow serves to slap her hand back in her lap.

"My wife offers the name of St. Paul for consideration," Doktor Freese speaks, "after the great missionary who sailed across many waters to preach the Way."

There are several polite appreciative nods around the circle, but Alma Werth tugs at her husband's sleeve. Friedrich dutifully clears his throat and says, "If we are considering personal names, then my wife and I would like to offer St. Alwin as an option."

Even single-digit Sarah understands that naming a church after a dead son is not so appropriate as after a dead apostle, but no human in the barn dares give voice to this disparity in the face of a mother's grief. Felix, however, yelps keenly in disapproval, though less from the suggestion and more from the appearance of a barn cat arching its back on an overhead beam. Baby Hans, disgruntled at having his milky repose so loudly interrupted, picks up his wailing once again, and the cows in their stalls start in on another chorus of maternal advice. Herr Werth moves to pitch fresh hay in the nearby manger to appease the lowing crowd, while Herr Blume applies some hat-in-hand diplomacy.

"It would be good to consider names of our Lord."

Yes, they all agree. Immanuel. Redeemer. But maybe St. Paul is the best name considering their circumstances after all, though there are other apostles to consider. Or perhaps St. Martin would be good.

Ideas, all of them sincere, are put forward, but none of them are chosen. None of them are quite right. None of them are Sarah's.

"Vater," she finally calls across the circle.

All eyes, wide with shock, turn toward her show of juvenile impertinence, but it is too late to take back her voice. She rises to her feet, crosses the floor, and leans into her incensed father's ear. When she pulls away, he is looking at her, seeing her, studying her. She blushes to be remembered so fully, but Vater's eyes are softening in a way she can see but cannot quite understand. She is only nine, after all. He pulls her hot cheek into his bushy beard and rewards her, not with a reprimand, but with a kiss. Then, not minding her being too tall, he pulls her onto his knee and says, "My daughter would like to suggest—"

Then he pauses. He smiles. He parts his beard with a hearty laugh. "Go ahead, child. Speak for yourself."

For while no one notices a little girl, she notices everyone and everything: a baby crying in a stable; cattle lowing around a manger; shepherds and farmers gathering in the night to witness a marvelous birth; wise men presenting gifts; and a particularly shiny star hanging overhead to point the way.

"We could," she starts, though she might die from being remembered by everyone at the same time. She takes a deep breath and tries again. "We could name the church Bethlehem."

None of them stay for long after that—the vote among the men is unanimous—but before everyone leaves, they all stand as one to pray the Our Father.

For good measure, and at Sarah's suggestion, they also sing "*Stille Nacht*."

Chapter Five

Saint Vivian

+ 2016 +

"All in favor say, 'Aye.'"

"Aye."

Only three voices assent, all of them female.

"All opposed?"

There is no opposition. No one expects there to be, for no one else remains in the pews of Bethlehem Evangelical Lutheran Church to object to the matter. Pastor Oglethorpe, on principle, never asserts himself on issues concerning the church's budget. Clem Lindel, chairman of the congregation, has no official vote. Clyde, his father, lies uncommunicative in a nursing home. Miriam Werth, while communicative as ever, sits homebound in assisted living exhibiting symptoms of dementia. Every other person associated with the business of the congregation is either shamefully absent, woefully apostate, or blessedly asleep in the ground.

"*But you, O Bethlehem,*" Pastor laments in his weary heart, "*who are too little . . .*"

Only now, after 50 years of pondering and preaching on this ancient text for Christmas dawn, does he realize the present irony of the Old Testament prophecy. Micah could have been foretelling the diminutive state of the clapboard church in Whistle Grove as much as the humble site of Christ's birth.

"The motion passes." Clem nods his head in absence of a gavel. "We will close the church."

The five of them—Pastor, Clem, his wife Honey, Iola Swart, and Lila Daniels—sit in mutual mourning. They are the remnant, the faithful few, and they have been keeping vigil at the deathbed of their frail church for years, praying and watching and listening and waiting for her to take her final breath. Now that the end is finally come, they sit as all the bereaved do: in stunned, silent exhaustion.

Eventually, Lila moves a blue pen to make an official note of the vote in the minutes, and Honey, known to be more comfortable proceeding through life accompanied by the sound of her own voice, takes this opportunity to speak.

"Well, this is just the worst. I feel terrible. I feel worse than when the DQ pulled out of Bramble, and I love soft serve almost as much as Jesus."

Iola's lined, drawn face grows, if possible, even more haggard. It has been a long few months, and not just because of the church's pending closure. The frequent meetings required to work through the dire finances of the congregation forced the mingling of certain family members who would otherwise have chosen to avoid each other altogether.

"I could cry. Seriously, I could, but I'm all dried up. I've been crying for years. *Years*, I'm telling you. Where are the people, y'all?" Honey raises her hands toward the raftered ceiling of the church, beseeching the very air. "I mean, seriously. Where are they? I haven't seen a Reinking step foot in this church since — "

"Vivian was faithful," Iola asserts.

"Well, sure. Vivian was faithful. But she's dead."

Lila closes her eyes, the dirt on her sainted friend's grave not even settled.

"And what good is her bequest to us? A measly five thousand? Y'all know she was sitting on some golden eggs in that nest of hers, but did she help us out in the end? No, she divided up her fortune between all of her traitorous family attending Glorious Praise in town. And now we'll have to close these beautiful doors and follow the lot of them to that amusement park every Sunday morning. Might as well move to Branson, now. The show's better."

Not all honey tastes sweet on the tongue, and no one understands this better than Clem. Pastor waits for their stoic chairman to intervene for the sake of his wife's — and everyone else's — reputation, but Clem persists in his active apathy, sifting through his papers and giving the appearance of not hearing the conversation at all. Pastor takes off his eyeglasses and rubs the irritation out of his eyes. Bethlehem may be dead, but Eve and her indifferent Adam are alive and well in Whistle Grove, apparently.

The grove aside, it has been years since their township resembled anything close to Eden. The Reinking factory closed back in the '80s, and half of Bramble's population shifted to Riverfield, leaving behind doorless sheds and unoccupied barns to decay in the middle of fields like so many county compost piles. In the '90s, suspicious transplants began moving into the vacant farmhouses west of the grove, and judging by the number of vehicles still burning rubber up and down the back roads at all hours of the night, that depraved lot makes their living in impious, unseemly ways. Certainly, none of them show any interest in keeping the Sabbath Day holy.

"Who's gonna tell poor Clyde?" Honey's exhale resonates like a growl. "This'll probably kill him, you know. Send him straight to his grave before his time."

"There is only God's time," Iola corrects.

Steadfast Iola. Ever the Deborah to her yellow Barak-of-a-nephew and his unrestrained wife.

"I will have to tell him, then," Honey decides.

"No," Clem finally speaks, and just in time. "I will tell my father."

"We both will," Iola amends, and Clem nods respectfully toward his aged aunt.

"What about Miriam?" Lila reminds.

Pastor clears his throat. "I'm headed over to Riverfield tomorrow morning to take her the Lord's Supper. I'll tell her then."

There is room for more words to be spoken, but he has already voiced them all, and repeatedly, over the last few months: the assurance that the Word of the Lord endures forever, whether the church's doors close or not; the promise that God will never leave them nor forsake them, though their family and friends have already done so; the exhortation to be in church every week, even if it is not their beloved Bethlehem in Whistle Grove; his personal pledge to remain in the area throughout his retirement to look after Clyde and Miriam and each of them as his very own family. But in this present moment, in this lowest of valleys, when a pastor should have his wisest and best of sermons prepared to comfort a defeated people, he finds that, once again, Micah already said it best.

"'And you, O Bethlehem,'" he recites, his voice bending under the weight of the moment, "'are by no means least.'"

Iola's shining tears are jewels adorning her quiet and gentle spirit.

The temptation for his meager flock in all of this dreadful business, of course, is to believe that a vote to close a church is a vote against Christ and His Gospel, but that simply is not the case. His people, poor in pocket, are merely voting to turn off the heat they can no longer afford and close a pulpit they can no longer supply. The Word remains, regardless of the fortress' failing might. Christ preserves His Church always, though most of it may exist below rather than above ground here in Whistle Grove.

"You," he reminds his congregation of four, "are by no means least, and neither are you alone. Remember, many have come before you, and while we are not promised that many will follow," he watches as Lila's eyes sweep involuntarily toward the door as they always do, forever looking for the son who never comes, "we remain one in Christ, whether here or in Bramble or before the Lamb on His throne. Wherever we are, we pray and sing as one body."

There is no time like the present. He clears his throat, opens his mouth, and—his own voice heavy with age and vibrato—sings with Simeon, Vivian, and all the host arrayed in white,

"'Lord, now lettest Thou Thy servant depart in peace
according to Thy word,
For mine eyes have seen Thy Salvation:
which Thou hast prepared before the face of all people.'"

All the saints of Bethlehem join in,

"'A light to lighten the Gentiles
and the glory of Thy people Israel.'"

Their heads bow.

"'Glory be to the Father, and to the Son
and to the Holy Ghost;
As it was in the beginning, is now, and ever shall be,
world without end.'"

As their amen wavers to a ponderous quiet, Honey sobs recklessly, "I love that song. And now we'll never get to sing it ever again."

The lines on Iola's face are forever deepening. "We will sing it on Sunday."

"Not at that circus-church, we won't."

Clem, to Pastor's surprise, condescends to take the hand of his wife, and Honey weeps gratefully into her husband's shoulder.

He raises his hand above the heads of his people, and they all shuffle to their feet to receive the benediction.

"'The LORD bless you and keep you; the LORD make his face to shine upon you and be gracious to you; the LORD lift up his countenance upon you and give you peace.'"

Clem adjourns the meeting shortly after, and each of them walks under the wooden rafters built by the fathers of their fathers' fathers. Pastor exits last, turning off the lights and locking the door behind him. They will gather once more on Sunday morning for a final service to close the church, but after that, Verl will turn off the water and the gas for good. At a later date, he and Lila will box up the Bibles, hymnals, paraments, communion vessels, and the hand-carved processional cross to ship to a seminary in Africa. Everything else will remain where it is, as it is. And Clem, whatever his weaknesses when it comes to managing his wife, is a farmer's son with a sharp sense of economy when it comes to managing land, property, and investments. He has agreed to handle the ongoing paperwork and correspondence of the church until all is good and done in the eyes of those who monitor such things.

The Lord provides in all things, even in death.

Pastor fondly pats the locked door of the deceased and turns in time to witness Lila placing something atop the headstone of Vivian's grave. He patiently waits on the front stoop like a dutiful father, waving paternally as she and all of his children settle into their vehicles and drive away. Only then does he turn to place the key above the doorframe of the church.

On the way to his car, he stops before Vivian's burial plot. There it is, Lila's gift. He bends in the waning twilight to inspect the item more closely, recognizing the blue pen Lila used that very evening to make her final secretarial notes. It is the same pen he saw Vivian pull out of her purse two months ago during Bible class when Lila had forgotten her own.

Sweet, soulful Lila.

He suddenly wishes he had spoken one more comforting prophecy of Micah's into this grieving daughter's ear.

"'O Bethlehem,'" he prophecies, stretching his hands over the gravestones of the baptized, "'from you shall come forth!'"

✝ ✝ ✝

The next day, Pastor pushes open the door to Room 217 of The Westmonte in Riverfield. Miriam Werth greets him from her armchair with a cheery smile of recognition.

"Pastor Engel!"

He has been serving the vacancy at Whistle Grove for the past twelve years, but Miriam, of late, continually mistakes him for her childhood pastor. No matter. The call and the cause are the same.

"Is Marta coming?"

Oh, dear. She is worse than last month.

"No," he kisses her cheek and lowers himself, with no little effort, onto the stool at her knees. He never knows, in these early days of dementia, whether it is best to let the past prevail or to continue walking in the present. In this moment, he chooses the present, though he treads softly. "Marta cannot come today," for she is dead, and from what he has heard, now scattered in the sea, though he does not say so to Miriam. He tries a different route to reality. "Do you remember when you attended her memorial service? Sally flew you to Maine, and the two of you went on a cruise to Prince Edward Island."

"I heard Marta playing the piano. Down the hall. I'll show you."

She tries to rise, but Pastor gently pats her back into her chair. "Show me later. I brought you something."

She is easily distracted, thankfully. He pulls out his black leather communion kit and Bible. "I thought we would read a bit of God's Word and then share Christ's Holy Supper."

"'. . . given into death for your sins.'"

Miriam's memories are jumbled and porous, but her understanding of eternal truths, thus far, remains inviolate. Pastor sends up a silent prayer of thanks to God for Pastor Engel's faithful catechesis in Miriam's youth. He will get to the Supper, but first, some hard news.

"Miriam," he takes her left hand in his right, "we had a funeral in Whistle Grove two weeks ago."

She could be looking straight through him for all he can tell.

"It was for Vivian."

She appears unmoved.

"Remember Vivian Reinking, your friend? You sat by her in church."

"I sit by Oskar in the balcony."

She is even worse than he thought. Maybe he shouldn't push the matter.

"Oskar holds my hand under the hymnal, but Mother doesn't know." Miriam giggles into her shoulder, then her eyes grow wide. "Don't tell her, Pastor. Please, don't tell her."

She is the worst he has ever seen her. "I won't."

"Marta won't hold my hand."

This, again. His heart breaks.

"Even when she wears her special gloves, she won't touch me."

He impulsively reaches for the lame right hand pinned between her hip and the arm of the chair. He kisses it tenderly. His cousin had polio.

"Miriam." Today is clearly not the best day for this, but he must at least try. He promised Lila and the Lindels that he would. "We had to close the church."

"That's Cherry's job. She always locks up after she's done cleaning."

He nods, resigned. He will have to try again another day, though at this rate, they may need to transfer Miriam to a nursing home faster than he anticipated.

"Cherry finds candy in the pews sometimes. She gives it to me."

Letting go of her hand, he opens his communion kit and smooths a white corporal on the surface of a nearby end table. One by one, he sets out the silver paten and chalice.

"Oskar is taking me into town tonight. For my birthday."

He nearly spills the wine he is pouring. *Please, Lord, not this memory.*

Miriam is talking of her new birthday dress when her lips open wide to scream, "Help!"

Even though he is anticipating it, his heart still races. He tries to set down the cruet without overturning it and pulls himself up from the low stool. Where is the button that alerts the staff?

"Help! Someone, help!" Miriam is in full hysterics, now, screaming as loud as her 78-year-old vocal folds will allow. "Why are you all standing around?"

There it is. Hanging around her neck. He grabs for the device and pushes the button hard, trying his best to calm her thrashing left arm.

"Miriam, it's okay. Look at me. You are in Riverfield. I am Pastor Oglethorpe. We play pinochle together, remember? Here, take my hand. See? It's Pastor. We're sitting in your living room. We're about to have communion." Out of habit, without even realizing it, he begins singing, "'*Create in me a clean heart, O God, and renew a right spirit within me. . . .*'"

She stares at him, mouth open and eyes wide, but her screaming stalls. He knows it is most likely from distraction rather than from comfort, but she keeps tracking him with her eyes, at least. He is still singing and holding her hand when Penny comes through the door with her nurse's cart.

"How are we doing this morning?" Penny calls out, assessing the situation with a single glance of her eyes. She walks straight to the kitchenette sink and fills a glass with water. "Well, look who's here. Pastor came to visit you, Miriam. How nice," she narrates as she moves toward the chair.

Pastor steps out of the way so Penny can better evaluate her resident, but Miriam reaches for his sleeve and holds him to the spot.

Her eyes are still wide but no longer from fright. She looks pitifully sad.

"Tell Sally I was wrong."

"About what?"

"I don't want her to be like me."

He doesn't understand.

"I don't want her to be alone."

She is talking about her niece, so she must be somewhere near the present again.

"Tell her, Pastor."

"Tell her what?"

"Tell her to get married. I don't want her to be an old maid like me."

So much sadness in those eyes.

"Tell her to marry Superman."

And madness.

Dear God, he sighs, *help*.

Chapter Six

Saint Bernice

+ 1958 +

Time measured precisely. Complex but recognizable patterns arranged on a page. Sonorous math worked out in the brain but realized in the ear. It is the good order of music that appeals to her. There are no secrets or surprises on a score that she cannot see coming. Every note, tempo, and dynamic, however troublesome, can be mastered with a bit of study and practice. All music is subject to the authority of her own hands in the end. That's why she likes to play the piano. That, and because Miriam can't.

"At the pick-up, please, Marta."

Miss Green looks her way and conducts a preparatory beat. Marta lightly touches her fingers to the keys of the church balcony piano. Her quick arpeggiation is a bird uncaged, a feathered motive soaring among the rafters, but all too soon the nasal singing of the choir casts its heavy net, capturing and pulling against her dexterous playing till it can fly no more.

Singers are the bane of all that is beautiful in music.

"Let's try that again." Miss Green cuts off the choir with the mere closing of her fingers. She likes Miss Green. The willowy woman thinks more than she speaks, watches more than she wavers, and feels far more than she chooses to show. Marta knows, because she is the same. "A little lighter this time."

In truth, the volunteer choir never sings lighter than Priscilla Blume's Guernsey bellowing across the Fireling Road. Only Oskar sings with any sensitivity, and the very thought of his full baritone warms her cheeks. She eyes him over the soundboard of the piano, but he does not see her. He sees only Miriam.

The front door of the church is thrown open, effecting a *caesura* in their rehearsal. Miss Green's hand hangs suspended in the air as they all wait for the thunder of footsteps in the stairwell to subside. It is probably Ralph Lindel, finally in from the fields, but a blonde braid, not a receding hairline, peeks around the balcony door. Miss Green lowers her hand, and several women in the choir turn in their seats and smile in happy expectation at the golden herald.

"Well, then. There's a new baby, I expect?" Drucilla Reinking asks.

The braid nods.

"Speak up, Iola."

"Yes," the girl says, stepping through the door but keeping her hands behind her back and against the wood. Her face is flushed from running, and her breath is coming fast.

"Boy or girl?"

"Boy."

"The name?"

Iola is still breathing hard, her eyes round and fixed as two eggs frying in a pan. "Clement Arthur Lindel, ma'am."

"Well," Drucilla nods authoritatively, looking around, "that'll get shortened to Clem by nightfall, mark my word." She turns back to the wide-eyed girl. "You must be proud as a peacock to be an aunt, Missy. And how is the new mother? Sleeping soundly, I expect."

Iola swallows more air, her voice a tremor. "I was sent to speak with Mrs. Werth."

Mother stands, her manner swift but calm. In moments, her hands are on the girl's shoulders, gently turning her out into the stairwell. The choir hushes, watching the closing door. Even Miss Green openly stares, appearing to have forgotten to hide her own concern.

When Mother returns, she is alone.

"What is it, Ruthie?"

Mother is averse to drama of any kind and always gets right to the point. "Bernice," but her voice catches on the following word, "died in childbirth an hour ago."

The gasps nearly shake the balcony. Marta feels her own hand fly to her mouth.

"Dear Lord!"

"What happened?"

"So young!"

"And this her firstborn!"

"Poor, Clyde!"

"Poor, little Clem!"

Mother waits for calm before speaking. "If young Iola has her facts correct, then I believe Bernice may have," again her voice catching, "bled out. Pastor Engel is with the family, now, but they have asked for our prayers. I am headed over there to help Viola care for the baby. Priscilla?"

With a single nod of her head, Priscilla Blume closes her music folder and stands to follow. Miriam stands, too, but Mother shakes her head.

"I told Iola to wait outside. Take her home with you."

The choir, after a tremulous prayer, promptly disbands to do what they can for the Lindel family, and Oskar walks Iola, Miriam, and Marta to the new house. Iola is quiet, one hand in Miriam's left, the other in Oskar's right, but Miriam chats easily for them all, telling stories of the gypsy tomcat that has taken up residence under their front porch. It isn't until Iola is tucked into Mother's armchair in the front room with a blanket folded around her legs and a mug of hot cocoa in her hands that the girl's shock melts into tears.

Silence is the problem, Marta suspects, so she sits at the piano and begins to play a hymn. "Jesus, Thy Blood and Righteousness" comes first to mind. She plays alone for a time, but by the second stanza, Oskar is singing along. She dares a glance his way and is surprised to find him looking straight at her, not at Miriam. The resulting thrill plays a *glissando* down her spine. Oskar stands at her back and sings, and she could make this music forever. Another hymn and then another. She stops only when Oskar moves to leave.

"I need to check on my mother. She might need someone to run errands for the Lindels."

He is looking at Miriam again, and her sister returns his gaze in full. Miriam abides in his look with such comfort and ease. She takes his eyes for granted. Marta would give her own right hand to live in Oskar's eyes like that. Jealousy sounds a cluster chord deep within her chest.

✝ ✝ ✝

Iola sleeps in Miriam's bed that night, and her sister pauses, waiting for an invitation to share Marta's bed. Marta simply turns away from the unspoken expectation. She once tried explaining to Miriam that her sister thrashes her legs in her sleep, but Miriam seemed wounded by the fact.

"I do not."

"You do, Miriam. You kick in your sleep. It keeps me up. You know I'm a light sleeper."

Neither spoke aloud what they both were thinking at the time—nerve damage from the polio—but Miriam couldn't help spitting out a quick accusation in self-defense.

"Well, you make a sucking sound with your tongue."

They never talk about it anymore. They never talk about much of anything. Marta keeps silent and to herself, and Miriam is forever turning her face toward Oskar.

Miriam pulls sheets and a blanket from the hall closet to make up the couch for the night. Marta is wearing her cotton gloves for the evening and heading for the stairs when her sister asks her to feed the vagrant cat under the porch.

"It's a stray."

"Don't be heartless, Marta. Even strays need to eat."

"Mother doesn't want us feeding strays from the kitchen."

"Mother feeds Barnaby and Twila from the kitchen."

"They're pets."

"C'mon, Marta. Old Tom is practically a pet by now."

"Then feed him yourself."

"I can't. I promised Mother I wouldn't."

She may be the youngest in the family, but her older sister is most certainly the baby. "I'm going to bed."

"Marta, please. Tom is hungry, and I've got to deal with these old sheets. Just do it."

She holds up her gloved hands in speechless explanation, one foot on the bottom step of the stairwell, ready for the final climb to bed.

Miriam rolls her eyes. "So keep your gloves on, and you won't get your precious hands dirty."

It is the easiest thing in the world to walk up the stairs, cheeks burning, without a single word of response. She doesn't bother turning off the light on the way up. Let Queen Miriam do it herself.

In her room, she seethes in the dark, unable to sleep. Miriam has no right to mock her gloved hands. Mother is the one who gave her the gloves in the first place.

"These might help, Baby. Rub some Vaseline into the nail beds every evening, and then wear these while you sleep. They'll help it soak in overnight."

Dry skin is her bane, and the perpetual weeding and washing and choring of the summer, coupled with hours of practicing the piano, is splitting the skin around her fingernails. It is painful and taking forever to heal, but she never breathes a word about it to Miriam. For one, it feels powerful to know something of which her older sister knows nothing, but it also feels unjust to complain about the overuse of her fingers when her sister can't use a single finger on her right hand.

But still, she spends the next hour composing a fugue in the dark, the subject her sister's annoying voice, the answer her sister's habit of making everything about herself, and the free counterpoint her sister's getting everything she wants.

✝ ✝ ✝

The next morning, after Marta returns from walking Iola home, she overhears Miriam and Mother arguing in the kitchen.

"I'm twenty, Mother. You were eighteen when you married Father."

"Things were different for us."

"Apparently. You had parents who trusted you."

"This has nothing to do with trust. This has to do with — "

"Bernice."

"Well, yes, in a way. Childbirth is dangerous business."

"That didn't stop you from giving birth. Twice."

"I didn't have polio."

"I *had* polio, Mother. I don't *have* it."

"And it has weakened you."

Miriam's exhale could break a dam. "You said Bernice hemorrhaged from a tragic tear."

"Yes."

"That has nothing to do with polio."

"But if a tear like that can happen to someone in the prime of health, think of all that you are vulnerable to in such a situation, Miri."

"Polio's weakened my nerves, not my womb."

"We don't know that."

"We don't know that my legs won't ever give out, but that doesn't keep me from walking every day. You want me to live my life as if I'm already dead."

"You know that's not true. I'm only trying to protect you, Miri. I want you to live a long, happy life."

"No, you want me to live a long, unhappy life without Oskar."

"Miri," Mother's sigh carries some force of its own. "Marriage comes with many responsibilities, one of them being children — "

"I know how it works, Mother."

"No, you don't!"

Mother's uncharacteristic shout reverberates even in the front sitting room. A strained silence settles over the entire house, but soon, Marta hears the soft stirrings of a heart-rending melody. Mother is shushing and shooing her own tears, most likely into a hankie.

"Mother," Miriam's voice is pleading yet firm, "Bernice is dead, and that is terrible. But I'm still alive."

The gentle weeping in the kitchen has the lilt of a lullaby.

"Oskar is the best of men, you know he is. I don't deserve him, but he wants me. He wants *me*, Mother, and he's been waiting two years for your blessing. That's longer than any man should have to wait for a woman already of age. And you know he's waited all of this time out of respect for your wishes. But they're your wishes alone."

She feels the conversation climaxing toward Miriam's final word. Every conversation spoken in the history of ever in this house cadences with a final word from Miriam.

"You think I'll die if I marry Oskar, but I'm telling you, I'll die if I don't."

She walks toward the piano. Mother needs to hear some music other than this same old pitiful tune.

+ + +

Bernice is buried on Monday, and judging from Mother's surrendered posture and Miriam's elated countenance at the funeral luncheon, Miriam got her way. Miriam always gets her way.

The sinking feeling in Marta's stomach bottoms out after supper.

"Do you think she'll like it?"

They are sitting on the front porch while Mother and Miriam are washing and drying the dishes in the kitchen. Oskar is holding out a golden ring with a small diamond set in the middle of it.

"It's perfect," she somehow manages, because it is. The solitaire setting is strong and true and unaffected, just like him. It would look so nice on her own left hand against the keys of the piano. Surely he must realize that.

He snaps the box shut and returns it to his pocket. She studies his frame in the fading light. When standing, Oskar is shorter than her—shorter than Miriam, even—but when they sit side by side like this, his eyes look down into hers. His back is as tall and strong as any man's, and his thick shoulders can carry the weight of the world. Certainly, they've been called upon to do so often, considering the financial strains of his own family and the physical deficiencies of her own. But it is his hands that she admires. They are brown and calloused from felling trees along Mr. Lindel's pastures. They are not afraid of hard work, just like hers. They do their part in this life, and they deserve to be admired and held and caressed as a pair, not always just one at a time, as with Miriam.

She can barely get the words out. "When are you giving her the ring?"

"Her birthday."

Next week. All of her hopes die next week.

"You'll be my sister, you realize."

She turns away, unable to restrain her wild grief. Surely he must see it. Surely he must know.

"You've always been my little sister, Marty." He ruffles the top of her bobbed hair. "This'll just make it official."

Miriam walks out onto the porch then, and Oskar jumps to his feet. Marta doesn't need to look to know that he is reaching out a hand to push back Miriam's dark curls. Now, he is folding his fingers around a lone lock. He always lingers in her hair.

She blinks back tears and rises in the dusk.

"Marta," Miriam calls after her, "stay. I brought Yahtzee."

But the screen door closes at her back, saving her from complete humiliation.

+ + +

On Sunday, Iola holds her baby nephew over the font at the front of Bethlehem's nave.

"Clement Arthur," Pastor Engel pours water three times over the infant's head, "I baptize thee in the name of the Father and of the Son and of the Holy Ghost."

"Amen."

The sadness surrounding the week's events somehow dims in the happy light gleaming from Iola's proud eyes. The young godmother stands tall between her older, newly widowed brother and Art and Viola Lindel, her smile beaming a radiant joy all the way up to the balcony, threatening to pierce even Marta's dark cloud. But it is not until after the service as Marta stands in the undercroft next to Vivian Leesmann, politely listening to Iola recount all of little Clem's perfections, that she feels the warmth of an actual ray of hope.

For the reverberations of a slammed door echo through the nave. Everyone pauses to ponder the cause except Marta who, from her place near the window, alone is privy to the plot.

Miriam is racing outside toward the open road, her mass of black hair whipping behind her like a cape. She catches the toe of her shoe on the old, half-buried wagon wheel bordering the church lane, but she regains her footing without a stumble and disappears through the trees.

Oskar, his neck stiff and aflame, stands alone just inside the closed church door.

Another day, another argument.

She checks the smile tickling her lips. Not all may be lost. Miriam's temper, swollen with pride, may prove too thick and unbending ever to fit a ring.

Chapter Seven

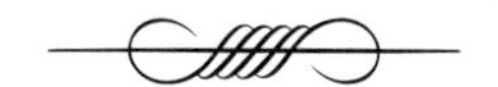

Saint Johann

+ 1867 +

Everyone thinks his tears are for Vater, but they are not.

Not that his father isn't worth a flood of tears. How will he ever get by this spring without him?

"No one could till a line straight as Old Johann."

"Nor till as long."

"He was always the first to his plow."

"And the last to his pillow."

The men nod their hatless heads and pat him on the shoulder before turning away from the grave they just filled, shovels on shoulders.

"Your father was the best of men, Ludwig." This comes from Frau Lindel. "I never met a man who said so much without saying anything at all. An 'in deed and in truth' sort if I ever knew one. The way he bent himself to every task, always helping whoever was in need."

"Yes, ma'am."

She pats him on the shoulder, too. "You're a good boy, Ludwig."

And this coming to him in his 32nd year of life.

They all take their time leaving the grove, and Ludwig waits for every last one of them. He has learned endurance from his father, though every second the Reinking girls linger over young Alwin Werth's grave tests his mettle. If Lesta hadn't promised she'd come at the worst, he never would be able to wait it out.

Pastor Uden alone remains at his elbow. "*Meine Frau* and I would like you to join us for supper, Ludwig."

"I thank you, Herr Pfarrer. But I want to be getting home."

"Then we'll send Maria down with a stew later this evening."

"I thank you, Herr Pfarrer."

Finally, everyone is gone, and he looses the breath he has been holding. He too can say much by saying nothing, so he grasps his father's tombstone with one hand. He will be back. Then he is running toward the tree line, across the road, and through the front door of the house he and Vater built from trees felled by their own hands.

"Lesta?"

"In here." Her voice is but a murmur, her brown head leaning over the table in the center of the room. "He's breathing. But Ludwig—"

She lifts her eyes to his. They are warning him.

"He is not right on the inside, I think."

Ludwig sobs then, his relief at making it in time equal to the grief at what is surely coming. He has never cried so much in all of his life, not when he hugged Oma for the last time in Hessen and not even when Vater breathed his last in the very next room. They were his only family, but Felix is his best and only friend. He buries his face in the dog's furry neck and, for the second time that week, commits himself to enduring the deathbed of someone he loves more than his own life.

It happened just before the funeral. The men were carrying Vater over to the grove, Ludwig's right shoulder directly under his father's, when Felix tore away from his side. The dog had been doing that of late, running toward young Sarah Lindel and her *Pickert*-filled pockets whenever he saw her. But the Reinking wagon was pulling into the grove at that exact moment, and the front left wheel proved stronger than Felix's hind quarters.

It was all Ludwig had been able to do not to drop his father. He cried out all the same, and when he was finally freed to run after his dog, Lesta was down from the wagon bed and on the ground, kneeling at Felix's side.

"Have mercy! Have mercy!" Frau Reinking kept whimpering from the wagon seat, and Lesta's sisters in the wagon bed were keening more loudly than the mourners of Jairus' daughter.

"Hush!" Herr Reinking quieted his daughters. "Elmer, jump down and give your mother a hand. Ludwig, I do apologize. I didn't see Felix coming."

But Ludwig was already carrying his dog across the road and into his house.

"In here," Lesta redirected. She had followed him through the front door and was waving him away from the bedroom and toward the table in the big room as she untied her bonnet's ribbons from underneath her chin. "The light is better."

Felix was whining, and Ludwig's shirt was wet with his blood.

"Never mind," Lesta said, as he started to take a bucket out into the yard to fill. "I'll do that. You change your clothes."

Felix howled, and Ludwig faltered. But Lesta grabbed him by the arm and squeezed hard.

"Ludwig Blume, listen to me. Your father needs burying. You must do this."

Ludwig balked.

"I will stay with Felix. I will wash him and bind him."

Still, he could not move.

"I will come get you if . . . you are needed. I promise."

How he finally was able to leave his friend suffering on the table, he cannot remember, but he now takes one of Felix's gray ears in hand and rubs the soft, familiar velvet between his fingers. Felix's tongue flickers out of his mouth in recognition, and his tail sounds one lone thump against the wood of the table.

Ludwig sees that Lesta has put an old quilt under Felix's body, and she has cleaned and stitched a gash above his right hip.

"There was a rib," she points at the gash, and he understands. "I did what I could."

And yet, Felix's abdomen is swollen to twice its normal size. And his gums are pale against his pink tongue.

Ludwig walks over to the far wall and lifts Vater's rifle from the pegs.

"No, Ludwig. That is not necessary, I think."

"He is in pain."

"Not for long. Here," she moves a chair in front of Felix and pulls Ludwig toward the seat. "Sit with him. It will comfort him. I will play for you both."

Lesta walks to the door and picks up her fiddle case leaning against the frame. The plan had been for her to play at Vater's grave. In seconds the fiddle is under her chin, tuned, and she draws her horsehair bow across the strings. She plays "*O Welt, ich muss dich lassen*," first, and then "*O wie selig seid ihr doch, ihr Frommen*." These hymns were meant for Vater's funeral, surely, but they calm both him and his dog all the same. She plays for as long as it takes, stopping only when Felix's labored breathing ends in a final, mournful howl.

✢ ✢ ✢

When Ludwig steps outside to wash his hands at the well, he finds young Sarah loitering in the yard. The whites of her big, round eyes glow in the light streaming from the open door.

"Is he dead?"

Ludwig nods, and before he can do anything to prevent her, the girl's wet face is buried against his middle and her arms are wrapped tightly around his waist. He stands stock-still, stunned, with his arms lifted uncomfortably in the air. It was only ever him, Vater, and Felix day in and day out. He does not know what to do with girls.

She pulls away to wipe her nose on her apron, and he asks, "Would you like to see him?"

She nods, and he leads her into the lamp-lit room where Lesta is wiping up the floor. She already has covered all but Felix's head with the blanket, and Sarah draws close to view him. Reflexively, she puts her hand up to his snout—an old greeting between the two of them—but Felix is cold to the touch, Ludwig knows.

"His eyes are open."

"Yes."

"But he is dead?"

"Yes."

"What are you going to do with him?"

"Bury him."

"Where?"

Ludwig has not yet considered such a detail, but he knows where Felix belongs. He asks Pastor Uden that very night.

"You want to bury him next to your father?" Pastor Uden blinks at him from the parsonage doorway. "The dog? In the cemetery?"

There are only two graves in the cemetery — Vater's and Alwin's — so there is plenty of room in the grove. And Vater and Felix are his only family. "Yes, Herr Pfarrer."

Pastor steps out into the night and shuts the door behind him.

"Come, sit with me, Ludwig. The air is warm, and there's a log good for sitting with a pipe on the other side of the barn."

They settle on the log and Pastor pinches tobacco from a pouch into the chamber of his pipe.

"You have had a day."

Ludwig never took to smoking and doesn't know what to do with his own hands without Felix there to lick them, so he squeezes them together between his knees.

"Herr Reinking sent Elmer by the house this afternoon to tell me about the incident with the wagon. I'm sorry, Ludwig. Felix was a good dog, I know. You had him . . . five years?"

"Seven."

A burst of flame then, and the sweet smell of smoldering tobacco.

"He came with you on the boat?"

"No. I found him along Dandy Creek. His leg was caught in one of our traps." It is easier for him to talk to men. "I carried him home to wash his wounds, and he never left."

"That's right."

He feels a sudden need to justify housing and feeding a stray dog. "Felix earned his keep, Herr Pfarrer. He chased squirrels and rabbits out of the garden."

"Of course."

The two sit in silence for a minute, and Pastor puffs on his pipe.

"He should be buried," Pastor confirms. "The thing is, Ludwig, the cemetery is for the baptized."

Ludwig is not wise about such things. Should he have had Felix baptized? Vater never said as much.

"A cemetery is a resting place for those waiting for the Resurrection Day."

He barely can abide this past hour without his friend let alone all of eternity, and grief shears him of all self-restraint. "Felix will not also be raised?"

"Ah, I see. I am not being clear. Forgive me, Ludwig." Pastor draws slowly on his pipe, taking his time. He is a considerate man always, but especially when he is smoking. "I speak of baptism, because it is man who needs the washing of regeneration. After all, it is he, not any animal, who brought sin into the world. It is he who needs the righteousness of Christ restored, but," and Ludwig hears a distinct note of kindness in the learned man's voice, "this does not mean the resurrection is for man alone. Doktor Luther himself wrote that he fully expects to see his own dog restored to him in the resurrection, and with golden skin and hair made of pearls. And why not, I say? Jesus promises to create a new heaven and a new earth when He returns, so why would He not also make new our beloved pets?" Pastor smiles around the stem of his pipe and nods. "Yes, I believe we can expect Felix to be restored on the new earth. Where you go, so will Felix."

Ludwig might cry again, this time from relief.

"But the cemetery," Pastor draws thoughtfully on his pipe again before continuing. "Here is a matter to contemplate, Ludwig. God created Felix, yes. God created all animals, and He called everything 'good.' But you and your father and every other person on this earth are the pinnacle of God's creation. It is you who are made in God's image. And Christ commands you to be baptized, that He might restore you with His image, His righteousness. This is why we baptize nations, not herds."

They sit in a fragrant cloud pondering creation and the curse.

"This is also why we bury your body in the cemetery to rest and wait until the Last Day when Christ promises to come again."

"Then what happens to all of the animals?"

"And what happens to all of the trees and the wheat and the stars and the fish? Good gifts from God, every one of them, and we thank and praise Him for such good gifts! But we do not baptize the stars, because they are not dead in their trespasses and sins. And we do not bury fish or trees or animals in the church's cemetery, because baptism is for mankind." Pastor knocks tobacco ash out onto the dirt at their feet. "Still, Felix needs burying, and there is nothing that says we cannot bury him in the grove if not in the cemetery itself. What about right here? By this log where you can come and sit any time you like? And I believe you can see this spot from your own front door across the road. Would that help you, Ludwig?"

He barely recognizes the feel of his own skin with all of these tears on his face.

"Yes, Herr Pfarrer. I thank you."

Pastor rests a hand on Ludwig's shoulder as he stands. "Did I ever tell you about the time I caught Maria feeding Felix *Strudel* from *inside* the parsonage?"

So young Sarah Lindel was not Felix's only girlfriend. This news does not stop his tears, but it does warm him to know that so many others saw that his dog was good.

Ludwig is almost to the Fireling Road when Pastor calls out, "Elmer also told me that Lesta stayed with Felix and cared for him while we buried your father."

"Yes."

"You are not so alone as you think, Ludwig."

✛ ✛ ✛

There is no point in delaying till tomorrow what needs doing today, so Ludwig wraps Felix tightly in the old quilt—stitched by Oma's hands—and carries him to the log. The digging does him good, as does the starlight and the fresh air and the sweat. This is a water that is familiar to him, and he feels returned to himself in a way that is reassuring.

Baptism may or may not be for Felix, but Ludwig prays the Our Father over his dog's grave all the same. Then, he shoulders his shovel and walks across the grove to lay a hand on Vater's tombstone—he had promised he would be back—before returning in the dark to a cold, empty house.

✛ ✛ ✛

He is drawing water at the well early the next morning when he hears a wagon turning toward the house. Lesta has the reins in hand, and he realizes he has been expecting her though she made no promise to come.

He meets her in the yard and offers her a hand to the ground. Her sister Thelma is with her.

"We've come to cook you breakfast, Ludwig."

His stomach fires into remembrance. He had not been able to eat the Uden family's generous stew from the previous evening. Lesta had fed some of it to young Sarah before sending the girl on home, and the rest she had left for him on the stove. But he had been too heartsick to eat much before falling into bed last night.

"Thelma, take this basket on in, and start the fire. Wood is out back." Lesta turns to him, hugging a folded quilt to her chest. "I need your help with something in the wagon bed, please."

He follows her to the back of the wagon and stares. There lies a wheel with a dark stain on the rim. He forgets his stomach again and involuntarily glances to the front left of the wagon. The wheel has been replaced.

"Felix was stronger than we thought." Lesta points to a crack in the stained wheel. "The wheel may have broken Felix, but he also broke the wheel."

Why is she showing this to him?

"You buried him, yes?"

Again, his eyes involuntarily glance away, this time toward the dark patch of spaded dirt in the grove across the road. Lesta follows his gaze and nods. Then she looks him full in the face.

"I asked Vater for the wheel."

He waits. He does not understand.

"It is no good to him anymore, and I thought, perhaps, you might want to mark Felix's grave."

He looks at the wheel then, and he understands. He will set the wheel in the ground today, at Felix's head, if Pfarrer approves.

"And you buried him in the quilt?"

He suddenly realizes his mistake. Oma's quilt. It was his only blanket. Other than Vater's.

"Yes."

She nods and hands him the quilted blanket in her arms. It is made of brown and white patches with long strips of green trim—his favorite color.

He follows her into the house, and he sees that she belongs there.

Chapter Eight

Saint Klaus

✢ 1879 ✢

Klaus Iken's favorite days are those when all fourteen children play in the grove together. Only half of them are his — the blonde ones — but he claims the brown-haired Blumes as his own whenever they wander across the road to eat at his table or take lessons in the *Schulhaus*. Herr and Frau Blume were the first to be married in the grove, and as local lore retells it, the entire congregation, in pious hope that God would soon bless the church with the gift of children, had gathered to lay a foundation for a new school the very morning after the wedding.

"It would be okay if everyone prayed a little less fervently in the days ahead," Lesta Blume had teased after the baptism of her third set of twins, but being father to one-third of the children in the congregation himself, his own ears could detect the weariness behind the wit.

"God teaches us to pray, always."

She had nodded and lowered her eyes.

"He teaches us to wait and yearn and ask for His blessings—"

"And then," she had finished his sentence, eyes glistening with a chastened, tearful understanding, "to ask for the strength to care for His many blessings."

"Yes."

How he loves his children! All of them. The ones born to him from his beautiful Inah and the ones reborn in the faith at the font. No father was ever so blessed as he. Well, except every other man in Christendom called to be a father in the church. He smiles at this fraternal thought.

Today, the sunshine in the grove is thick with cottonwood hair and dandelion seeds, and he takes his *Epitome* outside to study under the shade of a favorite sycamore behind the parsonage. He cannot see the children, but he hears their romps and roars as they chase each other in and around and over God-knows-what. His Inah will have a strong word to say about the state of their hands and feet before entering the parsonage for lunch, he has no doubt.

He is only three paragraphs deep in the affirmations of the third use of the Law when young Walther finds his way from his mother's skirts before the stove to his father's lap under the tree.

"Son," he greets the boy, opening wide his arms, book still in hand. Walther climbs into his lap, and he continues to read, this time aloud, "'For although they are regenerate and renewed in the spirit of their mind, yet in the present life this regeneration and renewal is not complete, but only begun, and believers are, by the spirit of their mind, in a constant struggle against the flesh . . .'"

But their pious contemplation of the Old Adam is interrupted by the sudden appearance of Martin and Philip, the middle set of Blume twins, from around the corner of the parsonage. His own

Peter is leading them, and the three boys land purposefully in front of the outhouse.

"Who's first?" Peter asks.

"Not me." Martin takes a step backward.

Philip throws a chin toward Peter. "You go first."

"I would," his son shrugs, "but I don't have to go. You guys aren't scared, are you?"

"No," in unison.

Peter moves to open the door, pausing a bit dramatically with his hand on the leather strap. "Because it happened ages ago. Long before the school was ever built."

Neither of the Blume boys step forward as Peter swings open the door.

"It's safe. I promise."

Philip shifts his feet as if to move but only asks, "Who was it who died in there?"

"Old Man Werth."

This is the moment when a wiser father would intervene, but he is too curious to hear the end of this tale to dare interrupt the teller.

"H-how did he die?" Martin asks from behind his brother's shoulder.

Peter shakes his head solemnly. "No one knows. But his wife came out one morning to broom the cobwebs and found him. Dead. Still sitting upright. With his eyes open."

He has to lean his lips against Walther's downy hair to keep from laughing out loud.

"And then," Peter is now whispering, "Frau Werth disappeared the very next night."

"Where?"

Peter shakes his head. "She just disappeared. Some say into the woods. Some say she walked the creek south in search of another husband. But others say . . ."

"What?"

"What do they say?"

Peter turns his head toward the open outhouse and silently nods toward the dark interior.

"What? She disappeared in there?"

"No." Peter takes his time. "But some say she never left the grove. I've never seen her myself. Johann says he's seen her once or twice in the early morning disappearing into the *Schulhaus*, but I don't believe him."

Martin shivers.

"Though one night, when there was no wind and no moon, I heard a woman's voice moaning outside our window, saying, 'Stay away, children. Stay away.'"

Philip's eyes are bigger than his ears, and Martin turns directly on his heel, saying, "I'm going home—"

"Scared?"

"No!" But the boy keeps moving. "I just want to do my business at home."

"Because no one has ever seen Frau Werth during the daytime," Peter calls. "The sun is shining. It's totally safe."

Martin stalls near the parsonage, and Philip clears his throat and steps forward. "I'll go. I'm not afraid."

Peter smiles broadly and gives his friend a congratulatory pat on the back, closing the door behind Philip and giving a strong, salutary knock on the wooden siding.

It is at this moment that he sees Anna Maria, his eldest daughter, creeping out from the line of trees just behind the outhouse. She crouches under the venting hole at the back of the privy, and in a voice too tall and wide for any nine-year-old — and with a rather impressive vibrato for anyone of any age — she moans, "Stay away, children! Stay away!"

Martin is gone around the parsonage faster than a mouse through a knothole, and Philip . . . Poor, Philip. The traumatized boy screams at the top of his lungs, banging his way out of the small wooden enclosure, his unbuttoned trousers tangled around his knees. He trips and falls flat on the ground, now whimpering, while Peter and Anna Maria flatten the earth nearby with their hooting, rolling bodies.

It is time for an intervention, but his Inah beats him to it. She is already at Philip's side, simultaneously pulling both the boy and his trousers upright.

"Philip, come with me," she gently croons, directing the sniffling boy toward the parsonage while waving a wooden spoon threateningly behind her back at her own children. "Let's find Martin. I have *Butterkuchen* and a bowl of blackberries on the table. I will pour us some milk, and you can tell me what those," she calls over her shoulder, "*criminals* just did to you."

But before she follows her guest into the house, she spins around, her spoon still poised in a threatening stance, and says, "I heard all of it, *meine Lieben*. Yes, I did. Every mendacious word. *Old Man* Werth is still very much alive and working on the railway in St. Louis, did you know? And seeing as how he never married, I can't see how that dear man possibly left a wife behind to roam the grove at night. I think I will invite Herr and Frau Werth from across the road over for supper tonight. That way, you can apologize to them for telling such a terrible falsehood about their brother. And after that, you will walk to the Blumes' house and scrub their privy for them before prayers. And since you wouldn't have a bed to sleep in tonight or any 'moonless night' if it weren't for the generosity of these wonderful people, I will let you sit in the outhouse — the one Hermann Werth dug himself — to count your blessings while everyone else eats lunch. And you — "

The wooden spoon turns and bares its teeth at him and Walther.

" — are no help at all."

He does not argue. He never does, not with his Inah, at least. There is no need. She is always right about such things. He merely smiles his admiration and bows his head, taking note of the twitch of her own lips before she turns away to minister to the poor in spirit.

"Children," he says, standing and folding Walther's hand in his own. "Come. Let's sit in the *Schulhaus* and study the Eighth Commandment. Again. For you seem to have forgotten what harm comes from telling lies."

Peter and Anna Maria rise soberly from the grass.

"And let us make one thing clear," he is looking directly at Anna Maria. "Frau Werth generously comes one afternoon a week to help scrub the floors of the *Schulhaus*, so that you and the other girls don't have to do it alone."

Anna Maria hangs her head in shame.

"And no one has ever died in that outhouse."

But he cannot help himself.

"Though Hermann Werth did once tell me that something bit him on his backside in there."

+ + +

The second scream of the day comes from the direction of the barn.

"Your turn," Inah says to him, not even looking up from the stove.

"Indeed."

He steps out into the afternoon sunshine in time to see his Katherine, mouth open wide in a continuous wail, running toward him from the direction of the garden. Seven more children spill out of the open barn door and follow the wailing to its source.

"My Kitty," he says, landing on his knees in front of her red, howling face and steadying her hot cheeks in his hands for a better view. The girl is crying the blue right out of her cornflower eyes. The children circle around them in the hot sun like soldiers on guard. "What is wrong?"

But it is Anna Maria who answers.

"She got stung! All over! And over and over again—"

"There's another wasp nest, Vater," Johann interrupts. "Under the west eave of the barn, just above the compost pile."

"And they're angry!" Dorothea Blume points toward a small, shape-shifting cloud forming just above the compost pile.

"How—"

But Loretta cuts him off. "It was Nathanael. He was poking at it with a stick from the loft—"

"—and Kitty was standing under it—" Dorothea continues.

"When it fell," Loretta finishes. The twin sisters nod at each other. They are always completing each other's sentences.

Nathanael crosses him arms in self-defense. "I didn't know Kitty was in the garden."

"Everyone, in the house," he urges, reaching out a hand to nab a passing Blume boy by the wrist. "Run home and get your father, Nathanael. Tell him there's another nest swarming. And tell him why."

The boy averts his eyes and blushes before nodding dutifully and taking off across the road, steering wide of the barn.

"Now, Kitty," he pulls his distraught daughter closer. Full sunlight will give him the best viewing. "Just how many kisses did those little beasts give you?"

He counts at least seven welts on her neck alone. Mercy! Thankfully, none of them are swelling out of proportion, and his daughter's sniffling is proof that she can breathe just fine. "Come with me, brave girl." He stands and leads her toward the parsonage. "Let's get in out of the sun and show Mutti what pretty stings you're wearing. I bet she'll have something cool to soothe your hot neck and something sweet to settle your sour tummy."

She does, and he leaves his exasperated bride with the hungry horde in order to help smoke the nest. "I'll take them all to the creek after lunch, I promise."

Ludwig Blume already has a fire built near the compost pile by the time he reaches the barn.

"Most of them seem to have settled or moved on, and those left are about to be drowned." His neighbor nods toward a bucket standing ready at his feet on the ground. It smells strongly of Lesta's soap and peppermint weed.

"Here." Ludwig hands him a long stick with a burning cloth tied on the end.

He shores his nerves and then steps forward beyond the smoke screen with the burning end of the stick pointed toward the open nest on the ground. Ludwig follows behind, reaching around him to upend the full bucket over the nest. The two of them race back to the other side of the fire before turning to look.

They stare and wait for a spell before Ludwig offers a somber, "Seems like it's time."

He nods. He is in complete agreement. He just doesn't want to be the one to suggest it.

"It's the third nest this summer." The tall man walks over to inspect the barn's walls behind the safety of the fire. He points up through the smoke toward where the nest had been hanging just an hour before. "See that hole up there in the wall? And that's not the only one. I can see at least four more from here."

So that's how Nathanael knocked the nest down from the loft!

"Not much to keep wasps from building more nests if the wood is rotting." Ludwig kicks at the base of the barn, puncturing a soft spot with his booted toe. "The barn's aging too fast. It's the low ground. Too much water drains this direction."

He gives the matter the respectful silence it is due. It is not his decision to make and he has not been invited to offer his opinion.

"Can't have school children running around next month with wasp nests hiding in every corner."

No, we cannot. He waits and prays.

"I will talk to Friedrich tomorrow. He won't like it," Ludwig sighs. "He and his brother built this barn. And we heard our first sermons here before the school was ever built. But," the words are slow to come, "it's time to pull her down and build us a real church, Herr Pfarrer."

The Lord's mercies are new every morning. And noon.

+ + +

The day's third burst of bawling comes from the direction of the cemetery.

All of the children, except for Walther and Josef who are napping, are splashing in the creek, and after leaving Johann in charge of the noisy crowd, he picks his way through snarls of sumac and cockleburs to see what new storm of distress is brewing in the grove.

Inah is already hovering over the little storm cloud when he arrives on the scene.

Loretta Blume, who minutes before politely excused herself from the creek to use the haunted outhouse, is now kneeling at Alwin Werth's grave, elbows on her knees and head in her hands. The girl is weeping.

Inah intercepts him before he can get too close to the girl and diverts his path a few feet away.

"What's the matter?"

His wife's eyebrows are arched almost to her hairline, and her red lips are purple from being pressed together too tightly for too long. He recognizes this expression. She is doing her utmost not to laugh. She pushes one fist against her lips and points with her free hand to the ground directly in front of Loretta.

There on the grass lies a pile of—What, exactly? He leans closer to get a better view, and then he immediately turns away.

"Are those squirrel tails?" he inquires under his breath.

But his wife snorts into her fist and walks farther away, bending over to study a nearby dandelion as if it is the rarest of flowers.

He turns back toward the grave and lowers himself beside Loretta.

It is indeed a pile of squirrel tails, as well as—he picks up a stick from the ground to move a few choice, fluffy tails aside—a bird's head. A snakeskin. A cat tail. Understanding floods over him, for the orange-and-white striped pattern on the cat tail looks remarkably similar to that of the Blumes' tailless tomcat, Frankfurt.

He rests a fatherly hand on Loretta's shoulder and soothes, "Well, now we know."

Inah's skirts swoosh past him toward the parsonage, her mouth buried deep in the crook of her elbow, and he has to bite his own lip to keep vigil proper to the girl's devastation.

But in all seriousness, who in their small world would cut off Frankfurt's tail and keep it as a trophy? And how did it,along with all of these other morbid keepsakes, end up on Alwin's grave?

He pats Loretta's shoulder and, gently leading her away from the bizarre pile, drops her off at the parsonage door for the consolation of the brethren. Then he wheels about and heads toward the creek to question his primary suspect. But upon passing by Alwin's grave, a much better idea comes to him.

The best way to catch a thief is to steal his credit.

He swoops down and gathers the grisly stash into his trouser pockets. Then, returning to the parsonage to beg some snacks from the keeper of the pantry, he takes the bait to the creek.

The children sprawl on the bank to eat their biscuits, and he starts, "Did I ever show you my collection?"

Nathanael Blume takes the bait. "What collection?"

"My pelts. From hunting."

"You hunted, Vater?" Johann asks.

"As a boy, yes. With my own father."

"Where?"

"In the fields and woods near our farm."

Anna Maria sits up on her knees. "Did you ever catch a bear?"

"Your Opa shot a bear once. I shot mostly squirrels and ducks. I even shot a snake out of a tree."

Thankfully, this is all true if a bit weak in detail and context. He begins to pull the trophies out of his pockets, one by one, laying them out on the ground before him. He is careful not to pull Frankfurt's tail into sight. No sense in upsetting the rest of the Blumes. When he lays down the bird's head, he catches his man.

"Hey!" Peter calls out, jumping to his feet.

"Yes, son?"

Peter looks him in the eye, first accusingly and then questioningly and then, after his cheeks and neck grow red, uneasily.

"Did you want to say something?"

Peter looks down at the ground. "No. I just . . ."

"You just what?"

The boy turns almost completely away, putting his hands in his pockets and shrugging. "I like your squirrel tails. That's all."

After the Blume children leave for home, he pulls Peter to the side and shows him Frankfurt's tail. "Did you do this?"

The boy nods.

"How?"

Moments of tormented silence pass before an uncomfortable, "With the hatchet. From the barn."

He will rehang the tools well above Peter's head tonight.

"But his tail was already half-off, Vater, I promise!"

"What do you mean?"

"I found him stuck in one of Herr Blume's traps near the creek. I found all of them like that—except the bird and the snake. The squirrels were already dead in the traps when I found them, and I thought, well, they didn't need their tails anymore."

"That was not for you to decide."

Peter looks away.

"What about Frankfurt?"

"I saved him, Vater! He was still alive, but his tail was caught. I set him free."

It is all too strange not to be the truth, though he is at a loss to find a punishment to fit the crime. "You stole from Herr Blume."

"He doesn't eat the tails."

"Animals are not sacrificed for meat only, son. Regardless, you took the tails from Herr Blume's traps. You stole them from him, and so you will return everything to him."

"The bird and the snakeskin aren't his. I found them in the grove."

"Perfect. Then you will offer them to Herr Blume as well, in apology for taking what was not yours in the first place."

It is already out of his mouth, so he cannot retract it. Peter's bird head certainly makes a better insult than an apology, but perhaps Lesta Blume will see the humor in it all. His Inah certainly will.

He is walking his son across the Fireling Road when he says, "Loretta found your loot lying on Alwin's grave. It upset her very much. Why did you leave them lying outside like that?"

"I didn't."

"Then, how did they get there?"

Peter shrugs. "Maybe the wind blew them out of the tree."

"The tree?"

"I store all of my tails and heads in that big hole in the cottonwood. Near the graves."

"Ah, I see."

He is appalled that his son has such a collection. But he cannot help himself.

"Honestly, I couldn't make heads or tails of the matter."

+ + +

The fourth and final cry of the day comes from the parsonage loft.

He doesn't dare suggest it is Inah's turn, not after evening prayers, and definitely not after her hardworking shoes are retired for the day. The night watch is always his.

"I'll go."

"And I will love you forever," she hums from her side of the bed. "Oh, Klaus— " she reaches out suddenly in the dark, "If it is Walther at the window again, put him right back to bed. No talking. No coddling. You reward that boy with too much attention, and he'll never learn to stay put."

"I coddle him," he yawns, "because he looks just like you."

The ladder to the loft creaks under his feet, and he fears waking up the other children. But all breathing remains steady in the night, and only Walther's small frame is silhouetted by the far window.

"Son," he whispers, kneeling by the boy. "You cried out."

"I did not," Walther responds full-voiced.

He begins to shush the boy but then stops. What is the use? Walther is too young to know how to whisper, and his siblings are accustomed to all manner of noises, night and day, at this point. If they wake up, they'll just turn over. He hears Katherine rustle and resettle under her blanket that very moment.

"If you did not cry out, then who did?"

"The night."

"The night cried out?"

"Yes."

He observes his young son standing in the moonlight, transfixed by whatever it is that stirs a juvenile imagination. He is certain he heard the boy, not the night, calling out earlier, but what is to be gained from proving the past at the expense of the present? He looks out the window toward the dark line of trees, trying to perceive what has captured the attention of his sensitive son. He breathes, he settles, he listens, and he smiles. Yes, there it is. A wild, familiar strain of music cuts through the crickets and the locusts. It is an omnipresent song. It has not been so long since he last heard it, but it has been too long since he last paid it attention. And what a pleasant song it is, so natural to this grove. And what a shame that his old, preoccupied ears have grown too accustomed to its sounding to appreciate it.

"Yes, Walther. I hear it. But the night is not crying."

Big, round eyes turn his way.

"Crying is for sadness, and the night is happy. Can you hear the trees smiling? They are happy to meet the wind."

Walther holds his ears at attention as only a child can. Then, in a moment of recognition, the boy bounces up and down on his toes. "Yes! They are happy!"

He scoops the boy into his arms and lays him next to Katherine on the cot.

"The night is whistling, son."

He tucks the coverlet under Walther's soft chin.

"We live in a whistling grove."

✢ ✢ ✢

Inah is not yet asleep when he reenters their bedroom.

"You coddle him," she groans.

Josef stirs in his crib at the foot of the bed.

"Shh. You'll wake the baby," he teases, brushing off the bottom of his feet before tucking them under the blanket.

"We have too many children."

"We can never have too many children."

She turns toward him, nestling her warm cheek in the crook of his shoulder.

"Good. Because God is giving us another one. In the new year."

The Church

Chapter Nine

Saint Perle

+ 1882 +

They pull down the barn, but they do not build the church on the low ground. There is no need, for the peak of the gently inclining land, the prime plot in the entire grove, soon becomes available.

"Herr Pfarrer," Alma Werth wins his attention with a gentle hand on his shoulder. She hands him a tin of cool water. "Drink this."

He is sitting on the half-buried wagon wheel, watching the smoke rise from what is left of the parsonage. Soot-faced men are sifting through ashes with pitchforks. Women are carrying buckets of water from the creek. His children are—Where are his children? He looks about.

"Noberta took them home with her," Alma explains.

The air stinks, and he knows he will take this stink with him to the grave.

When Doktor Freese approaches, the older man's solemn expression says it all. The flame of hope he had been fanning deep within his chest suddenly chokes, and he slides to the ground, winded, the rough wheel pulling at the back of his coat.

"She was resting in bed like you thought," Doktor Freese confirms. "She had Perle with her. I don't think either of them woke up. Or if they did, the smoke overtook them quickly before they could suffer much. That is a mercy, Herr Pfarrer."

Alma keens from behind him, "'The LORD gave, and the LORD hath taken away.'"

It is seconds before he can say it, and in those seconds, he is Jacob, wrestling with God on the ground. Finally, and with the stink burning his throat, he begrudges, "'Blessed be the name of the LORD.'"

He and the children spend the night with the Freeses. Noberta says nothing to him, only replenishes his coffee cup whenever he takes a sip and replaces on his plate whatever bits of cornbread he manages to swallow. She leaves the cup and plate before him long after the children and Doktor are in bed, and she lights an oil lamp on the table and sits with him, her knitting in her lap, long into the night.

"It is better not to have children," he finally says.

"Is it?"

And then he weeps. He weeps into his hands, into his arms, onto the table, and over his plate. He weeps, and she sits, and he weeps some more. When there are no tears left in him, she stands to pour him some water from a pitcher and then reseats herself exactly as before, knitting and purling soundlessly from across the table. It is her silence that draws him out.

"It would be better if Perle had never been born."

"Maybe for you," she concedes, "but surely not for Perle."

He thinks on this. He knows she is right, but he cannot find, let alone grasp, the truth in the cold, dark void that is pressing in upon him.

"You are thinking of your own loss, Herr Pfarrer, not of Perle's gain."

Yes. But, "To perish," he has to spit the words out, "in a fire."

"To live forever in Jesus." Noberta looks up from her wool, nonplussed. "Perle was knitted together by God in Inah's womb. She was born and loved and baptized, and she now rests from her labors, however short they were. Would you deny your child—anyone—the promise of life eternal simply because she might suffer for a few minutes in this world? Would you deny Perle her existence, just so you don't have to suffer the loss of her?"

He can neither deny nor confirm anything in this darkness, but he argues, "My children have no mother."

"Your children have a mother, but she has died."

So matter-of-fact is her response, but neither of them dare voice aloud, "Your wife has died," lest the darkness overcome him.

"Do not take from your children the joy of the last thirteen years, Herr Pfarrer. Their mother is still their mother even in death. Though your children now wait for the resurrection of the dead. So you must reassure them of this promise of God, that they will see their mother again. With their own eyes. Do not withhold from them the comfort that is rightfully theirs."

The flame poised above the lamp shivers suddenly in a draft, but the light is in no danger of extinguishing. Noberta is wise and keeps her lamp trimmed and full of oil.

The children will look to him alone, now that his Inah—he gasps for air. The darkness is closing in on him. It is stealing his breath. It is suffocating him.

"Drink this."

Noberta rises and retrieves a corked crock from a nearby shelf. She pours the amber liquid into a small glass and sets it before him. He obeys, swallowing the liquid-sting, gasping once again, and then falling onto his arms to weep anew.

She sits, knitting and purling and watching and waiting with him in the night.

He is finally spent, and he admits, "I cannot do this without her."

She neither confirms nor denies. She simply states, "The Lord teaches us to pray, always."

He moans to hear the truth from someone else's lips, and it is only when he lifts his wet face and sees her gray brow furrowing in the light of the lamp that he remembers what he never should have forgotten.

"Forgive me, Noberta. I'm so sorry. I should not have wished my children away."

She raises her eyes to his. They are dry of tears, but they radiate a pain and loss as magnificent as his own. "It is not better when they are never born, Herr Pfarrer. I promise."

Fourteen pregnancies — that he knows of — and still no children for her and the doctor to hold and raise and nurture and, yes, bury.

"'The LORD gave,'" he dares, "'and the LORD hath taken away.'"

She says it without hesitation, "'Blessed be the name of the LORD,'" and her immediacy chastens him.

\+ + +

Friedrich Werth and Ludwig Blume join him at the Freeses' table the next morning.

"We think a bird's nest fell into the stovepipe, Herr Pfarrer," Friedrich explains, bending and twisting the hat in his hands. "The fire spread from there to the roof. It happened quickly."

He tries to speak, but he cannot. Noberta rescues him with another cup, this one steaming. The scalding coffee shocks his tightening throat into opening again.

Doktor Freese adds, "We will not rebuild the parsonage in the grove."

He is surprised. He is also strangely relieved.

Ludwig clasps his hands together in his lap. "I've been thinking for some time about building a new house on some acreage further east. The boys are bigger and can manage the traps on their own, and I'd like to move my plow across the creek for good, nearer the fields. Now seems as good a time as any."

"You and the children will move into the Blume house across the road." Friedrich is still twisting his hat. "Ludwig's cabin is bigger than my brother's was, and the well is deeper. And the smokehouse out back will serve you well."

"I just put a new door on the chicken house," Ludwig adds, "and Lesta and the girls already moved Inah's hens into their new home."

The man speaks her name with such ease, as if the world doesn't turn sideways at the sound.

"We think it'll make a fine parsonage, Herr Pfarrer," Friedrich assures, finally daring to look up from his crumpled hat. "If you approve."

He nods. He does not care where they live. He cannot care about anything, presently.

Doktor Freese leans forward in his chair. "Noberta and I already ordered lumber for the church, and with your permission, we all think," he gestures toward his wife standing at the stove and to the men sitting around the table, "it best to build the church on the high ground."

On the ashes of his wife and child.

Noberta turns from the stove then, holding his gaze for support. She is so maternal. He marvels at how the Lord makes mothers even of the childless. Surely He will remember the needs of the motherless.

He takes another throat-opening swig of the hot coffee. "Inah said to me just last week that it would make her uncomfortable to walk out our door and look down upon the church. I think it fitting that, when our Lord returns to raise her from the grave, she will look up and see the church for which she prayed so long."

They gather what remains they can and bury Inah and Perle at the western edge of the cemetery, nearest where the new church will be built.

Chapter Ten

Saint Noberta

✢ 1891 ✢

"What are you making?"

Little Opal Iken perches on a stool near the open door of the Freeses' shed, licking sugar granules off the fingers of one hand while crushing a half-eaten doughnut with the fingers of the other. The smell of hot lard wafts in from the yard. Anna Maria and Katherine are frying doughnuts in Noberta's big copper kettle hanging over the outdoor fire pit, and all of the Iken children and grandchildren as well as a few stray Blumes, Werths, and Lindels are hovering in and around the outbuildings to be on hand for each fresh batch.

"I'm making a jewelry box," Doktor Freese murmurs, training his right eye along the plane of the freshly scraped pine board. The slightest hollow—more of a shadow than a depression—remains near the end of the board, and he picks up the scraper and applies himself afresh.

"I will put my necklace in it," Opal decides, her mouth around a too-large bite of sugared dough.

"No," he overrules, never breaking concentration down the line. "This box is big enough for one jewel only."

He runs his hand over the board. Yes, that will do nicely. He takes off his spectacles and pulls a hankie from his pocket to wipe at his forehead before turning to look at his young companion. "This box will hold the most precious jewel in all the world."

"A ring?"

"My wife."

His Noberta. She fell asleep in Jesus during the night, and after recovering from the terrible shock of waking up to her coldness, he waited patiently for the sun to rise before riding to the Werths for assistance. Pfarrer arrived within the hour followed by Lesta and her sisters who washed and dressed Noberta for burial. Now his bride of 45 years lies on a board on a table in the front room of the house, her arms crossed over the smocked bodice of her green dress, while the children, the Ikens and Blumes and Werths and Lindels and all of their children in the faith, play games and eat doughnuts in the yard. It is exactly as Noberta would want it.

"Frau Doktor is dead," Opal confirms, swallowing the last of her doughnut. "Vater told me."

"Yes."

"Oma is dead, too."

"Yes."

"Is Oma in a jewelry box?"

"Yes, she is."

Opal nods, satisfied, and having grown bored with both the scraping and the conversation, slides down from the stool.

"Herr Doktor," she turns in the doorway, "can I have a jewelry box?"

"Not yet."

"But who will make mine?"

"Someone who loves you."

"Vater," she nods. "Or Onkel Walther."

And then she is gone, most likely for another doughnut. He picks up a chisel and hammer from the work bench and turns back toward the smooth casket. His own stomach is too full of feeling for food, and he wants to carve a cross on each side of the casket before supper. As well as some begonias. Noberta loves—loved—begonias.

He is chiseling a petal out of the center of the coffin lid when young Frieda Lindel brings him a mug of coffee. Her tiny hands are capable, but still the dark liquid sloshes and spills as she lifts it above her shoulders and sets it atop the coffin. The coffee immediately stains the virgin wood, but he is not riled. This, too, is just as Noberta would want it. She was always wiping up Frieda's spills. How she loved the young girl's company in the house, though her juvenile help usually proved unhelpful in the end. He is slow in pulling out his hankie. One by one, he dabs at each inky splotch with the tenderness of a kiss.

"Thank you, Frieda. Did you make the coffee?"

She nods, unblinking.

He smiles. Frieda's coffee is better spilled than swallowed, as Noberta would say, and so he moves the mug and his tools to the workbench. "Would you like to see the inside?"

Another unblinking nod.

He lifts the unattached lid with both hands and stands it against the wall. The tingly aroma of pine refreshes the air.

Frieda, still unblinking, takes one step closer to the coffin and peers inside.

"Her head will go here." He pats the wider end of the coffin.

"How will she breathe?"

"She is done breathing. For now."

"I don't like this box."

"I do."

"Not me. It's dark. And tight."

She is right, so he does not counter. "I nailed the roof onto Frau Doktor's house to keep out the rain. I will nail the lid on her coffin to do the same. It is what husbands do."

This does not require her input, and she moves away and climbs onto Opal's vacant stool. "Tell me a story, Herr Doktor."

He knows what story she wants: the one about her father, Hans, Jr., the first baby born in the grove; the first baby he delivered in this strange, scruffy land; the first baby Noberta swaddled and kept warm through the night as the mother slept. He sighs. Noberta would do this time and time again in the years to come, though never for her own children. No, that privilege was withheld from her by God. He swallows and decides to tell Frieda a different story, one she has never heard. He replaces the lid on the coffin, picks up his chisel and hammer, and says, "I met Frau Doktor in Germany."

"She was a cook."

"No," he smiles, "she was a bell maker."

Frieda sits up straight. She has not heard this before.

"Her family owned — still owns — the oldest bell foundry in all of Europe."

"That's where bells are born," Frieda nods.

"Yes." His hands work the chisel and hammer, but his mind wanders back to a Sunday morning in Hessen. Noberta had stepped into his church, her thick, auburn braids adorned with pasque flowers, her gloved hand extended to caress the rope hanging from the bell tower — the very rope he was holding — like a mother her child. He had followed her movement into the church that morning, and he has been watching her movements ever since. From nave to grave.

"My church commissioned a bell from the famous Rincker family," he explains to Frieda, "and Frau Doktor accompanied her older brothers to the dedication."

"We hang bells on Jesse."

Jesse is the Lindels' pony. The poor child. Born in this backcountry, she has never seen a real bell let alone heard one ring. The closest thing in the entire grove is the metal triangle hanging outside the *Schulhaus* for the teacher to clang at the end of recess.

"A church bell is much, much bigger. It's as big as Frau Doktor's kettle in the yard, and it rings so loudly that even your Opa would be able hear it in his farthest field."

And that is when he makes the decision. Staring at his bride's coffin, he considers the entire matter within seconds. Yes. Yes, it is just as Noberta would want it. But first—he turns toward Frieda—he must tend to her many children. She would want that, too.

"Bring your stool over here, Frieda. We will carve a bell on Frau Doktor's coffin."

+ + +

He writes a letter to Cousin Heinrich that night, and Noberta's beautiful bell arrives by the end of the season. Too late for her burial, but not too late for ringing over her grave.

Peter Iken wants to be the one to do it, and he does not argue with the boy. Nor does he argue with Walther and Josef when they insist on the same privilege. In the end, six boys total will take turns ringing out Noberta's teller while Nathanael Blume stands watch and counts. This is just as Noberta would want it.

The next Sunday morning, they all gather outside the newly constructed belfry and Pfarrer prays and blesses Noberta's memorial bell, dedicating it for service to the Lord. Seven spirited young men promptly toss aside their hats and crowd around the trailing rope as Doktor Freese walks hand-in-hand with Frieda down to Noberta's gave. *One, two, three*—the bell begins to toll across the grove—*four, five, six*—such clear, vibrant tones! The sound waves tremble in and around and through him, and he closes his eyes so as not to miss a single note of Noberta's life-song.

10, 11, 12 . . .

Behind his eyelids, he sees her as he always sees her: ageless, looking over her shoulder at him, drawing him into her joyful self with her welcoming eyes.

Himself, he was nothing to look at. He was already worn and lined when he met her—nine years her senior—but she had spent her entire youth in the company of older men. She preferred him to every young, spry admirer.

"You suit me," was all she ever said about the matter.

27, 28, 29 . . .

Her own lines in life came with the death of each of their children, but he loved those lines. Every one of them. They etched the history of their shared losses into her every smile and laugh. They daily, hourly reminded him of the tender, motherly heart that was his to guard and protect, however empty his quiver. Those lines were the strange, blessed fruit of their union and made him bold to speak with enemies in the gate. He would gladly die for his family of two, and he would suffer every loss over again for the privilege of caring for Noberta's mournful lines just one more day.

41, 42, 43 . . .

Noberta rarely looked in a mirror. They never got around to hanging one in their home, and his small shaving glass was knocked off the table by—Was it an Iken child? Or a Blume? He cannot remember, but it does not matter. Noberta helped him shave after that, and he much preferred her attentive fussing over the convenience of any reflection.

But Noberta never saw the way her griefs were mapped on her face, and so she was not aware that there was anything to hide. She met every face with the bold interest of one who desires to see. She did not know to be afraid of being seen in return. Perhaps that is why so many children, young and old, told Noberta their troubles.

Who will listen to all of them now? And who will cut his hair?

52, 53, 54 . . .

Last year, she gave him a kiss for Christmas. She also gave him a tin of coffee and a new scraper and a green shirt made from the same material as her favorite dress—she loved when their clothes coordinated and matched—but it was the kiss he wanted. It is the kiss he treasures still. It is the kiss he cannot have ever again, not this side of glory.

60, 61, 62.

62 tolls for 62 years on this earth. He was blessed to spend 45 of them at her side, but now she is with Jesus for all eternity. He is jealous of the Lord and His nearness to her. He looks up into the heavens for a glimpse of their glorious reality, but he sees only as through a glass, darkly.

"Are you sad, Herr Doktor?"

Frieda is peering up at him keenly, still holding his hand.

"Yes. But only for me. I'm happy for Frau Doktor."

And he is. For his own days are written in the Book, and soon enough, the Lord will call him to join them both. That is just as Noberta would want it.

Chapter Eleven

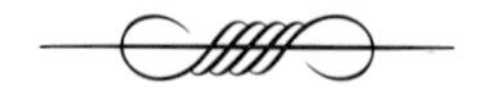

Saint Ernst

+ 1918 +

It begins with a fearful, easterly wind.

"My cousin in Cincinnati writes, they've draped *Germania* with the American flag."

"The statue? Why?"

"To keep the townies from burning down the neighborhood."

Renate Freese shivers behind the post office counter where she is sorting mail.

"There's trouble up north, too," chimes in another voice from the other side of the partition. "My uncle in Milwaukee sent us a clipping from their newspaper. There's a Wisconsin Loyalty League that's publishing sedition maps with all of the German districts labeled as centers of 'disloyalty.'"

"*Mein Gott*. They might as well be handing out torches and clubs."

"The trouble's much closer than that," offers a gravelly, deeper third voice. "My brother owns a bookstore in Chicago, and they've banned all German books in the city. Officials made him remove *die Heilige Schrift* from his shop window. The Holy Bible!"

But it is her own brother's announcement over dinner that makes the hair on Renate's forearms prickle.

"*Rosenstrasse* has been renamed 'Rose Street' in Bramble."

That is the nearest town.

Mama simultaneously sighs into her soup and beseeches the air with both hands. "I ask, what possible harm is there in a street name?"

"It's not the name, Mama. It's the language."

"Yes, *mein Sohn*, but what does it matter? So the street is named after a German? Campbell's Feed Store is named after an Irishman."

"But it's not the Irish who're shooting at Americans."

Mama's hands are pleading with the air again. "How can anyone possibly be offended by the name Rosen? Karl Rosen fought in the Civil War. He died a hero of the North. How much more patriotic can a German be?"

"American," her brother corrects. "Karl Rosen was an American, and so are we."

"American by birth, yes," Mama admits, "but German by blood. Or have you already forgotten that your *Opa* bought this land with *Gulden*?"

"That is the exact kind of sentiment that gets streets renamed in this country."

"All I'm saying is that America was settled by immigrants. Everyone here came from somewhere else at some point or other."

It is an exaggeration, but they let it stand lest Mama's hands tire out before dessert.

"Edgar Reinking told me it was the Johnson family who petitioned for the change."

This information is for Papa, but it is Mama who responds. "What in the world do the Johnsons have against Civil War heroes?"

"They live on *Rosen*—on Rose Street."

Mama's hands restate the question.

"They have to write it on every piece of mail, Mama."

Papa finally moves to reply, but he is not one to rush into any conversation. He pauses to take a long, contemplative drink from his glass before lifting his napkin to his mouth, folding it twice, and setting it on his plate. "The Johnsons' only son died in Le Hamel last week. Shot in the trenches, and by a German gun," he adds, looking directly at Mama. "The Johnsons are grieving, Cordula. Many of our neighbors are grieving."

Renate is relieved that Papa understands. She folds her own napkin and confirms, "They are afraid."

In truth, she too is afraid, though she does not say it aloud. Papa knows, of course—he always knows what she is thinking—and he turns his quiet, companionable omniscience upon her with a smile. She loves the way his bushy cheeks push up into hills, turning his eyes into two setting suns. He reaches out to brush a calloused knuckle against her cheek in the old way, the way he used to do when she was a child, and nods: a silent promise to discuss it with her later.

It is after the supper dishes are washed and put away that Papa asks her to help him sweep out the mill. Mama will not follow them there, not in the evening after she has already beaten the sawdust from her shoes.

"Herr König was asked to retire last week," he softly states as they walk side by side in the twilight. "After 30 years of teaching."

Herr König is Papa's longtime friend as well as her former *Gymnasium* teacher. He is the best teacher in the county, maybe even the state. "Why?"

"'Too aged to be effective,' is what I believe they told him."

This is nonsense. Herr König is sounder of body and sharper of mind than most men in Bramble, young or old.

"Who will teach on such short notice?"

"They've hired Jack Collins to replace him."

"But he's older than Herr König."

"Yes."

This is all Papa says, but Renate pushes the matter. "They wouldn't have fired him if his name were Mr. King."

His silence is confirmation.

"I'm afraid, Papa. I'm afraid of their ignorance. Are we safe in *Rauschenhain*?"

"In Whistle Grove? Yes. From our neighbors, at least."

But she can hear the concern in his voice.

"I will not pretend with you, Nata," he continues, his face hidden from her by the indigo of evening. "It is the people outside of our county who concern me. To our neighbors . . . Well, we are their customers and employees and friends. We are just as much citizens of this land as they are, and they know it. But to everyone else outside Whistle Grove, we are imports with umlauts, and we are related to the enemy."

"Everyone is related to the enemy of someone."

"Throughout time, yes. But today, it is our cousins who are killing their sons. This is war, Nata, and everyone wants to do his part. My fear is that, in their eagerness to defend the national cause, they will mistake our county line as the front line."

"But our sons are serving on the front line, too. And our brothers and our—" but she cannot say it without her voice breaking.

He stops then, turning toward her and wrapping her fear in the familiar safety of his burly arms. "Oh, *mein Liebchen*. I know, I know. 'The Lord is teaching us to pray,' as Pfarrer Iken always says."

✝ ✝ ✝

They see the storm coming, but they are horrified when it settles its cloud directly over the grove.

The very next Sunday, their beautiful church—the tall white clapboard edifice designed by her *Grossonkel*, built by her *Opa*, and constructed of boards milled by her Papa's own hands—is cowering under the trees, battered and bruised like the assaulted victim of some vile perpetrator. Every window has been bashed in with rocks, and the entire north side of the white-washed building is stained with the large, grotesque yellow letters, "S-A-U-E-R-K-R-A-U-T." Their beloved sanctuary, their ark built in faith to carry them safely through the dangerous waters of this hateful world, now stands wrecked and desecrated in the morning sun. Renate turns away from the scene, reminded of the Lord, flogged and bleeding, standing before the Sanhedrin on that Good Friday so long ago. Some things never change.

"*Herr, erbarme dich!*" Pastor Iken prays aloud, big tears rolling down his wrinkled cheeks.

"Lord, have mercy indeed," Papa whispers.

"This is the work of the Johnsons!" a woman cries out.

"No!" Papa counters, raising his voice to equal the woman's. "This is not the work of anyone who knows us. This was done by someone who does not have to suffer looking us in the eye in the daylight. Remember that. Acts of shame are performed by shameful people, not by the Johnsons." He turns away from the violent scene, honoring the church's modesty in her present humiliation. "Come, Edgar. Nathanael. Help me pick up the glass. Simeon, Lowell, all of you boys, run home and grab some buckets, soap, and rags. We can all work together to set things aright as best we can, and then," he turns to Pastor Iken, "we can have church out here on the lawn. If that would that be all right, Herr Pfarrer?"

As the congregation disperses to attend to what they can, Renate follows Papa and holds out her skirt for him in which to collect the shards of glass.

"If Ernst comes home to this — " she starts, but she cannot finish the thought. She is too angry.

"Ernst is serving in the trenches, Nata." Papa bends to pick up another shard. "The depravity of man will come as no surprise to him."

Her thoughts run to the frontline as they always do. She sees the mud on his boots. She smells the gunpowder on his sleeve. She hears his voice saying, "Will you marry me?" and her throat tightens with emotion. She has only ever read those words in a letter and in the secret silence of her room. What she would give for Ernst to come home and say those words aloud to her, right now, and in the safety of this grove! But the grove — she looks around, seeing the glittering wreckage anew — it is no longer safe. Reality slaps her hard on the face, and her cheeks burn from the disgrace.

"All of your hard work, Papa," she mutters. "Ruined."

"Ruined?" He straightens to his full height, holding her to the spot with the strength of his stare. "Hardly."

She feels her color deepen, though she does not understand why.

"You think windows and siding are the only fruit of my hard work?"

She is missing something important, she knows, but her brain comes up with nothing.

"Nata, a man builds more than just walls and a roof when he builds a church. He builds muscles. He builds," Papa beats his fists against his chest, "character. He grows in knowledge. Of his trade, yes, but also of himself. I was a boy when my Papa laid Bethlehem's foundation, and I grew into a man building this church."

His eyes are on her face, but they are seeing someone — something — beyond her.

"'Tribulation worketh patience; and patience, experience; and experience, hope; and hope maketh not ashamed.'" Papa grins suddenly, his beard parting to make way for the fruit of hope. "No mere rock can shatter what is built from such materials. It is eternal. It is beyond the hand of any other man."

His voice is exultant, as if this morning is Bethlehem's Easter Sunday rather than her Good Friday, as if the litter scattered on the ground is wreckage from the stone that has been rolled away by angels rather than the garments of Christ cast aside by hateful men. He spreads his hands wide. "I milled these very boards alongside my Papa. From the ground up, he helped me build a man as much as a church. I tell you, Nata, no time is wasted when you work alongside your Papa, serving the Lord with gladness. This entire building could be razed, and I would have no regrets."

She tries not to regret the yellow letters profaning their church. It is hard.

"I enjoyed building this church, and I'll enjoy building another one if I have to. Only this time," his eyes are seeing her again, "it will be you and me who put in the new windows. You will learn to build some character of your own."

She cries at this. Her hands are occupied with the refuse of her father's labor, so she lets the tears run down her cheeks and baptize the broken glass.

"Do not think a mere man can take so much from us, *mein Kind.*" That tender, calloused knuckle nuzzles her wet cheek, and Papa throatily sings,

Nehmen sie den Leib,
Gut, Ehr, Kind und Weib:
lass fahren dahin,
sie haben's kein' Gewinn . . .

The world is at war, and Papa is singing. No time is wasted when singing alongside Papa, so she joins him,

. . . das Reich muss uns doch bleiben.

✢ ✢ ✢

They replace the windows, and they whitewash the church. They even raise an American flag in the yard of the grove, but it is not enough. A mound of horse manure is left on the steps of the church the following Sunday.

"Perhaps they wish to help us fertilize our fields," Frau Sarah Werth suggests.

Renate likes Frau Werth, and not only because she is Ernst's Mutter. The woman is feisty and friendly, especially to the youth in the grove. And Frieda Lindel once confided that it was Frau Werth who named the church all of those years ago. Knowing the patriarchs in the Lindel family, it must have taken a good portion of that character Papa likes to talk about for a young girl to win the ear of her elders.

The men make fast work of clearing the manure, and as they leave to spread it over Oskar Blume's nearest field, the women apply themselves to scrubbing the stoop.

"My brother Karl in Dubuque," Frau Werth begins, lowering herself onto her knees and rubbing a bar of Ivory against the bristles of a scrub brush. "He writes, they can no longer have *Kirche auf Deutsch*. It's now illegal to speak or sing in German in public places."

"Surely not, Sarah," Mama counters.

"It's true. And Iowa's not the only state to pass such a law."

"But what will he and *Grosstante* Käthe do?" asks Frieda Lindel, her head down, both of her hands pushing and pulling at a brush.

"They'll start singing in English," Frau Reinking grumbles, "or they'll keep singing German in jail."

"What about in Illinois?"

"We're too civilized here for such nonsense," Frau Werth assures, and the other women nod in agreement, missing her sarcastic tone.

The very next day, a threatening letter is published in the *Riverfield Post*, and the elders of Bethlehem gather in the church to discuss an appropriate course of action. The women sit outside the new open windows with their knitting, listening in.

"They've threatened to tar and feather Pfarrer."

"They'll do no such thing."

"They'll do it if we don't stop praying in German."

"It's an empty threat. There's no law against praying in German. This is America!"

"And it's Americans who're passing laws against us right and left."

"Not in Illinois."

"Not yet, you mean. Did you hear about that girl with pneumonia just two counties south of here? They pulled her from her sickbed and dragged her into the public square and made her kiss Old Glory, just because her name is Liesl."

"No one's going to pull our children from their beds in Whistle Grove. And no one's going to tar and feather Pfarrer. Our neighbors won't stand for it."

"Our neighbors won't stand for anything or anyone these days. That's the problem."

"I'm telling you, we should've switched to English the day the Lusitania sank."

"But *Kirche* can't be changed. It's Scripture."

"I'm not suggesting we change *Kirche*. I'm suggesting we sing it *auf Englisch*. Get the synod's new English hymnal. My family's been living in this grove for 70 years, now. We're Americans. It's time for us to start praying and singing in English."

"But God doesn't understand English."

Frau Werth snorts violently into her wool.

"*Meine Brüder*," Renate recognizes the calm, steady voice of Herr Lindel. The excitement quiets down in the pews, and Frau Werth swiftly manages her laughter at the sound of her older brother's voice. She also sits a little taller. "It is Pfarrer Iken we must think of. He has been our *Seelsorger* these past 50 years. It will be difficult for him to change how he prays and preaches at this point in his life."

What Herr Lindel is kindly not saying aloud is that Pastor Iken does not speak English.

"Yes, Hans," this affirmation is from Papa, "you are right. We must think of Pfarrer and do what is best for him. It is he who is being threatened."

The men murmur their agreement and resettle into a ponderous silence. It is a difficult matter.

"You know, Renate," Frau Werth calls easily from across the circle in the lawn, "I think you're right about the seminary."

She looks up in alarm, confused. What is this? She has never thought about the seminary let alone talked to Frau Werth about it. She glances quickly at Mama and the other women, but they are as baffled as she is, their needles stalled in midair.

"They do turn out fine young men these days," Frau Werth continues easily as if this is the most natural time and place to be talking about such things, and so loudly, too. "Think of it, all of those young men with German in their hearts and English on their lips. Though I do sometimes wonder if their education is too short in the end."

Renate's cheeks burn with shame. She wishes her own name had not been singled out by Frau Werth, not when they all should be praying instead of talking. Surely, the elders can hear this idle chatter!

"It seems to me, it would be mutually beneficial for a young pastor to be called to a church where there is an older, experienced pastor on-hand. The senior could mentor and support the younger, even as the younger assists and supports the elder. Did I tell you that Ernst considered entering the seminary? No? Well, he did, years ago, before the war . . ."

Frau Werth continues chatting easily, and only when the men resume their deliberation inside the church do the other women relax and resume their own industry, though many of them cast furtive, sidelong glances at the open windows, visibly distressed at no longer being able to hear what the men are saying. Thankfully, Frau Werth pauses in her storytelling when Herr Lindel stands and moves toward one of the open windows. The older man takes his time, casting an amused look onto the lawn before turning and addressing the men.

"I think we can all agree, that it is time for us to get our dear Pfarrer some help."

The moment passes too swiftly for her to be certain, but Renate thinks she sees Frau Werth cast an amused smile onto her needles, as well.

+ + +

No one in the county harms Pastor Iken, but neither do the people in the grove warm to Pastor Milhahn's urban ways. Much of the young man's preaching is lost in translation, and not simply because his sermons are in English.

"I never realized I could learn so much about so little," Mama carps on the walk home from the grove following one of Pastor Milhahn's particularly long sermons on eternal election. Nevertheless, she and Papa proudly board the young pastor in their own home, and despite the man's tendency toward intellectual ramblings regarding the writings of some theologian named Pieper, Mama considers him to be the catch of the grove. Renate suffers constant humiliation in the form of frequent gesticulations made from behind the man's back by Mama's opinionated hands, but Papa is always swift to the rescue.

"Cordula," he intones from whichever corner he is occupying at the moment, "no matter how hard you try, you will never fly like that. God gave you hands, not wings."

A letter from Ernst arrives in the autumn and with the news that he is coming home.

"He was shot," Frau Werth explains, her eyes red from crying. Ernst is her only son — her only child, an Isaac given to her and Herr Wilhelm Werth in their old age — and she has borne his absence with a courage that comes only from the Lord. "In knee-deep mud, in Saint-Mihiel. But he is alive, and he is coming home."

Renate prays to the same Lord for the same courage, for knowing Ernst is alive and coming home seems to double her fear of loss. There are oceans to cross and connections to meet and letter-less silences to endure. He is not home until he is home, and no amount of previous waiting tempers the torture of these final days, these final hours.

Frau Werth understands perfectly, for she says, "God gives us only today, Renate. Tomorrow is always in His hands, though sometimes it feels like He's holding Ernst forever in tomorrow. We must help each other be patient for the blessed day God turns tomorrow into today."

+ + +

Today finally comes with a frigid, northerly wind.

She is at the mill when he finds her, wrapped in Mama's coat and muffler, her cheeks stinging from the cold. She can barely feel her fingers let alone the broom in her hands, when he opens the door and meets her eyes.

He is the same, but he is changed. He is the same height, the same build, the same eyes; but he stands taller, wider, and wiser. He looks no different, but he looks at her differently. She has known him her whole life, but she is meeting him for the first time.

"Nata," he says, and the sound of his voice unlocks a wild grief in her. She moans at the violent release, and he is near her in an instant, taking the broom from her hands, pulling her heart against his own, kissing her wet cheeks and her dry lips, laughing and crying and singing her name.

Ernst is home.

Tomorrow is finally today.

Chapter Twelve

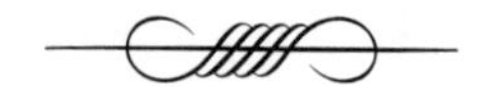

Saint Orville

+ 1944 +

It is another war, another today, with another son held at tomorrow's length, though it is Ruthie Werth whose mind wanders to the frontline every hour, visiting the sight, sound, smell, and taste of her husband lest she despair.

"We must help each other be patient," Mother Renate says as the two prepare salads for this evening's bazaar. Ruthie and the girls are living with Orville's parents. They moved in the very night he boarded the train for France. That was two years ago.

"The work of war is waiting on the Lord," Mother Renate continues. "Every night I pray tomorrow'll be the day the boys are lifted 'out of the miry clay.' Though, it's different for Frank and Orville than for their father. Ernst is still trying to rub the clay from his skin after those God-awful trenches."

But Orville and his older brother are seeing their fair share of clay, too. Orv's last letter relayed they were digging foxholes in the frozen forest floor to stay warm, though Ruthie suspects the holes have more to do with safety than the weather. She shivers.

"Pass me a spoon, and I'll get these nuts stirred in while you dress the girls."

Ruthie finds Miriam and Marta cuddled on the Werths' bed—the very place they were instructed not to be—with a large picture book open on their laps. She will scold them later, but for now, she stands just outside the door, listening as Miriam recites more than reads *The Three Bears* to her younger sister.

"Goldi-wocks was still as-weep," Miriam narrates, her finger moving faster along the lines than her narration. "Den she waked up an'," turning the page, "she wan outa da house an' Baby Bear cwied, 'No, stay! Pway wid me!'"

She really must find time to work with Miriam on her phonetics. The harvest got in the way of reading lessons this fall, but the two of them will be able to make up for lost time once Orv comes home and takes over the milking.

Marta's big, unblinking eyes follow her older sister's finger faithfully, her tiny treble asserting, "Again," the moment Miriam turns the final page. Marta's diction is always exact.

"Daughters of mine," Ruthie makes her move, "you are not allowed on Oma's quilt. And with your shoes on, too! Come down, now. Miriam, hand me the book."

Miriam's fingers and eyes linger on the colorful pages, but she allows the book to be taken from her hands. Marta, without hesitation, obediently rolls onto her stomach, pointing her soled toes toward the edge of the bed and expertly regulating the rate of her descent with fistfuls of the prohibited quilt. She is far too practiced in her dismount, but Ruthie lets the evidence pass unmentioned. There are worse things than her daughters' repeatedly hiding in plain sight, and she would prefer the precocious elder lure the amenable younger onto her grandmother's *verboten* bed than onto ladders, roofs, well-tops, haymows, and a thousand other more perilous perches outside. She takes Marta's hand and narrates over her shoulder down the hall, knowing full-well the promise of new information will motivate Miriam to follow her far more than any parental directive, "There'll be popcorn balls at the bazaar tonight. And Mrs. Daniels is making her peppermint divinity."

Miriam cheers from behind, and Marta adds an extra hop to her every other step.

Dressing the girls is easy work with the promise of sweets ahead, and within the hour, Papa Werth is driving all of his ladies, small and tall, to the grove in the shiny green Willys – Overland.

"Look, Maw-ty!" Miriam cries from the front seat in between her grandparents, pointing ahead at the glowing church through the windshield. "Candles in da windows! An' a Cwis'mas twee!"

When the car pulls to a stop, Ruthie swings open her door and lowers Marta to the frozen turf with a crunch. She can hear the Daniels boys clamoring in the dark amongst the tombstones in the cemetery. They are throwing snowballs at each other and shrieking at the resulting spray. She smiles, remembering. She used to do the very same thing with her brothers when she was young, but still, "Stay close to me, girls."

Matthew and LJ Daniels are good kids if a bit rambunctious, and who can blame them? Their father, too, is off fighting in the war but with the Pacific Fleet. Last they heard, Mark Daniels is somewhere near the Marshall Islands, wherever those are. She must remember to ask the boys to point out the islands on the map the next time she visits the old Werth farmhouse where the Daniels family boards. For when Mark first joined the Navy, his boys asked Papa Werth if they could hang a map of the world in the front sitting room. Papa not only said yes to his farmhand's precocious sons, but the sentimental WWI veteran bought the boys a box of red, white, and blue pushpins with which to track their father's progress across the ocean.

How Cherry can sleep at night knowing Mark is bobbing along on top of some foreign wave, Ruthie doesn't know. But then, her own husband is passing his days and nights under some French snowbank, and she still manages to get some sleep. She sucks in the familiar, reflexive breath that always rushes past her teeth with such stomach-roiling thoughts, and she breathes out her usual responsive, whispered prayer: "Lord, help!"

The church basement is warm with light, life, and love. Women and children and elderly men are all moving and talking at once, some wiggling out of coats, hats, and scarves; others arranging cakes and breads and handmade wares on tables; still others tuning fiddles, guitars, and horns near the piano; and everyone greeting and hugging each other as if they have not just seen each other in the pews that very morning.

The words "Bethlehem Bazaar" are painted in bright red letters across a bedsheet hung over the soundboard of the upright piano. It is new this year, this homegrown fundraiser of sorts, and it is a recent enterprise of the Ladies Aid Society which itself is not that old. Kickstarted at the beginning of the war by Miss Frieda Lindel and Mother Renate with the noble intent of beautifying the church, the guild of resourceful women in the congregation continue to muster monthly to polish precious metals, oil pews, plant flowers, scour the schoolhouse, and chase blue jays from the cemetery. Only when the war succeeded in extracting every able-bodied man from the grove did the glossy goal of beautification dull to mere routine maintenance. "Plumbing" and "pliers" began replacing "paraments" and "paraffin" in the secretarial minutes, and now every woman in the Ladies Aid makes sure to tuck a pair of work gloves in her purse ahead of every meeting.

Just last month, Ruthie and Cherry, with the assistance of a small but cat-like Oskar Blume, managed to replace the mouse-eaten rope in the church belfry with one woven by Viola Lindel's own hands, and Grandmother Freese, with the help of her attentive husband, fitted, planed, sanded, and finished a new door for Pastor Engel's splintered book cabinet. But it was when Frieda successfully replaced the toilet in the men's restroom all by herself that Papa Werth teased Mother Renate over supper, "I don't remember voting Frieda Lindel in as head trustee of the congregation."

"She's only taking care of what no man's bothered to do," Mother quickly defended her friend.

"That toilet wasn't bothering any man."

"Nonsense! It hasn't flushed properly for months."

"Which is why we all agreed to do our business at home and save the church a few dollars until the fighting's over."

Mother Renate pursed her lips at that. "Well, someone forgot to inform young Matthew Daniels of the fraternal fast. It took me two hours to clean up the mess."

That was when Papa threw back his head and laughed from his belly.

"Be serious, Ernst. It isn't funny."

"Oh, but it is!"

Ruthie remembers Mother's creamy cheeks drowning in a dangerous, crimson flash flood. "We wouldn't be having this conversation if you'd fixed that toilet yourself!"

Papa sobered quickly, straightening in his chair. "And why would I do that? When you women are so eager to do it for me?"

Whatever private conversations divided households that night, the public discourse in the back of the church the next morning proved complaisant. The men and women of the congregation never felt so unified in doctrine and practice as when rainwater collected in puddles on the church floor, pews, and altar. Every child was sent running home for towels and buckets, and the women busied their hands with mops and rags. The older men enlisted teenaged boys to climb up onto the roof for a proper assessment of the damage, and by the time everyone drove home after church that day, the men had a plan in place for repairing the roof and the women for raising funds: a Christmas market for the congregation and surrounding county complete with crafts and games and food and music.

Now that the evening of the bazaar is finally here, it is the sound of coins dropping into empty pails that pleases Ruthie the most, more than the candles, more than the festive games, more than the sugared goodies. "Raining" coins into buckets is Cherry's idea, and children from all across the grove appear to have saved egg and chore money in mason jars for this very purpose. Granted, it will be extraordinary if coins alone can fund a new roof, but the convivial clatter heartens Ruthie in a way that little has over the last few, dark weeks. She always struggles this time of year when the days are so short and the nights so long, but facing a second Christmas without Orville is a dark sunrise even sunshine can't fix. She sucks in another reflexive breath and whispers, "Lord, help!"

The girls follow her to Great-grandmother Freese's table to deliver their confectionery contribution, eyes wide with wonder at the long line of frosted layered cakes, molded gelatin salads, candied nuts, platters of cookies, bowls of puddings, and—there it is!—Cherry's plate of peppermint divinity.

"Oh, Mother—!" Miriam starts, but Ruthie swiftly squelches her eldest's outburst with some light redirection—"Quick hugs for Great-grandmother, and then coats and hats before anything else."—steering both daughters toward Cordula's open arms and then back around the table toward the hooks lining the east basement wall. Behind the girls' backs, she passes last week's mending money and expeditiously points her finger. A corroborating nod and wink from Cordula, and a silent transaction is made.

Mother Renate kindly offers to make paper snowflakes with the girls while Ruthie assists Cherry with supervising the ring toss game, so Ruthie settles the girls amidst paper scraps and scissors and makes her way to the west end of the basement.

"Flossie's sellin' popcorn balls, but have you seen the boys?"

Ruthie ties an apron around her waist and smiles knowingly at Cherry. "In the cemetery."

Raising the girls apart from Orville is difficult enough, but raising growing boys without the help of a father—this is a sacrifice Cherry is making for the American cause that is greater than most women in the grove, including herself. She and the girls have Papa Werth's stabilizing, comforting presence, at least. Cherry is miles from any family who can assist in the home or on the land. "We manage," is all she ever says when Ruthie inquires, and she knows her hardworking friend really does manage. Cherry's resolve and stamina are outperformed only by her eternal optimism.

"They're playin' war, aren't they?"

"Naturally."

Cherry shakes her head and passes three rings to a young boy from Bramble. "You'd think it'd get old, but ev'ry mornin', noon, an' night, those boys 're launchin' snow grenades at each other's faces, yellin', 'Sayonara, sucker!'" Her dark eyes sparkle with an easy humor. "I admit, I cheer 'em on."

Ruthie takes a ticket from a well-dressed woman who must be the boy's grandmother. "And better to launch grenades outside than in, I say."

"'Xactly," but Cherry's confidence balks. "You don' think Miss Frieda'll be offended by their stagin' an attack on top o' her ancestors?"

"Last I heard, the boys are fighting in the Blume section of the cemetery. The Lindels are safe tonight."

"The Blumes, huh? Maybe I'll enlist Oskar for the defense. My boys could use a good whompin' from someone stronger'n 'em." She bends at the waist to collect the rings a second time and hands them to one of the Westen twins next in line. "So, what did you make for tonight?"

Ruthie smiles. She's been waiting for this. "Cherry fluff salad."

Her friend's reaction is immediate and deeply satisfying. Cherry whips her torso around and stares at Ruthie's grinning profile. "How did you know—?"

"Mother Renate told me."

Today is Cherry and Mark's tenth wedding anniversary—Ruthie has known that for months—but according to Mother Renate, Cherry served fluff salad to her wedding guests after the ceremony all those years ago. And judging by her friend's reaction, Mother is right.

"Oh, Ruthie," Cherry openly admires, but then, quite unexpectedly, her eyes spill over with tears. In seconds, she is full-on crying behind her hands.

Alarmed, Ruthie takes her friend by the elbow and leads her to a chair along the wall, motioning an S.O.S. across the basement to Cordula for some assistance managing the stunned line of children queuing for the ring toss. She settles Cherry into a chair, and blocking the curious glances of others with her own body, leans down and whispers, "I'm sorry, Cherry. I didn't mean to make you sad."

Cherry blows her nose in the hanky Ruthie hands her and taking a deep breath, shudders out, "It's not you. It's the water."

"The water?"

"I hate water," she blows her nose again. "An' Mark knows it."

Ruthie stands still, utterly baffled. This war does horrible, strange things to people, even keeps husbands and wives apart on wedding anniversaries, but Cherry's reaction makes no sense. "Fluff salad has too much water in it?"

"No," Cherry shakes her head. She reaches for Ruthie's hand and clings to it. "You're so good to me, Ruthie. The fluff salad—it's a sweet gesture, really. Thank you. It's just," she reaches for the words, "I'm tired. I'm really, really tired. I'm tired of goin' to bed alone each night. I'm tired of wakin' up each mornin' an' havin' to be both father and mother to my children. What good're anniversaries if Mark's not here to share 'em?"

Apparently, even Cherry's optimism has its limits. Ruthie feels oddly relieved by this and turns and sinks into a neighboring chair.

"I hate this war."

"Me too."

"An' I hate water."

Ruthie wrinkles her nose. "I don't understand. About the water."

Cherry looks up and stares at her as if she has just spoken Japanese. "I hate water, an' Mark joins the Navy."

She still doesn't understand.

"Ruthie, the man can't swim!"

Comprehension straightens her spine.

"It's the stupidest, meanest thing the man's ever done to me. Do you know what's worse than worryin' ev'ry minute of ev'ry day that your husband's bein' blown up by some bomb? It's worryin' that he's drownin' in the ocean before a bomb can even catch 'im. He *knows* I hate water."

Ruthie doesn't mean to, but the laughter bubbles up in her throat and escapes her lips before she can cover her mouth.

"No. You don't get to laugh about this, Ruthie Werth."

But it's too late. Ruthie is already snorting into her hands and sucking in air like a hyena.

"No. No, no, no," Cherry asserts, squeezing Ruthie's elbow with her free hand, but the corners of her lips are twitching. "It's not funny. It's not funny at all."

"You hate water," Ruthie gasps, "and I hate foxes!"

"What do foxes have to do wi—?" but Cherry is faster on the uptake than Ruthie. "Ah, foxholes. Oh, yes, that's too bad. How hard that must be for you, Ruthie Werth."

And then they are both hysterical.

Only when Cordula brings them cups of punch a few minutes later do they clear their throats and wipe at their eyes. Ruthie feels deliciously tired and sighs, leaning back against the wall and forgetting for the moment all of her grown-up responsibilities. "Did you talk to Papa Werth?"

Cherry is doing her own bit of leaning and sighing. "I did."

"What did he say? Will he sell you the old house?"

"After the war. He said he'll consider it after the war, once he's talked it over with Frank an' Orv."

Ruthie reaches out and takes her best friend's hand. This is everything Cherry wants in life, to make a home with her husband, and not just on the land he works but on the land he owns. She was hoping to secure the house as a surprise before Mark's return. "Before or after the war. What difference does it make in the end?"

"I s'pose none." She leans her head against Ruthie's shoulder. "Jus' think. We'll fin'lly be real neighbors."

They already are neighbors, but Ruthie understands Cherry's true meaning. Her friend is proud, and owning the home she lives in is something no one in her family has ever done. Not her parents, not her grandparents, and certainly not any relative before the Civil War. This reminds her of the persecution she read about in yesterday's newspaper. A fresh shot of adrenaline shoots through her veins and she sits up, upsetting Cherry's head. "Did you read yesterday's *Post*?"

Cherry frowns. "Haven't had time. Not with the bazaar an' all."

Ruthie feels her cheeks growing hot with renewed passion. "Well, most of it is Lester's usual drivel, but his latest article on Poland — Wait, I brought it with me. You have to read it." Ruthie stands to retrieve her coat — the paper is rolled up in her pocket — but Cherry holds her back with a firm hand.

"Show me later."

"I'll only be a moment. You have to see what he says about — "

"Then jus' tell me about it," Cherry sways. "We've already been away from the ring toss longer'n we should. Besides, you always say things better'n Lester, anyway."

Ruthie swallows genuine irritation. Cherry is continually brushing her off whenever she talks about the news. If she didn't know better, she would suspect her friend never read anything about the war. She once confronted Cherry on the matter, and in her usual, deflective way, Cherry responded, "Of course I read the paper. When

I have the time. But I don' ever have any time, so Flossie ends up readin' it to me in the evenin's while I pitch hay."

Ruthie doesn't ever have to pitch hay in the evenings, thanks to Papa, and she tries to remember her blessings, even now. Cherry has it much harder than her at home, always has, and she should have more patience. It is no real trouble to tell her about Poland herself, so she opens her mouth to explain what a work camp is when Edgar Reinking announces from the door, "Please, rise for our national anthem!"

The hustle and bustle in the basement quiets immediately, and everyone, Ruthie and Cherry included, rise to their feet as Anders Lindel blows a bugle call on his horn. Papa Werth, in full military regalia and marching to the steady roll of Dick Weston's drum, leads a small parade of Oskar Blume, Ralph Lindel, and Matthew and LJ Daniels with an American flag outstretched between them. The multi-generational procession lands before a pole standing beside the piano, and the moment Papa gets the flag properly hung, Miss Frieda arpeggiates an introductory chord to "The Star-Spangled Banner" on the keys. Mother Renate maneuvers the girls over to Ruthie in time for the second couplet, and they stand as a family, hands over hearts, united in body, voice, and spirit. The Werth women are all thinking of Orv and Frank in France, Ruthie knows, and Cherry is thinking of Mark on those dreaded waters. And certainly Edgar Reinking is picturing his son Simeon somewhere on the sands of north Africa, and the Lindels must have an image of Art parachuting out of a plane in their mind's eye. When Oskar Blume begins singing "God Bless America," his voice cracking with the first pangs of adolescence, they all think of the boy's father, Lowell Blume, flying somewhere over Germany.

Lord, help!

What happens next surprises Ruthie. Her girls step forward, ushered by a grinning Mother Renate, and tiny Marta climbs onto Miss Frieda's lap to play the melody of "Silent Night" with her right hand, the older woman fleshing out the accompaniment with her left. Then, effecting a warm chuckle from the crowd and an elbow or two from Cherry, Oskar takes Miriam's hand in his own and begins to sing with her, "*Silent night, holy night . . .*"

"When did those two turtledoves start singin' together?" Cherry whispers at her side.

Ruthie feels her face flushing from the astonishment. "I'd like to know when my baby girl learned to play the piano!"

"When you were milkin', of course. Or on the privy. That's when our children get to their real business."

They both hide their laughs behind their hands, lest they offend the musicians, young and old.

The horns and violins join in next, leading everyone in singing "O Christmas Tree" and "Hark! the Herald Angels Sing" and "Lo, How a Rose E'er Blooming" and a whole slew of favorite hymns, carols, and jingles, restoring the festive mood for Ruthie and Cherry. Though it is Miriam who threatens everyone's peace and joy for a rather tenuous minute at the end of the evening when she walks past Great-grandmother's waning food supply and pitches herself, with a loud and laborious howl, onto the floor.

"Good heavens!" Ruthie calls over the keen. "Daughter of mine, what on earth is wrong?"

But Miriam will not be consoled, and she calls upon gravity as her accomplice to keep all lamenting low to the ground. It takes Papa's brute strength to lift her hot, limp body off the floor, and when she finally calms down in the Willys enough to wail, "The divinity is g-o-o-one!" Ruthie quickly restores hope for humanity by pulling Cherry's peppermint platter out from under her coat.

+ + +

It is two days before Christmas when Mother Renate interrupts Ruthie in the barn during the evening milking. Mother is wearing only her kitchen apron—no hat and no coat, though it is snowing.

"Ruthie, there's . . ." she starts, but she must swallow before continuing. "There's a boy. On the porch." Mother's eyes are unnaturally wide. Her voice is tight and frightening. "From Western Union. He has a telegram for you."

Ruthie cannot remember what happened to the bucket of milk that night or to the engorged cow. All she remembers is the boy's downturned face, the yellow of the paper in her hands, and the impersonal rectangular block of five typed lines:

THE SECRETARY OF WAR DESIRES ME TO EXPRESS HIS
DEEPEST REGRET THAT YOUR HUSBAND PRIVATE ORVILLE
WILHELM WERTH WAS KILLED IN ACTION ON SEVENTEEN
DECEMBER IN BELGIUM. LETTER FOLLOWS=
ULIO ACTING THE ADJUTANT GENERAL.

+ + +

They bury Orville's remains in the grove, and Mother Renate weeps over his grave, "The Lord heard and answered my prayer."

"What pwayer?" Miriam inquires from her side.

"To lift your father out of the miry clay of France."

Ruthie is drowning in the ocean of her own grief, and she cannot help but add, "Yes, but only to return him to it in the grove."

But Mother Renate's eyes are lamps, and she shines them directly into Ruthie's darkness as she speaks, "And he will rest here in peace until Christ raises him on the Last Day." There is more pity in her voice than reprimand, but Mother takes the hands of both girls and walks them away to the safety of the Willys, away from the rising tide of Ruthie's dark ocean.

Only Cherry remains graveside, but Ruthie will not look at her. She will not meet the eyes of a woman whose husband is still alive. She will not suffer the pity of a woman who still has everything that matters in life.

The church bell begins to toll. 26 times it rings, one for each year of Orv's short life on earth. Only when the bell and the birds and the trees fall silent in respectful mourning does Ruthie raise her chin to Cherry, eyes still on the broken ground at her feet, and say, "Thank you."

Ruthie is certain one of Cherry's sons is still hanging at the other end of the bell's rope. Or Oskar Blume. Whichever boy, Cherry is behind the funeral toll, Ruthie is certain. She loves the old teller tradition, and Cherry knows it. She feels the warmth of a small sun dawning on the horizon of her dark ocean, and perhaps its golden rays would have crested the churning waves if Cherry hadn't chosen that very moment to say, "I've got a loaf of cinnamon raisin bread risin' in my kitchen."

My kitchen.

"Come to my house—"

My house.

"—you an' the girls, and we'll get my ol' oven fired up and eat us some warm bread."

My oven.

Cherry's possessive pronouns sink the rising sun, and Ruthie, drowning anew, turns abruptly to leave. But first, "That house is Orville's, not yours. No amount of dirt on his grave changes that."

\+ + +

Later that night, Papa pulls her into the living room to talk.

"Cherry's offered to buy the old house and the five acres surrounding. For a start."

Not this. Not now.

"And given everything that's happened. Well, life is short, and I've a notion to let her have it."

Ruthie feels like she is falling through the floor, though her head remains upright, her shoulders steady, her feet flat on the boards. Still, having nothing to hold onto, she squeezes her fingers into tight, little fists.

"Frank's got no need of it with his business in Aurora, and Orv— Well, you and the girls'll always have a home with us here. And this house'll be yours when Renate and I are gone. Seems right to let the old house go to a thriving family."

And that is when she feels it, the stinging slap of reality across her cheek. *A thriving family*. Her husband is dead. *A thriving family*. Her girls have no father. *A thriving family*. All of these years, she's been so concerned for Cherry and how little her friend has in life, but—*a thriving family*—that's not true. Cherry has Mark and three healthy children and—*a thriving family*—the opportunity to have more. She and Orv will never have any more children. *A thriving family*. They will never have any sons. *A thriving family*. Cherry is rich, when it is she who is poor.

"No."

"No?" Papa's eyebrows raise like the spines of two startled cats.

Ruthie purses her lips. Cherry and all of her sons have no right to what is Miriam and Marta's. "No."

Papa's two cats lean together in consultation. He is conflicted, but she knows him. He will not deny her, not the widow of his dead son, not the mother of his only grandchildren.

She lifts her chin and makes the decision for him. "Orv would want the girls to have that house, that land."

Cherry and all of her children can find someone else's inheritance to buy.

Chapter Thirteen

Saint Woodrow

+ 1978 +

Art Lindel is not a fan of Pastor Woodrow Seefeldt, but he would never dream of leaving the church where he was baptized. His own father was baptized, married, and buried in Whistle Grove, as was his grandfather, and he has every intention of doing the same.

"Lindels keep to their own pasture," his father told him the year before when Glorious Praise in town started a folk service and half of Bethlehem's congregation migrated to Bramble on Sunday. "Remember, no good ever came from one sheep following another."

When Gene Reinking stood up at the next voters' meeting and suggested they start a folk service of their own, Art had thought maybe that wasn't such a bad idea. The music was catchy, and guitars sound worlds better than their old, wheezy organ. But Pastor Seefeldt had insisted that "heathen music" was "from the devil" and would lead them all to hell.

"Maybe he's right, maybe he's wrong," Art's father had said the next morning while packing flakes of second-crop hay in the ewes' feeders. "But I know sheep, and sheep're dumb. Follow the shepherd. Ev'ry time."

Still, when Pastor Seefeldt suggested the elders start wearing long white gowns when assisting with communion, Art had pressed his father, "But what if the shepherd's a fool?"

His father had taken his time stacking the bags of pellets along the inside wall of the shed before answering, "Far's I know, honoring a fool's still honoring. No sin in honoring."

"But what if he's chasing the sheep out of the pasture?"

"Then," his father had thrown another bag against the wall, "pray the sheep outlast the shepherd."

That was the last conversation Art had with his father before finding him facedown in the south pasture, and he took his sainted father's final words to heart. So much so, that when most of the Reinkings left Pastor Seefeldt "and his fussy ways" to become disciples of the new, young pastor at Glorious Praise — and taking half of the Freeses with them — Art advised Viola and the rest of the family to stay put.

"But they've got a new youth group," his son Clyde had argued. "Clem's fifteen, now, an' I'd feel better havin' him in somethin' like that. You know, surrounded by good kids."

"He's surrounded by us," was all Art had said.

Thankfully, his Viola supports him even in the hard times, and she told their son, "But we've already got Catechism class at Bethlehem on Wednesday nights, and those kids who join us from Trinity–Covenant are of good stock."

"Yeah. They're real nice. All two of 'em."

"Well," she had given their son one of her smiles, the unrelenting kind, "'where two or three are gathered together in my name . . .'"

Viola is generous in all things, and when they are alone at home later that evening, she spills a few words into his lap along with the popcorn she pours into his bowl.

"Ruthie's going to Maine tomorrow. Marta had her baby. It's a girl. Sally Augusta Grisbone."

"Where's the Augusta come from?"

"Oh, that's from her mother. Ruthie gave the girls middle names same as the month they're born, remember? Marta's following suit."

"I thought the last name was Brisbane."

"No, Grisbone. Marta married a Grisbone. I remember," giving him one of her smiles, the amused kind, "because I thought of a grisly bone when Ruthie first told me. Gerry, I think is the husband's name."

"I thought Marta was married to a Bryan."

"That was her second husband."

Art lifts a handful of popcorn to his mouth.

"Ruthie needs you to talk to Pastor. About Sunday's sermon."

He lowers the hand, still full.

"She tried talking to him yesterday, but he was out making visits. And now, she's going to be out of town for at least three weeks. That's too much time to pass without saying something."

"She can't call him on the phone from Maine?"

"She could. But she thinks this kind of thing is better in person, and I agree."

He drops the popcorn back in the bowl. He no longer has any appetite for it. It is his least favorite thing to do in all the world, talking to Pastor Seefeldt about church stuff. He'd rather castrate a thousand lambs, and he hates that nasty business. But Ruthie is a widow, and he is an elder of the church. There's no other man left to speak for her; not one she trusts, anyway. Every worthy Werth is already buried in the grove, and the unworthy Werth that still carries the family's seed is hours north of here and in a skyscraper on Sundays rather than a church. Art remembers his father speaking up for Aunt Frieda in the church, because she never had a husband to do it for her. He will do the same for Ruthie.

"I'll talk to him tomorrow."

Viola gives him one of her smiles, the thankful kind.

+ + +

The next morning, after moving the ewes to a new paddock, he knocks on Pastor's study door.

"Arthur, come in."

It reminds him of old Pastor Milhahn, the way Pastor Seefeldt calls him Arthur. He once invited the younger man to call him Art like everybody else in the church, but Pastor Seefeldt's only response was, "Arthur's your baptismal name."

"Is this a quick matter?"

"What?"

Pastor Seefeldt waves a hand toward the chair opposite his desk. "Do you require only a yes or no from me, or should I invite you to sit down?"

He knows the reverend has no claws, but so often the man's words come at him like a batting cat paw. It's as if he can't help but choose the disagreeable way of saying something every time.

"I'll sit, if I may?"

Pastor Seefeldt nods and leans back in his own chair, resting his folded hands atop his rounded belly.

Art sits uneasily. He never knows how to start these things, so he does what all sheep do: chooses the path of least resistance. "It's about the sermon."

"What about it?"

"Your comment about marriage."

"I don't remember making a comment about marriage, specifically."

"You talked about divorce and— "

"Ah, you mean to say 'remarriage.' Yes, I did speak about that. There is a difference between marriage and remarriage, of course. What's the problem?"

"The problem is . . ." What exactly is the problem? He tries to think of the matter from Ruthie's point of view. "The Werth family."

"I don't see people as problems, Arthur."

"Yes, but when you say that getting remarried is against God's will, well, that comes down pretty hard on people like Ruthie."

"Ruthie's never remarried," Pastor Seefeldt points out. "And I made perfectly clear in my sermon that widows are free to remarry, though Paul advises against it. Why should Ruthie be offended by my sermon?"

"Her youngest daughter is remarried."

Pastor Seefeldt nods his head. "So I've been told. It's unfortunate the way young women exchange spouses these days, as if a husband is an off-shade scarf or a too-tight belt."

"It's not just young people, Pastor. Frank Werth is remarried, too."

"Frank? Oh, you mean the older brother in Aurora?" Pastor Seefeldt thinks on this. "What happened to his first wife?"

"Nothing. That I know."

"Divorced, then?"

"Yes."

"And the wife left him?"

"I believe it is Frank who left. His first wife, I mean."

"For reasons of . . . ?"

Art knows where this is going, and he knows Pastor Seefeldt is right. He just wishes the reverend were better at being right, the way Pastor Engel used to be. Pastor Engel had a way of pointing out the good, right thing in such a way that invited you to agree with him, not put up defenses on every front. "Winsome" was the word Viola always used in describing Pastor Engel. Viola has no such descriptor for Pastor Seefeldt.

"From what I understand, Frank left his wife," Art sighs, resigned, even disgusted, "to marry his second wife."

"And that is wrong. Wrong for Frank, and wrong for his second wife. And a sin against the first wife."

"Isn't there a way to say it," he wants to add the word *better*, but he settles for "differently?"

"The text is clear." Pastor Seefeldt does not even need to open the Bible on his desk to quote, "'And I say to you: whoever divorces his wife, except for unchastity, and marries another, commits adultery.' Our Lord Jesus said that, of course. Frank and his second wife are adulterers. Plain and simple."

"Yes, Pastor, and I believe it," but Art tries a different way. "It's just, well, publicly calling out remarriage from the pulpit like that. It shames Ruthie."

"It does not shame Ruthie. It shames Frank."

"Yes, but Frank's the only brother of Ruthie's dead husband. It gets personal, Pastor. And we're a small church. What's personal for Ruthie is personal for all of us. Shaming the Werths publicly like that—"

"Remarriage is a public matter, yes, but so is preaching. I cannot hide the Word of truth from God's people, Arthur. I will not. And if any of you are offended by the Word of God, then," he throws his hands up in the air, "what can I do about it?"

Always with the batting, claws or not.

Art sighs. Maybe he's just not saying it right. He tries one more time. "With all respect, Pastor, I don't think it's the truth that's being questioned here. At least, not by me, and not from Ruthie, I believe. It's the question of how to help Ruthie."

"Are you saying that Ruthie's in trouble?"

"No. Well, yes. In a way. What I mean is, in all of this talk about remarriage, is there no word of comfort? For Ruthie, I mean?"

"Of course there's comfort!" Pastor Seefeldt moves his hands to the arms of his chair and squeezes. "Did Ruthie not hear the blessed words of forgiveness in the Absolution? Did she not receive Christ Himself on her very lips in the Supper? Did not everyone else in the church receive the same? How can any of us ask for more comfort than that?"

Art realizes that he is looking at a shepherd who cannot see the sheep for the flock. Or won't see the sheep.

"It's just, we've already lost so many people, Pastor. Practically all of the Reinkings — "

"Simeon is still in the pew. And Charlie and Vivian are faithful."

"And so is Ruthie," Art adds. "Ruthie is more faithful than all of us, probably, but she's hurt by all of this business. And embarrassed, I think, about Frank. Maybe even Marta. I think she needs a visit from you, Pastor. She needs a comforting word . . ." And to see you use your staff for something other than beating at the wolves. But Art leaves that last part out.

"I fear, you place too much stock in method and manner, Arthur. It's an easy thing to do, but remember, the *how* doesn't matter as much as the *what* when it comes to the Word of God."

Art is not entirely convinced of this. In his experience, how he speaks to his sheep makes more of a difference in his pasture than what he says. But people aren't sheep. But they also are. How can he say this?

"God assures us," Pastor Seefeldt quotes Scripture directly from memory again, "'so shall my word be that goes forth from my mouth; it shall not return to me empty, but it shall accomplish that which I purpose, and prosper in the thing for which I sent it.' The Word is 'living and active, sharper than any two-edged sword.' And Christ Himself says, 'Do not think that I have come to bring peace on earth; I have not come to bring peace, but a sword.'"

Art knows a few verses from memory, too. He recites his confirmation verse, given to him by Pastor Engel—kind, patient, caring Pastor Engel—the first year he served Bethlehem. "But Christ also said, 'I am the good shepherd, and know my sheep, and am known of mine.'"

He wants desperately for Bethlehem's shepherd to know his sheep. He stares at Pastor Seefeldt, silently willing him to know Ruthie and talk to her and comfort her. He feels certain that in being known, Ruthie will follow her shepherd readily and willingly. All of them will. What few sheep are left, that is.

"He is the Good Shepherd, this is true," Pastor Seefeldt nods.

The pastor is faithful, Art knows this, and he appeals to the man's faithfulness. "Ruthie is in need of a pastoral visit, Pastor Seefeldt. Will you please call on her?"

"Yes, of course," he nods vigorously. "Gladly. It is my privilege to do so. Once she gets back from Maine."

"Thank you, Pastor."

"And I appreciate your insight in all of this, Arthur. I do. Talking through these situations, it helps me see just how important it is to reassure Ruthie of the truth in the sermon. Clarifying these matters is the thing."

Art sighs, discouraged. Pastor Seefeldt is a faithful pastor, but he is a poor shepherd.

+ + +

"How did it go?"

Art doesn't have the words, not even for Viola.

"That bad?"

He takes a paper grocery bag down from the top of the fridge and shakes it out. "He said he'll pay Ruthie a visit."

"Good!"

But he is not convinced. Their small congregation may get smaller and smaller, one pastoral visit at a time. He opens the freezer and takes out two frozen packs of butcher paper-wrapped meat.

"What're you doing?"

"Taking chops over to the Seefeldts."

"As a thank you?"

"Pastor said his wife's been suffering her headaches again."

"Is she still seeing that doctor?"

"Weekly."

"That must cost a pretty penny."

And there are fewer pennies in the offering plate these days. "I thought they could use a bit of help."

Viola doesn't answer, and so he pauses, a pound of frozen chops in each hand, and looks her way. She is giving him one of her smiles, the proud kind.

"You're a good man, Arthur Lindel."

This is when he doesn't mind hearing his full name so much.

"I don't know about that," he says, his cheeks warming pleasantly under Viola's sunlamp of a look. But he is a good shepherd, thanks to his father. And maybe — looking down at the chops in his hand — not such a bad sheep. At the least, he knows in which pasture he belongs.

Still, he might start praying that Bethlehem's little flock outlasts this particular shepherd.

Chapter Fourteen

Saint Edgar

+ 1986 +

All faith is lost in her husband when the ice cream melts.

It doesn't matter if a tombstone breaks a blade on the mower or if lightning strikes a tree in the grove or if too many crockpots in the church kitchen trip a breaker the morning of Edgar Reinking's funeral—it's always the pastor's fault.

Of course, none of this would have happened if Lila Daniels had done her job last night. All the fellowship coordinator of the Ladies Aid needed to do was disseminate reminders to the women of the society as to who was bringing what for today's funeral luncheon, but Lila botched the simple directive. Instead of telling the A through H's to bring salads and the I through P's to bring a main course, Lila told the entire first two-thirds of the alphabet to bring a main course. Making matters worse is the fact that several of the women, inspired by New Year's resolutions recently made, decided to forgo their usual calorie-laden pans of mac-n-cheese and lasagna and, instead, pull a shoulder of pork from the freezer, dump it and a packet of

Italian dressing seasoning into a pot, and call it a day. Meaning, a total of 13 slow cookers are now plugged into Bethlehem's weary outlets, and as the final bell of Edgar's life toll dissipates through the branches of the leafless trees in the grove, Georgia Sterling is aware that something is terribly wrong: she cannot smell a single thing.

Neither can Miriam Werth, and the older woman sighs, "Why is it that the good things in life are the first to go? Why can't belly fat or water retention decrease with age? Why must it be my hair, my hearing, and my sense of smell?"

"It's awful," Viola Lindel commiserates from her side. "I can no longer hear Art talking if he's facing away from me. Even if we're in the same room. And he can't hear me, either. I sometimes wonder if he turns away from me on purpose."

"No, not Art," Miriam assures. "That man's as crazy about you as ever."

But Georgia frowns down at a roast in a nearby crock. It is soaking, not simmering as it should, in its juices. She touches the pot: stone-cold. In a frenzy, she looks around and sees every inch of the kitchen counter real estate covered with crockpots and roasters of varying ages and efficiencies, none of them generating any heat. No one can smell anything because nothing is hot enough to smell. "Oh, no."

"What is it?" Miriams asks.

Georgia runs to the refrigerator and opens the upper door. No light comes on, and no cool air comforts her hot cheeks. She lifts her mudslide ice cream cake from the freezer and is horrified to see it actually slide in the pan.

"The power," she explains, "to the west outlets. They must all be off."

"Did Pastor trip a breaker during the funeral?"

Georgia, still facing the open, balmy freezer, rolls her eyes at the ceiling. Of course, her husband must be blamed first, even for an electrical failure in the church basement when he's presently standing outside in the cold cemetery burying their beloved dead.

"We all tripped a breaker," Iola Swart corrects. "Or a wall of them. Look at this mess! Who decided to have so many people bring pork roast today?"

They all look at Georgia, and she looks at Cherry Daniels. Lila is absent, as usual, most likely still asleep in her bed. Or someone else's.

"Did Lila make the calls last night?" Georgia presses.

Cherry is hard of hearing, but she is quick to recognize an accusing tone. She promises up and down like a squirrel on a cottonwood that her daughter is overtired from working the graveyard shift at The Stewpot, but they all know Lila likes to barhop late into the night with that no-good Larry Johnson. And with one out-of-wedlock child at home, already!

They hear the doors open overhead. Soon follows the stomping of snowy boots on the vestibule rugs and the tramping of feet down the stairs. A pack of boys push into the basement first, and Iola calls out to her son, "Brett? Quick, go get your father and flip the breakers to the kitchen."

Miriam throws her hands wide and asks of the world, "What will we serve?"

"Cold meat and warm Cool Whip," Georgia sighs.

Old Simeon Reinking enters the kitchen, his wool hat still pulled down over his ears, and calls out fondly to the women, "Ladies of the Society! Queens of the kitchen! I and my family thank you for your generous hospitality."

"Y'all might want to hold off on thanking us till after you eat," Honey Lindel advises. "The pork's a little cold today."

"Well, turns out, so am I." The old bachelor is cheerful and chivalrous as always, though it is his father they just laid to rest under frozen clods of dirt. The Reinking patriarch was just short of turning 100 when he died in hospice two nights before.

"Just think, Uncle Si," Miriam offers, "instead of birthday cake, your father's enjoying the Lamb's high feast today."

"Indeed. Though, my father lived for funeral luncheons." Uncle Si flashes one of his signature toothy grins, and then he laughs at his own morbid joke. So does Miriam. Georgia can't quite muster any gaiety in the moment, not in this graveyard of roasts.

"Do I smell ham?" LJ Daniels booms merrily, stepping behind Uncle Si and laying both hands filially on top of the older man's shoulders.

"No," the women answer as one.

LJ balks, surprised by the unanimous chorus. "Sweet potato casserole, then?"

"Most likely not," Miriam shakes her head.

"You're smellin' nothin'," Honey confirms, "'cause there's nothin' to smell."

LJ's lean, lined face grows wide with boyish alarm as his mother explains their present plight, and as he hightails it to the closet with the circuit breaker box, Cherry explains to the kitchen at large, "That boy lives for the Lord and sweet potato casserole. If anyone'll right this wrong, it's him."

But Georgia will not trust a Daniels ever again. She recruits several youths out of their metal chairs to unplug and redistribute the many slow cookers to various outlets throughout the church, and once power is restored to the west wall of the kitchen, she convinces the women to go ahead and set out the tepid desserts as an appetizer.

"But where's Pastor?" Miriam asks, craning her neck around the basement. "We shouldn't start until he says grace."

Georgia sighs for the thousandth time that day, nods once, and turns in search of Jacob. No doubt, he was waylaid by a mouthy Reinking on his way to the sacristy to disrobe. The only thing that passive man does worse than initiating a task is following through with one.

"Leave it to Georgia," she hears Honey murmur from behind as she moves toward the stairs. "If Pastor ever can't manage himself, she'll find a way to manage *him*."

Georgia feels outrage creeping up the back of her neck even as a heavy grief sinks her stomach to her knees. Such miserable people! If they aren't criticizing her husband for working too little, then they're shaming her for working too hard. She nearly dies every day trying to serve the ungrateful lot—practically running the Ladies Aid single-handedly, laundering the linens weekly for the non-existent altar guild, superintending the Sunday school of six children for the actual superintendent who has yet to make it to church on a Sunday morning, managing and rehearsing the handful of amateur musicians who persist in populating the praise band, and keeping her dazed husband fed and watered morning, noon, and night.

Six years before, when the seminary placed her husband at this little country outpost, she felt certain they would easily win the hearts of every person in the pews. How could they not? With Jacob's broad shoulders, handsome smile, and witty preaching to dazzle the countryfolk along with her multiple diplomas in business management and finance as well as a lifetime of piano lessons under her belt—the two of them were and are a ministry dream team for any congregation. So much so, the seminary still uses their picture on their recruitment brochures.

But no sooner had they moved to Whistle Grove than Georgia discovered the church didn't have a secretary or a tax accountant or women voters or even a Risograph. She did her best to help the congregation move toward acquiring all four at once—What could rally middle-Americans more than moving toward efficiency and democracy all at once?—but there was a surprising amount of resistance from the blue hairs in the pews on every point. Mr. Lowell Blume even went so far as to say to her face that a pastor's wife should not concern herself with such things.

Unfortunately, her husband proved to be of no help in any of these matters. Whatever his gifts in smiling and preaching from the pulpit, his talents in diplomacy from any platform remain sadly wanting. There were times in the first years of their ministry that the men of the congregation bested Jacob so fully in debates that Georgia had to step in and mediate affairs herself. And then everything blew up at the end of their first year in Bethlehem when Brett Swart and Kelly Upkin, upon learning Georgia could read lead sheets at the piano, brought a guitar and a tambourine to choir practice and made a rather impressive pitch for the three of them to start a praise band. Jacob was fine with it, of course—everyone knew that praise music was the proven way to throw open the shutters of dead orthodoxy and let fresh air into an old, dusty sanctuary such as this. But Mildred Potters, Bethlehem's organist and choir director of the past fifteen years, didn't take too kindly to the insurrection and left the church for good, taking every stubborn traditionalist Blume with her.

The choir disbanded soon after that, but any displaced singer who missed warbling in the balcony quickly took up residence with the praise band at the front of the church. They even picked up a few extra musicians in the transition: Roman Daniels turned out to be pretty good with a harmonica, and Vivian Reinking could play a few folk tunes on an old family fiddle. Overall, the congregation didn't complain too much during the transition, though Viola Lindel characterized the "affected peace" as a mere "symptom of exhaustion and grief." Georgia shrugged off such passive aggression as easily as a silk scarf, for she knew instinctively that the congregation's silence was relief, not grief. Her arpeggiated piano chords were a welcome vacation for all ears after Mildred's militant homophony.

But real trouble hit last year when Lila Daniels was incarcerated for 48 hours for drunk driving, and Jacob failed to visit her in jail. The entire Daniels family threw a holy fit, and Miriam made some noise before the elders about "pastoral negligence," but the whole thing was a simple misunderstanding. Jacob had taken a few days off to go fishing with his father and brother, and their cabin in Minnesota had no telephone. But grouchy, arthritic Mark Daniels almost succeeded in running her husband out of town, tarred and feathered on his fishing pole. Thankfully, Simeon Reinking suffered a heart attack and distracted everyone from the awkward business for a full two weeks. And when the congregation witnessed her husband's faithful, daily devotion to Uncle Si's bedside for the entirety of the man's stay in the hospital, everyone sort of forgave Pastor Sterling's dereliction of duty toward the Daniels' delinquent. Now no one even brings up the conflict in conversation anymore. Well, Georgia brings it up regularly to Jacob at home in the hopes of effecting a change in the docile man, but it never does. No job review she offers her husband ever gets through to him.

She is walking past the open utility closet, when she overhears Mark Daniels saying, "Maybe he's a Jonah."

She smells mutiny in the air, so she stops outside the closet and listens, unobserved.

"A what?"

"A Jonah. Like in the Bible."

"You mean a prophet?" LJ sounds just like his father.

"No, I mean a coward. A person who brings bad luck. We had 'em in the Navy. Jonahs brought storms an' droughts an' all kinds of nasty troubles with 'em. We threw 'em overboard."

"In the U.S. Navy?"

"Well, it never really came to that in the Pacific—not with our own boys—but we were ready."

She rolls her eyes and moves to leave. Forever, the old men in the congregation are retelling war stories, and she has heard them all. But the next words from Brett Swart's lips stop her mid-stride.

"You think Pastor Sterling's a Jonah?"

"I do. Think about it. First there was that business with the choir when all the Blumes left. An' then Sterling forgot about my Lila in her time of need. Nearly drove her to leavin' the church. Us, too. And now, in the middle of the funeral of the deepest pockets in the grove, the power to the kitchen goes out just before the meal. Ev'ry Reinking in the county'll think we don't care about 'em. They'll leave their memorials to Glorious Praise or the park district or anything other'n our church. We're sunk with that man in the boat, no matter what we do."

"And so you think we should—What? Throw Pastor Sterling overboard?"

This came from Brett's father, and there was a grand note of incredulity in his voice. He even chuckled at the end.

"Now, no. I don't think it'll come to that. It's just fishy, that's all. There's a pattern, is what I'm sayin'."

Georgia is ready to break against the traitors like a foaming grinder when she hears Art Lindel's unmistakable tenor chiming in.

"You fellas remember when Pastor Seefeldt died?"

"He choked on that bone."

"Yes, well," Art clears his throat, "I'm the one that gave him the chop that killed him."

The men are silent for a good five seconds. Georgia can barely breathe, herself.

"You meant no harm," Mark assures.

"See, that's the thing," Art amends. "I meant him no harm in feeding him, yes. But at the same time, I was praying to the Lord to send him on his way. The very night Pastor Seefeldt died, I prayed that prayer."

"What're you sayin', Art?"

"I'm saying," the elderly man's voice is shaking, "be careful what you pray for, Mark. All of you. Be careful what you wish, for that man or for anyone. The Lord hears your prayers, and He answers them. And He disciplines all of us in the answering."

Georgia hears a pair of feet shuffling toward the open door, so she turns and vacates the hallway as quickly as she can. Art's confession is both terrifying and comforting to her, and the last thing she wants to face is a man that honest and vulnerable, especially when she is so stirred and confused herself. Such moments are when people can get the better of you. She makes for the sacristy and is surprised to come upon her husband's open study door.

"Jacob, what are you doing in there? And why are you still vested? Hurry up! The people are waiting downstairs for you to start the meal."

He is sitting at his desk with his head in his hands, and when he looks up at her, she sees that he has been crying.

"Good heavens, what's wrong now?"

He has that slow look about his eyes. She hates that look. It usually means missed deadlines and more work for her.

"Nothing's wrong," he says, "and everything's wrong."

She rolls her eyes toward the ceiling. She's been busting her tail all morning long, all so that no one will blame them for anything, and he's sitting here playing the part of Hamlet. She could wring the man out for all of his soppy philosophizing.

"We can talk about it later," she huffs, moving toward the desk to prompt him out of his chair.

"I love you, Georgia."

He stops her in her tracks with his tenderness. He does that to her sometimes, stuns her with words and actions she does not expect. Early in their marriage, she was attracted to his ability to surprise her—so few people ever can—and even grew to admire his curious insights and observations, especially in his sermons. But 11 years later and in the wake of an entire congregation's hungry expectations, she finds his perspicacity distracting and cumbersome, like a strong current flowing against her own stride.

"I just buried a man in the ground, Georgia. His children and grandchildren and great-grandchildren surrounded the grave. There were so many of them, and I thought," his red-rimmed eyes beseech hers, "who will surround our graves?"

Not this. She will not listen to this now. He is asking too much of her to stand here and think about . . . to talk about . . . She will not. "Come on, Jacob."

"Do you ever think about our children, Georgia?"

She feels the heat climbing back up her neck. How dare he? To speak of such things with her here and now? When she must hold it together and walk back down to that hellhole and serve those subversive people?

He steps toward her and reaches for her hand, but she shrinks from him.

"I'm so sorry, Georgia. I don't mean to hurt you. I just can't help but think of them at burials. We've lost so many. So many."

The insufferable man! There are some things even she cannot control, cannot make right. Must he point it out to her face?

She glares at him, fuming, and spits, "Fine. If you won't pray with your people, I will."

And she leaves him to his precious pondering and does his job for him.

The School

Chapter Fifteen

Saint Ludwig

+ 1868 +

LUDWIG ASKS HER FATHER in the evening and with both feet to the fire. The women are washing the dishes at the stove, but he knows they are listening. Neither man is in the habit of talking much, so the conversation is brief. It is the handshake that is long.

The matter settled, he excuses both himself and Lesta from the house, silently taking her drying towel and handing it to her twin sister. He leads her blushing cheeks out under the stars and walks her down the lane. He wants to hold her hand, but both of his are in his pockets. He is embarrassed by his hands around Lesta. They are always scabbed and bleeding from clearing brush near Dandy Creek.

"Lesta," is all he manages at the start.

She waits. He loves that about her. She fits perfectly into his silences. She fills his quiet, not with talk or noise or fuss like her sisters or the Lindels' silly wives, but with presence and patience.

He stops when they reach the line of pines and tries again. He cannot see her face in the darkness, but he feels her gaze on him all the same. "Lesta, I want to marry you. If you'll have me."

"I will."

"Tomorrow."

"Tomorrow?"

He is surprised at her surprise. Is it that she can bear to live apart from him for another day? He can't. "Is that too soon?"

"Well, no. Yes."

"My house is ready."

"My trousseau is not."

He knows nothing of such things. "When will your . . . it be ready?"

The dark is hiding her eyes from him, but he hears her breath quickening. The sound starts his own heart racing. He would like to—

"I could be ready by Tuesday. Maybe Wednesday."

That is only two days away. Three at most. He can wait three days, though her absence from his house this entire week might undo him. But if she needs more time, "Would it help you if we waited till Friday?"

"That would be helpful, yes."

"I will talk to Pfarrer."

It is settled. He should walk her back to the house, but she is waiting for something. He can feel her anticipation. Could it be that she is waiting for him? He pulls his hands from his pockets.

"Ludwig, where will we be married?"

He hesitates. He blinks at the question. He honestly does not know. He cannot picture it. There's never been a wedding here before. "Where do you want to be married?"

"In the grove."

"Okay. I will talk to Pfarrer."

"And my family will come."

"Yes."

"And the Freeses. Noberta is already making my dress."

Already. He thrills at the thought of Lesta and Noberta making plans ahead of his own planning. He wants to say something, to give words to the happiness he feels at abiding in Lesta's plans, as she abides in his, but all he says is, "Won't everybody come?"

"Yes."

She is waiting again. She stands still as the pine behind her, but she is breathing and waiting. His hands are back in his pockets where he can trust them. He takes in a slow, long draught of the evening air to calm his thumping heart. Surely she will speak again, but she doesn't. She simply waits. His forearms twitch, threatening to loose his hands. "Lesta, may I — ?"

"Yes."

And his arms are around her. He pulls her tiny frame up into his own. He buries his face against her neck, kissing her little ear, then her warm cheek, then her smooth forehead, circling around the other side of her face like an explorer mapping new territory. Finally, he meets her lips, pulling her breath into his own, and he cries out. He sets her down, almost dropping her in his haste. He must walk her back to her house, now, or he may shame her.

"I promise, I will take care of you," he gruffs, stuffing his hands back in his pockets and sniffing. "I will die taking care of you."

"No!"

This shout does not come from Lesta. It comes from somewhere within the line of pines, and it is followed by the rustling of boughs and the running of feet. Suddenly, two scrawny arms encircle his middle, and a pair of braids sprout from somewhere beneath his chest.

"I will not let you kill him!"

Sarah Lindel is hissing and spitting under him like a tortured cat, and her fingers are digging into him like claws into a tree.

Lesta steps back, the darkness swallowing her, and his stomach lurches to be separated so soon after their embrace. But she does not leave him. She simply stands back, watching and waiting and breathing again. When she finally speaks, her words curl at the ends with what sounds like a smile. "I'm not going to kill Ludwig, Sarah. I'm going to marry him."

"It's the same thing! He said so himself!"

He looks up at the stars and sighs. He is ever at a loss for what to do with Sarah Lindel. The girl is wildfire, and she's always burning at the edge of his fields.

"You said you'd die!" she accuses.

He reaches behind his back and grabs at Sarah's wrists, peeling her from him like skin from a potato. She does not peel willingly, but he is bigger and stronger. "Now, stand back."

"Be gentle with her," Lesta reminds from the darkness.

"You shouldn't be listening behind trees."

"I wasn't! I was here first. I can't help it you two came along."

"What were you doing in the pines after dark?"

"What were *you* doing in the pines after dark?"

He feels Lesta's laughter vibrating the night air, though she makes no sound. He sighs again. "Go home, Sarah."

"She bit you! I saw it. Is that how the dying starts?"

"She didn't bite me. She . . . I . . . Well, we . . . I asked Lesta to marry me, and then we . . . we made a marriage pact."

Lesta's laugh sounds low to the ground. She must be bending at the waist.

"It's not funny!" Sarah shouts.

He happens to agree, so he takes Sarah by the elbow with one hand and Lesta's arm by the other.

"What are you doing?"

"I'm taking you both to the house."

"Oh, Ludwig," Lesta exhales another laugh from his side, working her way out of his grip. "Please, stop. Please. Just for a second. I need to catch my breath, and Sarah needs . . ."

"What?"

Lesta leans against his arm and whispers in his ear, "I think Sarah needs you."

"Me?"

"Yes."

He stands there, listening to Lesta's musical breathing in the darkness, utterly baffled and beaten by the moment. "I don't understand."

"Sarah needs you to walk her home."

This child? This she-cat that can see in the dark?

"She needs you to talk to her."

"I have nothing to say to her."

"Then let her talk to you."

"About what?"

Lesta leans against him again, and his heart races. His beautiful betrothed. Just moments ago, he tasted her sweetness for the first time, and in five days, his name will be hers. He almost forgets about the wildcat pulling at the end of his other arm, but Lesta explains to him, "I think Sarah wants to be the one to marry you."

He stalls in his dreaming. He considers this absurd notion for one grotesque moment, but a savage aversion rises in his stomach and chokes him like bile. He almost drops Sarah's sinewy arm, but Lesta stays him with a whispered promise, "I will marry you on Friday, Ludwig Blume, and then you can die taking care of me. But first, take Sarah home. And be gentle with her. She has a broken heart, I think."

Lesta disappears down the lane, and on this night of nights, he is left alone under the stars with only a mad girl and his bile for companions.

"C'mon," he sighs, dragging her toward the road.

"Where are we going?"

"Home."

She pulls at his hand. "I know the way."

"That you do," he admits, "but I'm still taking you."

No one knows the grove better than Sarah Lindel. The girl is always hovering on the edge of everything, day and night, rain or shine, and usually alone. Where she comes from and how, no one ever figures, but that she arrives is almost always a given. Her nose can sniff out any person's trail better than Felix's ever could.

"How old are you, anyway?"

"Eleven."

"Double digits, already?"

"Yes." There is a note of hope in her voice, and that gross aversion fills his throat again. He swallows hard and tries to remember Lesta's final admonition.

"Why don't you play with the other children?"

"What children?"

He considers this as they trudge along. It's true. There are no other children in the grove, not near her age, anyway. It must be lonely, growing up in a new country with no playmates other than farmers and milkmaids and animals. He softens a bit toward the girl.

"I miss Felix," her voice is simultaneously tight with frustration and soggy with tears.

"Me too."

"He was my best friend."

"Mine too."

"Why do you want to marry Lesta?"

He does not talk about such things, not even with Lesta, and he will not start talking about them now. Not with a child. He redirects, "Do your parents know you're running around in the dark like a wild animal?"

She doesn't answer, and he finally lets go of her elbow.

"Will you and Lesta have children?"

He smarts at her relentless impertinence. "You shouldn't ask such things."

"Why?"

"Because it's not your business what adults do when married."

"You don't want any children? I want ten children. Will Lesta give you that many?"

He honestly doesn't know. He would never dare ask such a question of a woman. His own mother only ever had him, and Noberta Freese still has none. All of that pain is a mystery. It seems cruel to ask a woman for an answer only God can give.

"Why won't you marry me?"

Be gentle. She has a broken heart. But the girl's child-love makes him uncomfortable. It sickens him. "I'm marrying Lesta, and that's final."

"But if you don't marry me, who will?"

"Whoever God chooses."

"That's easy to say. You've got lots of women to choose from. But me . . . If you don't marry me, no one else will."

"What about Willie Werth?"

"He's so old."

"He's younger than me."

"How old're you?"

"Older than Willie," is all he admits, but then, maybe knowing his actual age might help cool this unnatural wildfire. "I'm 33 years."

She walks along, silently considering this reality. "That's the same age as Jesus when He died. Hey, you're the same age as the Lord!"

He searches the night sky, scandalized. Will the Lord strike them down right here, in this new, wild country? He cannot decide if the girl is pious or wicked. Or both. He closes his eyes and scrubs his face with both hands. "Willie's only 20 years."

"That's nine years older than me."

"I'm 14 years older than Lesta."

She stops in her tracks. "You are? And she still wants to marry you?"

He does not point out the disparity between their own ages, though he is tempted.

"Why not marry Mathilda? She's the prettiest Reinking."

"That's enough of this nonsense, young lady. If you don't start showing respect to my betrothed, I'll leave you at this very spot to walk home alone."

"It's all right," Sarah continues, undaunted. "I already know why. Mathilda's too silly for you. I once saw her throw a fit after church and all because she stepped in horse manure. She sat and cried like Hans, Jr., even though she's a grown-up, and all because her slipper was a mess. Mutti explained later that we all have a certain number of tantrums in us, but some people are spoiled by their parents and go untested for too long and don't get enough of their tantrums out before they grow up. Mathilda, she must've been spoiled. You're right not to marry her. Lesta's got all of her tantrums out, I'm sure of it."

He doesn't know what to say to that.

"You're really gonna marry her, aren't you?"

"Yes."

"Even though it'll kill you?"

He might die from this child's incessant talking first. "You shouldn't say such things."

"I didn't. You're the one who said it."

He grits hits teeth. He will check for Sarah behind every tree before he says anything to anyone ever again. "I'm marrying Lesta on Friday."

"Lord willing."

"What?"

"Lord willing. You should always say, 'Lord willing.' Mutti told me."

She is right about that. "I'm marrying Lesta on Friday, Lord willing."

She sighs. "Can I come?"

And that is when he thinks of it.

"We need you to come."

"Me? Why?"

"To sing."

"Sing what? When?"

He is thinking as fast as he can, but he can barely keep one thought ahead of her quick wit.

"A song for Lesta. For my bride. As a gift."

"*I'm* the gift for your bride?"

"No. The song is the gift. You know how much she loves music."

"What song?"

"'*O Welt, ich muss dich lassen*.'" He smiles, remembering Lesta playing that hymn on her fiddle for him and Felix.

"No, no. That won't do."

"It won't?"

"No, the words. They're all wrong. I mean, they're all right for a funeral, of course, but not for a wedding."

He frowns. Maybe the girl is right. "What, then?"

"Lesta used to play a *Schottische* from the old country. Remember, in the grove in the summertime? She played it the night of the big meeting, when the families gathered to start a church. Remember that night? She played it for you."

"For me?"

"Yes. You just don't remember, because you're a boy. But I remember."

"What's the name of the song?"

"Doesn't matter."

"Why?"

"'Cause I'm gonna give it a new name."

"Why?"

"'Cause I'm gonna write new words for the song. For Lesta. For the first bride in Bethlehem!"

Lesta will be the first bride in Bethlehem. He smiles at the thought.

"Wait, who will be your *Hochzeitsbitter*?"

He is happy in his thoughts of Lesta, and he shrugs, unconcerned about anything else.

"But you must have a *Hochzeitsbitter*! Or how will anyone know to come to your wedding?"

He stops in the middle of the lane. The girl is right. He is neglecting his duty in appointing such a man, and Lesta deserves every joy in life. But who of his hardworking neighbors can he possibly inconvenience to ride around to every home in the grove on his and Lesta's behalf, reciting a silly poem and inviting everyone to their wedding? And who of these men would possibly deign to having invitees pinning long ribbons to his hat?

"I'll do it."

"Nonsense." He begins walking again, agitated. He should have thought to discuss this matter with Lesta earlier, but he is not attentive to such things. Honestly, he has never even been to a wedding. He feels a surge of panic. What else is he forgetting?

"I can do it! I have a black hat."

"No. The *Hochzeitsbitter* must be a man."

"But there's no other man in your family. Not in America, at least. You don't have any brothers, and your father is dead."

He frowns. Again, she is right. "Lesta's brother will do it."

"Elmer?" Her voice communicates full disapproval of his choice.

"Herr Reinking," he corrects.

"But he's so," she sighs, "ugly."

Such a mouth! Whatever he promised Lesta regarding this braided irritant, some things are not to be tolerated from any youth.

"You will hold your tongue before me, Fräulein. Herr Reinking is a good man and worthy of a little girl's respect. He will be the *Hochzeitsbitter*, and that is final."

She is silent at this, but only for a moment.

"What will you name your first child?"

Truly, he might die before Lesta can kill him properly. Right here, this very moment, he might have a heart attack from this wildfire's relentless burning. *Be gentle.* He sucks in a long, steady breath and takes his time releasing it. "Lord willing."

"What?"

"You should say, 'Lord willing,' about such things. You said so yourself."

"Oh, yeah." He hears a smile in her voice. "What will you name your first child, Lord willing?"

"I don't know."

"You know, Sarah's a nice name."

✢ ✢ ✢

Friday morning dawns clear and bright, and Elmer Reinking, wearing a hat pinned with ribbons from every corner of the county, hoots and hollers up the grove's lane ahead of Lesta and her family. Others are following behind, Ludwig knows, but he sees none of them, remembers none of them. It is his bride that fills his every sense, crowding out all other sights, smells, and sounds. Except one.

"I made this for you." Sarah appears at his side and hands him a blue cloth folded into neat quarters. "It's for your pocket. You're going to cry when Lesta says her vows. I know it."

He is standing next to Pastor, waiting for his bride. Distracted, he nods his thanks and hastily moves to tuck the handkerchief in his coat pocket.

"No, look at it, first."

"What? Oh," he looks down and turns it over in his rough hands. That is when he sees it, the dog embroidered on the corner. It is Felix. Tears immediately sting his eyes.

She grins up at him and pats his arm like a mother her son before turning and running off to join the noisy crowd quickly approaching where he and Pastor stand beneath the big cottonwood. Elmer grins at him, turning and making way for Lesta on her father's arm. She is sweet and welcoming as a robin in spring in her best brown-and-red dress, and stopping just before him, Herr Reinking places his daughter's steady hand into Ludwig's quaking paw. They both turn to face Pastor who prays for them, exhorts them, and then prompts their vows. Ludwig proves Sarah right. The moment Lesta turns to face him, speaking aloud her oath before God and man to submit to him, he begins to blubber like Hans, Jr., drowning Felix in his tears. He gladly will die taking care of her.

The congregation, men standing on the right and women on the left, enthusiastically joins in singing a hymn, and at the end of it all, as the grove explodes into cheers and hollers and congratulations, Elmer Reinking produces Lesta's fiddle from behind a tree and scratches out a familiar tune. Ah, yes. Ludwig does remember it. It was when he was walking toward the Werth cabin to gather the women. That is when this song filled the night and accompanied the stars. His throat tightens with grateful abandon. Even then, Lesta was fitting perfectly into his silence, and he didn't even realize it.

Sarah is quieting the crowd, saying something about a gift from Ludwig to Lesta, and then she opens her mouth and sings,

On this good, green earth 'neath trees of cotton,
pine, and maple
near a stable,
Bethlehem's first wedding is begotten
by a farmer
and his charmer.

Elmer joins in with his fiddle, the jaunty sawing only heightening the sweet sincerity of Sarah's lyrics. Ludwig bites his lower lip to keep from openly bawling again.

Vows exchanging, they will live together,
he protecting,
she expecting.
At all times and in all kinds of weather,
harvests reaping,
children keeping.

Let us pray, till death they hold each other
never fighting,
never biting.

And now he buries his face against Lesta's hair lest he laugh out loud and offend the girl.

God, in mercy, make this wife a mother.
Make our small grove
into Thy trove.

The congregation erupts into appreciative acclamations, encouraging Sarah to sing her song once again and then yet one more time that they might dance to it.

Men carry boards and sawhorses from the barn, setting up makeshift tables under the trees upon which women drape printed cloths. Lesta's sisters carry baskets and bowls down from the parsonage, loading the tables with the most delicious-looking fare. Herr Reinking settles himself on a stool before an open wagon and merrily serves his wife's home brew out of a barrel, while Thelma and Mathilda slice and serve cake to the laughing guests on Frau Reinking's delicate Meissen porcelain. But Ludwig is neither thirsty nor hungry. He has been feasting on Lesta's glowing eyes for the past hour, and he is thinking of their home. It is finally Friday, and she is his to have and to hold, from this day forward. He will take her to the house soon, but first, "I have another gift for my wife."

The families quiet down, turning curiously toward Ludwig's booming voice and towering frame. He is as tall as a tree today, and he may grow roots this very night. His heart is full of Lesta and the fruit they will bear together, and he walks toward his own wagon, nearby.

"Andreas, Karl—Hans, too—help me with this."

Between them, the four men lower and roll a giant stone, hand over hand, over the ground and to a spot of Ludwig's choosing near the lane. Then, walking back to the crowd and wiping his hands on his trousers, Ludwig settles in front of Lesta and explains, "It's a gift for my wife."

"A rock?" Lesta asks.

"A cornerstone. For a school. I found it alongside Dandy Creek, and I thought, my children are going to need a school someday. I'm going to build a school in this grove for all of our children." He turns suddenly and looks for Sarah, catching her eye and adding, "Lord willing."

Chapter Sixteen

Saint Helmut

✠ 1922 ✠

"Children, you may take your seats."

Viola Freese is not a child, and she does not appreciate being called one.

"Frank and Drucilla, open your Bibles to Genesis, chapter 22, and read the story of Abraham and Isaac aloud to Miss Lindel. She'll question you both at the end. You may begin."

Frankie and Cilla are most definitely children. They still bring milk to school, but Viola is ten years old. She drinks water from the tin cup hanging from the pump like Simeon and Lowell and Frieda and all the other big-and-growns.

"Arthur, Viola, open your Catechisms to The Creed and write out the First Article gifts in the same order as Dr. Luther. No variations. Hand your tablets to Miss Lindel when you are finished."

Pastor Milhahn never checks their penmanship himself. It's beneath him, or at least, that's what Artie Lindel told her last week. Their teacher only ever examines their English essays, and of that, only the work completed by the eldest and best students in the school. Everything else gets handed back to Frieda Lindel for grading. She's not a teacher, but she's not a student, either. She's some kind of in-between. She's too old to learn anything new in school, but she still comes by after pasturing the sheep, to hear the lessons.

"It's 'cause she's got no husband," Frankie Werth keeps saying, which raises Artie's mercury every time.

"Aunt Frieda doesn't need a husband! She's got Pa. An' she's got me!"

"Yeah, then why's she still comin' to school?"

"'Cause she's nice. She likes helping people."

"It's 'cause she's sweet on Pastor."

Which usually results in Artie swinging a fist toward his best friend's nose. Viola thinks it might be worth getting a husband someday just so as not to have to come to school every morning and sit across the aisle from Artie.

"Simeon, Priscilla, Lowell, Eugene," Pastor Milhahn calls from his desk at the front of the room, "at the board, please, and leave your Catechisms at your seats. We'll take turns writing out your memory work assignments from yesterday. Lowell, first."

Lowell is always first. Priscilla, or Eugene, is usually second, and Simeon is always last. Simeon Reinking hates memorization. He also hates English, history, and music, but he likes arithmetic and baseball. Viola likes arithmetic, too, but not as much as music. And not as much as she likes Simeon. She secretly monitors the tall, dark-haired boy over the top of her Catechism, but Artie jabs her with his pointer finger from across the aisle.

"Ouch!" she hisses.

"Hey," he grins, tossing a folded piece of paper onto her desk, his whisper not quite a whisper, "take a look at this!"

She rubs at the assaulted rib and ignores her perpetrator along with his dumb note. Simeon would never treat a girl this way.

"Open it," Artie urges. "Open it and read it."

"No."

"Aw, c'mon, Vi. Please? I found it outside in the cemetery. On top of ol' Johann Iken's grave."

This gets her attention. She glances down at the folded paper and condescends to open it behind her Catechism.

"It's just a list of names."

"Look closer."

"No." She stares faithfully at Simeon—it's almost his turn at the board—and wads and throws the paper back onto Artie's desk.

"Vi, just look—"

"Children!" Pastor Milhahn calls from the front of the room. He is turned around and looking directly at the two of them. Everyone else in the room immediately hushes and stares. "Are you having trouble locating the correct page?"

"No, sir," Viola and Artie answer as one.

"Perhaps I was unclear. You are to write out the First Article gifts, not recite them."

"Yes, sir."

Satisfied, he nods his head and returns his attention to the board. Lowell resumes his measured cursive on the board, and soon, Frankie and Drucilla recommence their reading lesson at the back of the room. Artie tosses the paper back onto her desk, but he overshoots, and she lets it fall to the floor. She will have nothing to do with him or his vile note. Not now, not ever.

Only when the class is let out for recess and Simeon, Eugene, and Lowell are all standing before her, each playing sentry to an imploring Artie, does she finally stretch out a reluctant hand to receive the paper willingly.

"See?" Artie says, before she even has a chance to see anything properly. "It's a list of names."

"I already know that."

"Yeah, but look at the bottom."

That is when she sees it, and her heart skips a beat. Her own name is scrawled at the very bottom of the list.

"So?" she shrugs, handing the paper back to Artie, but she can feel the concern creeping up her neck. Soon, it will paint her face red for everyone to see.

"Vi, it's your name!"

"I can see that Artie. So what?"

"I found it on Johann Iken's grave, and—" Artie swings out a hand and slaps Lowell on the stomach, "Tell her, Lowe!"

Lowell Blume is a serious boy. He works hard and studies hard and plays hard. He's not as tall or as handsome or as rich as Simeon, but he's smarter and kinder and more steady than any boy in the bunch. He doesn't usually go for Artie's juvenile plots, but this time around, even Lowell seems charged by some unseen power source. He takes his hands out of his pockets, shakes them, and faces Viola like a man. "That list. I'm pretty sure it's Tante Loretta's handwriting."

Viola's face and neck suddenly grow cold. She wants to reach for the list again, to see with her own eyes what terrible doom lies before her, but she's afraid to touch it. "W-what's it mean? Why's my name on her list?"

No one speaks. No one moves. Drucilla, who is crouching behind the boys along with Fauna and Frankie, all of them listening in, begins to cry.

"It's probably just some shopping list," Viola scoffs, tacking a laugh at the end of her sentence for show, but it sounds more like a gag than a giggle.

"Look again," Artie presses, finally and miraculously achieving a whisper when and where it no longer matters. He holds the list before her face. Everyone is looking at her, watching her, waiting for her. She gulps and leans forward, studying the paper anew. There, at the very top of the list, is Johann Iken's name. Crossed out.

"It's a drop-dead list."

Viola looks at Artie first, then Lowell, then Eugene. But it is Simeon's face that alarms her the most. He is staring at her, truly seeing her—perhaps for the first time in her grown-up life—and those brown, dreamy eyes are looking at her in horror and repulsion.

Viola blinks repeatedly and tries to swallow, but her tongue sticks to the back of her throat. Drucilla is openly bawling now.

"Quiet, Cill!" Artie hollers, throwing out an elbow behind him for good measure. This kindles Viola's fire.

"Arthur Lindel, don't you dare lay a hand on my little sister!" Viola jumps up from the log on which she was sitting and sticks her furrowed brow directly under Artie's chin. She is shaking from ribbon to boot, but she does not care. She's going to die soon, anyway. What does it matter if Simeon sees her afraid?

"But Vi, you know as well as I do that when old Johann Iken drowned in that well, it wasn't an accident." Artie's hazel eyes are not so handsome as Simeon's, but they are just as big and round and rimmed with the same horror. But she also sees concern in his eyes, and it's adding fire to the flecks of green swirling in his ponds of muddy brown. "Looney Loretta pushed her own husband in the well and killed him."

"We don't know that," Lowell loyally defends his aunt, though his tone isn't convincing.

"And look at this!" Artie's eyes might pop out of their sockets any moment. He pushes the list under Lowell's nose and points, "Elizabeth Blume. Philip Blume. All dead. All crossed out. She killed them too. And now she's gonna kill Vi!"

Viola is near her breaking point, and so she controls the only thing she can. She grabs the list and starts running. There is shouting behind her, maybe even some pounding of feet, but she doesn't care. She's fast—faster than most of the boys, even—and she outruns their echoes. She runs down the Fireling Road, across the creek, through one of Artie's father's pastures, over ditches and under fences, all the way to the mill where her Papa is planing and sanding boards. But she does not go inside. She stops just outside the door, panting and sweating and shivering, and then she turns and vomits into a nearby bush.

"My, oh my!" a deep voice rumbles from behind. "So much running, and now so much sickness!"

Viola stands and wipes at her mouth. She is too exhausted and humiliated to turn around, though the voice is friendly, even familiar. But it is not Papa's voice, and she wants to speak to Papa.

"Come, Fräulein Freese. Sit and rest out of the sun."

She turns around to see Herr König sitting on the old iron bench in the shade of the big silver maple. He smiles at her, and the gray-black hairs of his mustache splay like the wings of an exotic butterfly resting upon his upper lip. He pats the seat invitingly beside him.

"Come and sit. I have some of your Oma's mint tea here in my cup. Yes, yes. You shall have the rest of it, and it will soothe your stomach."

She wants to sit, but she wants to talk to Papa more.

"He will be out soon," Herr König reads her mind. "I am waiting for him myself. He is finishing my table today."

His table. Yes, she remembers a table. It is for a family wedding. A gift for a niece or something. Papa will be awhile, still.

Of their own accord, her feet trudge toward the tree and deliver her onto the bench. The paper is still clutched in her right hand, but the mug somehow appears in her left, and soon the cool, calming mint washes the sour from her mouth and soothes her burning throat.

"You run too far and for too long, I think. But then," his voice box rattles in his throat like dice in a tin can as he pats his round middle, "I run too little and not nearly often enough, so who am I to judge?"

She sips and rests and then sips some more.

"You ran here from school, I think."

Herr Helmut König is a teacher. Or he used to be. Before the war, Mama said.

"I think, you are a false start."

"A what?"

"A racehorse out of the gate before the gun." He pulls a gold watch from his vest pocket and opens it to check the time. Satisfied, he returns it to the correct pocket. "Your running here, it is ahead of the school bell, yes?"

She takes another sip and hides her face behind the mug.

"What is this in your hand?"

She is far from the grove, but she is still close to her fear. Tears spring from her eyes. She has no hands left to catch them, and so they fall freely onto her lace.

"'Weep you no more, sad fountains!'" Herr König recites, pulling a handkerchief out of his pocket. "Did you know that our

Lord collects tears in a bottle? But alas! I have only this handkerchief, if I may?"

She nods, and he gently drapes the cloth over her blouse. The manly scents of tobacco and peppermint warm her nose, and she returns the empty mug. "Thank you."

"You are most welcome, Fräulein."

Fräulein. Herr König never calls her 'child.' Sometimes 'young lady' or 'my dear,' but never 'child,' like Pastor Milhahn. She sits a little taller and dabs at her eyes with the handkerchief the way her mother does.

"The last time I ran home early from school, it was because a group of men asked me to leave. Did the same men chase you away from school?

She thinks of Artie and Simeon and Lowell standing over her. "Boys, not men."

"Ah, yes. Perhaps sons of my men, yes?"

She giggles at this. Herr König talks funny. No, not funny. Straight. Straighter than most.

"And what, my dear, did these foolish boys say to chase a lady such as you from where she belongs?"

She looks down at the crumpled paper in her hand and, swallowing, opens it and smoothes the wrinkles out on her knee. She hands the paper to Herr König.

"This is not your handwriting, I think."

She stares ahead at the door of the mill, listening to the familiar scraping of blade on wood.

"Ach! And here is your own name, Fräulein. At the very bottom." Herr König turns toward her. "The boys gave you this?"

"Yes."

"Why?"

"Because they think I'm in danger."

"Of what?"

"Of being killed."

"Well," his voice is matter-of-fact but not disinterested, "that is serious. Very serious, indeed. And so, the boys got this list from a policeman?"

"No, Artie Lindel found it on Johann Iken's grave. And then he gave it to me. You see, Loretta Iken wrote this list. It's her handwriting, see?"

"No. I do not see."

"Oh. Well, Lowell Blume said it's her handwriting, and she's his aunt."

"And this Lowell Blume. He's to be trusted?"

"Yes. He doesn't lie."

"And this list, it means you are in danger?"

"Yes."

"Lowell Blume said this?"

"Well," she frowns, "no. Artie Lindel said this."

"And he's to be trusted?"

"Not necessarily."

"I see. And this Artie Lindel, he thinks you are in danger, because . . .?"

"Because Loretta Iken wrote it, and her husband's name is crossed out."

"This is significant, because . . .?"

"Because she killed him."

Herr König is quiet for a moment. "That, Fräulein Freese, is a very grave accusation, one that is not supported even by the local police. For I believe I saw Frau Iken just this morning at the butcher's. She was buying a ham hock, it seems, when she should be in jail."

Viola sinks a little lower in her seat.

"This Lowell Blume whom we trust. What does he say?"

"He doesn't say."

"I see. Well, without his fine testimony, we must consider the evidence at hand. These other people on the list. I see, yes, I see Elizabeth Blume and Philip Blume. They are crossed out. What does this mean?"

"Well, they are dead."

"Like the husband, I see. Oh, dear." All music leaves Herr König's voice. "I do see. Yes, I see the crux, I do. Elizabeth Blume. That tragic business regarding Frau Iken's niece, Lowell's little sister, yes? We are to believe that Loretta Iken pulled the barn down onto young Beth, then?" He clicks his tongue. "Such a big job for such a small woman. I wouldn't have thought."

Shame takes a seat between the two of them and blocks her view of the stately man.

"And Philip Blume, her younger brother. His heart attack was caused by—I do not know about such things. What do you think? Arsenic, perhaps?" He gives the paper an emphatic shake and continues reading down the list. "Ernst Werth, Katharina Blume, Dorothea Reinking. Now, these names have no lines through them. Oh, and there you are, my dear. Viola Freese." He turns and stares straight through Shame's shadow to study her profile. "And think, that excitable Arthur Lindel is convinced you will be the next to be lopped off like some character in a book. But why not Frau Reinking, next, instead of you? It seems to me," and he chuckles, "this boy is much distracted by your charm and beauty to move you ahead of Loretta's own twin sister."

To hear it discussed out loud like this and in the bright of day and on her Papa's own land: Viola bows her chin to her chest. She is too embarrassed to pull her elbows from her ribs, though she wants nothing more than to reach for the paper and tear it into a thousand pieces.

"You are a good student, I think," Herr König nods, refolding the paper and tucking it into one of his many hidden pockets. "Tell me, Fräulein. Setting aside the generous omniscience of this boy who would be your suitor, who is the one person in the entire world who can tell us why your name is on this list?"

Deep down, she knows that he knows that she may die of shame long before anyone else can kill her. "Loretta Iken."

"Frau Iken," he corrects. "And yes. You answered correctly, as I knew you would. Just as I know that you will do the right thing and help me return this paper to its proper owner." He stands and bows deeply at the waist, rising again to offer her his arm. "Good news. I have reason to believe that Frau Iken is in her kitchen this very minute stewing some beans along with her ham hock. I wonder, my dear, if you think some flowers might also be appropriate for the occasion? Yes, then we shall ask your Oma if we might peruse her garden. After we return her mug with our compliments, of course."

+ + +

Herr König protects her by doing all of the talking, and as he walks her back out onto Frau Iken's front porch — a steaming bowl of pork and beans in hand — he pats her hand that is gripping his left arm.

"Let me tell you something true, Fräulein Freese." They manage the steps together, cautiously and deliberately, making it safely to the ground with no slops or spills. "There are smarter boys walking this earth than Artie Lindel."

She is not a child, but she can still laugh like one.

"But mark my word, my dear, you may never find a boy so attentive. He must want you to stay alive more than reason itself to make such a fuss over nothing."

She considers this. When she pictures Simeon, she always sees him refilling the coal bucket or working figures on the board or swinging a bat in the grove. When she pictures Artie, his eyes are always on her.

"Another true thing," Herr König opens the passenger side door of his Studebaker and ushers her inside. "Run toward school, not away from it. Read every book Pastor Milhahn gives you, even if it's boring. Keep singing your hymns and memorizing your Catechism and reciting your poems. You are bright as well as beautiful, and that little school of yours in the grove is the final, unharvested gem in this cave of a county. Don't let any miner or mayor or man or monster take it from you, ever. One more true thing, Fräulein," just before he shuts her door. "There are few privileges higher in life than having someone pray for you."

For that piece of paper was not Loretta Iken's drop-dead list. It was her prayer list.

Chapter Seventeen

Saint Frieda

+ 1948 +

FRIEDA'S HANDS ARE SUBMERGED in hot dish water, but her ears are tuned to the pair of fine-feathered friends cheeping noisily on the far side of the church kitchen.

"Look at this cake."

"One layer only. I bet it's not even chocolate."

"Well, I won't take a slice when it comes to it. I'm having a dress fitted tomorrow."

"Who brings cake to a luncheon, anyway? Custard is best for midday."

"I'd settle even for a simple pudding. But a cake?"

"I guess some people can't think past a fork."

"Well, if my dessert *must* be served on a plate, give me an assortment of cookies, at least."

"Not me. If I even look at a cookie, I gain a baker's dozen."

The peacock feather angling from the blue straw hat bobs dangerously close to the red finch perched atop the nearby yellow cloche, and the two dead birds titter and jounce obnoxiously, drawing a reproving glare from Opal Lolling who is pouring lemonade into three lines of cups ordered neatly on a tray. The silent chastisement succeeds in settling their feathers, but the moment Opal picks up the tray and pushes a hip against the door to walk the beverages out to the tables, the birds resume their trilling and fussing.

"Did you see that look she gave us?"

"It must've taken a supreme effort for her to turn around in that dress."

"The side seam alone looks like it's about to burst from the strain."

"No doubt, she'll be eating the cake."

The peacock shakes anew with laughter, but the wary finch throws out an elbow and peeps, "Here comes the old dishrag, again."

As Opal reenters the kitchen — "I forgot Dorothea's water" — they busy themselves with studying their white gloves and picking lint off their three-quarter sleeves, all the while holding Opal's hand-made frock in contempt with sidelong glances. Frieda reaches for a nearby towel and dries her hands. Either these foul fowl have lost their way, or they've chosen the wrong tree in which to roost. Regardless, her vocation is clear. She aims a polite smile at the un-welcome warblers and, extending a warm hand, greets them with a cordial, "I don't believe we've met. I'm Frieda Lindel."

"Oh," the peacock dips and turns, keeping her elbows close to her ribs and lightly touching Frieda's fingers with her own, "hello. I'm Betty Potter, and this," turning the finch around by the shoulder, "is Gina Reisinger."

"How nice to meet you both. Are you here for our Ladies Aid Society meeting?"

But the visitors are too busy monitoring Opal's second exit from the kitchen to answer. Frieda clears her throat and tries again.

"I do hope you'll join us for lunch. Won't you sit at my table?"

"Good heavens, no!" the finch squawks, turning back around and pinching her cheeks into a tight smile. "We're with Retha Reinking."

"Yes, we're sitting with her."

"Of course," Frieda nods, relieved. She is not required to manage this pecking order, after all. She opens wide her arms and steps toward the door, effectively shaking the kitchen's limbs of vermin. "Well, then, won't you please have a seat? Lunch is served."

What Retha intends by inviting her townie friends to their church society meeting, Frieda doesn't know, but she is certain the move is tactical and, most likely, has something to do with last night's voters' meeting. She motions to Opal through the kitchen door, and the two carry platters of chicken salad sandwiches to the tables as well as three large serving bowls filled with pea salad, cottage cheese Jell-O salad, and ambrosia salad, respectively. That is one salad too many in Frieda's humble opinion, but what can be done? Retha arrived just ten minutes before, dropping off the two strange birds in the kitchen along with a glass bowl heavy with canned fruit, marshmallows, pecans, and shredded coconut smothered in marshmallow whip before rushing off to confer privately with Pastor and Theresa Engel in a corner of the basement. It isn't even Retha's turn to host! Most likely, an attempt is being made to purchase their affections with maraschino cherries, but that might be putting the worst construction on the matter.

They all take their seats, and Pastor leads them in a blessing. Then, the ladies pass pleasantries back and forth along with the food. Conversation centers mostly around the sweet antics of the three lap-babies in attendance — Viola Lindel's angelic Iola, Drucilla Reinking's fist-sucking Charlie, and Cherry Daniels' bubbling and babbling Roman, a mere fraction of the congregation's bountiful, post-war harvest — though all maternal cooing stalls when Dorothea Reinking drops her cup of water on the floor. But Opal, ever attentive to her elderly aunt, has the mop out within seconds, and soon the slippery mess is as good as gone and Aunt Dorothea's cup of water restored.

When the time for dessert draws near, Ruthie Werth jumps up to clear the tables, and Priscilla Blume brews coffee to serve along with her modest slices of vanilla tea cake — both politely declined by the visiting birds. Only when everyone else's beverage has been refreshed does Frieda stand to call their meeting to order, and before the long hand on the wall clock can approach the next number, both Ruthie's secretarial minutes from their last meeting and young Mildred Blume's treasurer's report are approved. Frieda smiles, satisfied. There is not a single dawdler in her well-ordered lot. Assuredly, both Cordula Freese and Dorothea Reinking can turn a good ship sideways with the gust of their personal opinions, but neither matriarch has enjoyed good health this entire year. Cordula is not even well enough to be present today. And while she wishes no one ill, Frieda is not above admitting that the older women's bane has been the society's blessing. Today, especially, it is a boon not to have to weather Cordula's wind, given what it is they need to discuss.

"Ladies, you'll notice on the agenda that we have only one item listed under 'New Business' for today. I know, I know, there's much more we need to discuss — the church picnic is just two months out, the annual sock drive for the seminarians is fast approaching, and — Yes, Dorothea, I see your hand, and I've made note of your concern regarding the bathroom mirror. I'm putting it on the agenda for next month's meeting—"

"I may not be alive by then," Dorothea harps from her chair, but Opal succeeds in quieting and consoling her agitated aunt with murmured assurances and a single, hovering, generous forkful of cake dipped in coffee.

Frieda nods appreciatively at Opal and continues, lest time be wasted, "We all feel the weight of pressing organizational matters, I understand, but I do believe the threat of our school closing requires our sole attention today."

All women, birds too, grow silent at this statement.

"I've asked Pastor Engel to give us a report from last night's voters' meeting," Frieda continues, "to bring some clarity to the issues at hand. Pastor?"

As the man rises from his chair, Frieda sits in her own. It is a fitting picture, she thinks, both of the church and of their present plight. Make no mistake, she knows her place—God's Word is clear on the matter of headship—but look where it has gotten them, women being seated and silent. If the women in this room don't stand on their feet, and soon, the men might vote to close Bethlehem's morning school for good.

"It's a simple matter, really," Pastor begins. "Enrollment in the school has been down for years—"

"Because of the war, Pastor," Renate interrupts, "but the war is over."

The point is well made, but Frieda feels a flash of irritation at her friend's impertinence. How will they ever make it through this meeting if Pastor is not allowed to finish even one sentence? But the man merely nods and affirms, "Indeed."

"Thirteen babies born in Whistle Grove alone this year," Opal amends.

This is not good order. Not at all. Frieda points a stern look down the table.

"Yes," Renate agrees, "enrollment's about to increase, and everyone knows it. But even if there were only one child in the grove, isn't that child alone worth teaching?"

"Yes," Pastor is quick to assure, "and teaching our children the faith is one of the great privileges of my vocation."

"Then, why—?"

"The man's trying to tell us why," Dorothea thumps a reprimanding hand on the table, "if you girls'll let him!"

A smile tickles Frieda's lips, and so she stares fiercely at her hands folded in her lap. She should not be so hard on Dorothea.

Renate, flushing, "Forgive me, Pastor. I'm just so upset. All of us are. I can't believe we'd ever vote to close our school, not when we have such need of it."

"*We* will never vote to close the school," Opal clarifies.

"I assure you, one child alone is worth a school," Pastor sidesteps, completely avoiding Opal's planted landmine. "It's not simply an issue of population. Or rather, it's more about what the present population wants."

"What the *men* want," Opal corrects.

Frieda swallows a sigh. Opal is to be pitied, no doubt about it. The woman endured a 30-year-long object lesson on the depravity of man at the hand of her cheating husband, but that is no excuse for speaking out of turn and in such a tone. She stands and places both hands on the table. "Ladies, I asked Pastor Engel to relay to us the content of last night's meeting, not to interpret it or judge it or defend it. I must ask that we all refrain from asking any more questions until he's had the opportunity to speak his piece," *or we'll be here all afternoon*, she wants to add. She waits and listens, nodding approvingly at the responsive silence, and then sits, inviting, "Pastor, please, continue."

He addresses Opal directly, "I understand your concerns. In fact, I share them. We all do, I believe. There's not a single voter in our congregation who doesn't think our children's education is the chief concern. The truth is," and here he pauses, seeming to form his words carefully, "we do not all agree on what kind of education is best. Or rather, it's looking as if most of the voters would prefer their children and grandchildren have," he pauses again, treading cautiously, "the opportunity to attend school in Bramble."

"But they already can," Renate argues, "in the afternoons. Our children have the best of both worlds: Catechism, music, English, and history at Bethlehem in the morning and mathematics, geography, and science at Bramble in the afternoon."

"Frieda, if I might have the floor," Retha calmly interrupts, not waiting for any confirmation before rising from her seat and pulling a piece of paper out of her handbag. Frieda barely has time to open her mouth before the stately woman continues, "Of course, you all know my husband serves on the Bramble school board, and the availability of excellent education is his primary concern for every family in the county."

The ambrosia salad. It is campaign food, then.

"Of course, we love our little Bethlehem school, but if the war taught us anything, it's that we're stronger when we join together with the larger community." Retha's friends, the peacock and finch, begin to nod their heads reverently and in perfect time. It is no longer a mystery to Frieda as to why the strange birds are there. They are to serve as Retha's Greek chorus in this staged tragedy. "And it is a proven fact that education is more efficient and works to the best advantage of every student if formalized."

Frieda feels her face flush. She was mistaken, apparently. There are women in the congregation who *want* to close their school. Still, she will not question or interrupt Retha or any other woman in the society. That is not her way, though she is sickened by this obviously planned speech of manipulation.

"Edgar was just saying to me the other day, 'Retha, our grandchildren deserve the best this great nation can give, and that includes a better school system.'"

Renate is not bound by the same personal ethic as Frieda, so she leans forward and asks, "What could be better for our children and grandchildren than being taught the *reine Lehre* by Pastor Engel?"

The birds' feathers are visibly ruffled at hearing the enemy's tongue spoken so easily and openly on American soil, and Dorothea bellows an assurance at them, "That means 'pure doctrine,' ladies. Not '*Heil*, Hitler.'"

"Certainly," Retha soothes, "nothing is more important than teaching the faith." She smiles grandly first at Pastor and then at his wife Theresa who is seated on the other side of Priscilla, her hands folded in her lap, her eyes downcast and unreadable. She is probably praying. They all should be praying. "But Pastor Engel's already so overworked. And with all the new babies this year," she smiles affectionately at the lap-trio present, "how can Pastor possibly teach them all and keep up with everything else? No, with a growing congregation like ours, it's high time we give help to our pastor where we can, take the unnecessary bits off his already full plate. There's no need for him to teach our children every morning when Bramble Elementary is already offering morning classes to every child in the county."

"Bramble's going to teach the children the Catechism?"

Retha's smile radiates patience. "Edgar was just saying to me last night, 'Why should the elementary school bother teaching our children what we already teach them at home? That would be a waste of everyone's time and resources.' No, we're not suggesting that the public school teach in our place. We're suggesting that it'd be beneficial to everyone if the public school supplements what we can't give our children ourselves. Like bringing in experts to teach physics and geometry and the biological sciences and everything else that might give our kids a leg-up in this," Retha pauses a moment to refer to her paper, "fast-changing, technological world."

More head-nodding from the birds.

"You make it sound like progress, our school's closing," Viola speaks up for the first time, her voice thick with emotion, "but to me, it feels like a death in the family. We've already handed over our children to the public school for half of every day. If we close our school altogether, well . . . it's like turning our backs on our parents and grandparents. It's like saying 'no, thank you' to the stewardship of everyone who came before us."

"I understand, I do," Retha assures, "but who of us here isn't capable of cracking open a Catechism at home and reading it aloud to our children and grandchildren?"

"Pastor Engel does a little more than that," Renate reproves, though she tosses a swift look of concern down the table toward Cherry.

"Certainly, he does," Retha casts her unflappable smile upon the man seated at the end of the table, "but—and forgive me for pointing this out, Pastor—neither he nor any of us, really, is qualified to teach mechanical engineering."

"Mechanical engineering?" Renate laughs, but there is no music in it. "I'm sorry, Retha, but even Bramble won't be teaching elementary school children mechanical engineering."

Frieda opens her mouth to put an end to this discussion bordering on derision, but the finch suddenly peeps her head out from under one of Retha's wings and chirrups, "My son told me just the other day, 'Mommy, I want to be a physicist.' I said, 'Tommy, what in the world is that?' And do you know what he said? He said, 'Someone who studies physics.'"

The women are made mute by this underwhelming observation.

"What Gina means," Retha rallies, mustering a diplomatic smile, "is that little schools like our own aren't equipped to meet the curricular demands of a thriving national workforce."

"Our little school may be a diamond in the rough, yes," Viola counters, lifting a fussing Iola up to her shoulder and patting her on the back, "but it's still a gem. There's nothing else like it in the county. And here, we're considering tossing it in the bin like some worn-out hand-me-down, all because a few people in Bramble want to try on a new science class for size. No offense to present company." She turns and nods courteously toward the flock at the end of the table. "But it's our own children who're losing out here."

"Hear, hear!" Renate cheers.

But Retha will not relent. "Our children will not lose anything. They'll gain more education and opportunity. Don't you agree, Theresa?"

This is taking it too far, baiting the pastor's wife, and so Frieda stands to intervene. "Thank you, Retha. It's helpful to hear what you and Edgar and, um, your friends think about the matter—"

"Oh, my! Forgive me," Retha interrupts with a little clap of her hands, "I completely neglected to introduce these fine ladies to all of you. Yes, this is Gina Reisinger from Bramble," one hand designating the finch and the other the peacock, "and Betty Potter from Greyville. Their husbands serve on the school board alongside Edgar, of course, and they generously agreed to accompany me here today to listen to all of you and support you and take your concerns back to the board. Betty, you've been taking notes, yes?"

The peacock feather bows in dutiful deference.

"Wonderful. Then, before we close, are there any more questions?"

This comes from Retha, not Frieda, and the overt lawlessness is simply too much for the society president. Frieda restates the question word-for-word so as to make absolutely clear her opinion of such gross disorder. "Are there any more questions?"

Retha maintains her proud stance for an awkward moment, maybe two, before acquiescing and slowly lowering herself and her paper into her seat.

"What'll happen to the school building?" Viola's voice relays resignation.

Pastor, still standing, bends a bit at the waist as he answers, "Yet, undecided. Though there is talk of possibly renting it. Or even using it as a storage shed for equipment, for ongoing care of the cemetery."

"If I may, Pastor," Frieda asserts, "I have something to say about this very thing."

"Of course."

Frieda takes the time to look at each woman in turn, though skipping Retha and her portable aviary. She is not married and never has been. She has no husband, no living father. She is part of no mysterious "we," as Retha so often identifies in her little speeches. Other than her older brother Anders and astute Pastor Engel, no man in the grove shows any interest in hearing or representing or guiding or protecting her in congregational matters. She holds out very little hope that her personal concerns over the school's closing will be represented in the voting assembly, but regardless of what the men decide in the coming days, months, even years, she will joyfully serve this church. For she knows to do it as to the Lord. But here, in the Ladies Aid Society, among this little band of sisters in Christ, Frieda has a place and a voice and a seat at the table. She has the attention and the respect and the affection of these women, and she knows she can ask them anything. She knows they will help her with anything.

"Heaven forbid the morning school closes, but," she nods her head, "I think there is something we can do that may help the children."

"What?" Dorothea is the one who voices the question, but every other woman is asking it with her eyes.

"We can start a Sunday school."

"No," Renate is quick to dismiss. "Absolutely not. This will serve only to convince dissenters that we don't need the school. My mother, if she were well enough to be here, would tell all of you how she and Papa had to fight in years past against this very movement for this very reason."

"But Retha is right," Frieda explains, which earns a surprised expression of pleasure from the anarchic queen, "our children *will* be missing out on a daily review of the Catechism with Pastor Engel if the school closes. A Sunday school can help with this."

Renate shakes her head. "Pastor already leads *Christenlehre* after the sermon every Sunday morning, and there is nothing better."

"But Trinity in Covenant's been offerin' Sunday school for years," Cherry dares to counter over Roman's head.

"What does it matter to us what Trinity does?" Renate shrugs at her farmhand's wife. "Trinity doesn't have a school. We do."

"For now," Viola tempers. She looks up at Frieda. "I see the good in what you're suggesting, Aunt Frieda, I do. But I just don't see how Sunday school is a good enough substitute for what our children can learn from five days a week with Pastor."

Frieda bows her head for a moment in deference to Viola's point. The younger woman is the wife of her only nephew, and she is right. It is the children who are being cheated in all of this. "I open the floor to anyone else who has a better idea."

The women sit in silence. Even Retha's tongue appears to be stalled before the dilemma.

Surprisingly, it is Renate, shifting in her chair and sighing, who resigns all of them to the best of the worst. "*If* the school closes—and I maintain that we are far from any such an atrocity; certainly, my husband will never vote to do such a foolish thing—we still cannot ask Pastor to teach Sunday school. He is already so busy on Sundays."

"Agreed," Viola nods. "But if not Pastor, then who?"

"We already know the men won't do it," Opal grumbles.

"Now, hush about the men!" Dorothea barks. "None of us have any peace on earth without some goodwill toward men. They always go together, or have you girls forgotten what the angel said?"

Frieda quickly diverts, "Why not, us? We can teach the children." She turns to the one woman in attendance who already understands, the one who will be the easiest to convince. "Ruthie, don't you already read the Bible to your girls at home?"

Ruthie, who has been silent throughout this entire debate, is a widow. She, too, has been stripped of her mysterious "we" in life. She keeps her silence, but she nods.

"Then why not read to the other children, as well? Think of it. Between you, Priscilla, Theresa, Renate, Opal, Viola, Cherry, and — "

"I don't think Cherry should teach Sunday school," Renate asserts.

Frieda is stunned by this public, strangely specific calling out. She steals a look at Cherry who is hiding her burning cheeks behind Roman's curls.

"What I mean is," Renate rushes to explain, looking apologetically at Cherry, "none of the mothers with little ones in diapers should be asked to do this. They already have their hands full. We older women should bear this load."

Frieda notices that it is now Ruthie's cheeks that begin to redden.

Pastor Engel swiftly intervenes, "I think your Sunday school idea has merit, Frieda. I do. Thank you for suggesting a way to help both the children and me should the school close, though," more of his measured, careful thinking, "I'd like to take some time to discuss the idea with the elders. Perhaps, we can wait until a later date to discuss the matter of volunteer teachers — "

"These will not be paid positions, then?"

This interruption comes from Drucilla, Retha's daughter-in-law, and it is one interruption too many in Frieda's accounting. Also, it is one thing for an older woman with a weak upbringing to interrupt her younger pastor, but for a younger woman to interrupt her older pastor? Such impudence will not be tolerated, not on her watch. She turns a disapproving eye toward Drucilla.

The young woman falters a bit. "I'm just asking, you know, if we can expect to be paid. As teachers. Teachers are usually, um, paid. And — " Her voice fails, and she must swallow before finishing, "Pastor is paid."

"So are chefs and maids and nannies. But do you ask your husband to pay you for cooking and cleaning your own home and caring for your own children?"

Drucilla, looking miserable, shakes her head.

"Neither will we ask to be paid for reading the Bible and the Catechism to our own church family in our own church." But Frieda's conscience pricks. She is speaking too pointedly, too harshly. She will chase the younger women away from the joy of service if she is not careful, and if Drucilla's weary eyes are any indication, the woman is already serving her family plenty hard, day and night, at home. Frieda checks her attitude and face, softening her demeanor toward the younger woman. "It's been the privilege of women throughout history to work full-time both in the home and out of it."

"Just not usually for pay," the finch trills under her breath.

"True," Frieda tries shining some of that goodwill Dorothea mentioned down the table, "but we women are created to be helpmates. What better life is there than to help and serve others, pay or no?"

"I can think of a few things."

Are there none left who have not bowed unto Baal? She, even she only, is left! But Frieda was born a woman for this moment, and she is in a church, not a cave. She lowers herself into her seat and offers these women her very best.

"I wish," she begins, "you could have known my Aunt Sarah."

Renate raises her eyes and nods appreciatively at the mention of her sainted mother-in-law. She appears to know where this is going.

"Aunt Sarah was feisty and smart and often getting into trouble. But she was faithful, and she once said something to me that I'll never forget."

She has the women's full attention now, young and old, and she determines not to waste it. Though it means breaking two of her personal rules: no deviation from an agenda, and no personal stories in public. But if she doesn't say something now, Retha's birds certainly will, and not for everyone's good.

"Aunt Sarah said, 'It's a blessing to be a woman.'"

Frieda thinks on her sainted aunt and grows bold in her sharing.

"I was angry when I was young. I didn't have a husband to shear my sheep or spade my garden or carry my bags or make my way any easier in life, and I didn't have any children to milk my cow or set my table or take out the bath water or lighten my load. I was lonely, and I was feeling sorry for myself for having to work for my brother and spin wool all day and launder sheets for other peoples' families and for very little pay, only to have to do the very same work for myself when I was done. And Aunt Sarah said to me, 'But everyone has to work all of the time. Do you think a husband or a wife has it any easier than you? Do you think a man doesn't have to feed his animals and discipline his children and fix his roof when he comes home from work? Do you think a mother doesn't have to clean up her children's vomit in the night?'"

Drucilla, holding her baby to her breast, wipes at a tear on her cheek.

"'Everyone has their struggles,' Aunt Sarah said, 'and everyone has their blessings. One of your blessings: You get to sleep through the night. One of your struggles: You have to face an empty breakfast table. But everyone has to work all of the time, just like you. At least, they are blessed if they do. For what good ever came from sitting around more or looking in the mirror more or having more time to eat and drink? I tell you, it's a blessing to work all day long. And it doesn't matter so much where you work or what kind of work you do or for how much, but that you work. And if God gives you the health and ability and opportunity, then you will be blessed if you get to work your entire life.'"

Pastor Engel is studying her carefully—Is that admiration or concern in his eyes?—but every woman is looking down at her plate, tending to her own thoughts. For her own part, Frieda is surprised at how easy it was to say all of that aloud, and she leans back in her chair, content, even excited. No wonder Retha likes talking in public so much. It's thrilling having everyone look at you and listen to you that way. But Frieda knows not to dwell on such feelings, lest she learn to like them, need them, and even seek them out.

"Maybe the men will vote to close the school," Frieda acknowledges, "maybe they won't. I don't know. But I do know this. If they do close the school, we women will have more work to do. And we will be blessed because of it."

Chapter Eighteen

Saint Jacob

✛ 1991 ✛

He's been watching his mother die for seven months now, mostly from a distance, though these last two weeks have been from the wingback chair next to her bed. Her decline has been steady, her alert periods intermittent and waning. But this morning, after three sips of orange juice and a chocolate bar, she is somewhat revived. There is heat in her cheeks and a sparkle in her eyes, and she is chatty, even wily, more like her old self.

"Wait till you see it, Eddie," she is saying, talking of some back-road paradise Dad discovered on one of his many driving adventures. "It's the most darling little church. Your father was fishing in Dandy Creek over near Bramble with Si Reinking when he first saw it. You remember Uncle Si? His old buddy from the Air Force? Well, it's a tiny, whitewashed church and has a little steeple at the front that looks just like a pinky finger poking up from a fisted hand. And that bell! You've never heard such a sound, Eddie. It could make a saint out of Aristotle Onassis. And the whole thing is surrounded by the prettiest circle of trees, like ruffled lace on a country skirt. Whistle Grove is what they call it. The church is called Bethlehem, I believe. Bethlehem Lutheran. And they're the funniest, darling-est people. They still sing out of hymnals, Eddie. Can you believe it? Anyway, I've decided to be buried there."

He blinks, completely taken aback. "Not with Dad?" His father, career military, is already buried in a national cemetery. "But you have a plot in Danville next to Dad, Mom. You and he bought it years ago."

"I *do* have a plot there, yes. But I don't want it."

"You don't want it? You don't want to be buried next to Dad?"

"Oh, honey, it's not that. Of course, I want to be buried next to your father, but he's been gone for thirteen years now, and, well . . . It's too sunny there."

"Too sunny?"

"Yes."

"For a grave?"

"For anyone visiting the grave. Trust me, sweetheart, I know. I've been visiting your father come rain or come shine — mostly, come shine — and it gets so hot in the sun. And the wind there is like . . . well, it violates you, that's what it does, always ripping off your hat and scarf and undressing you in public. It's like being assaulted, standing out there at your father's grave."

He is looking at his mother through his fingers, mortified to think that a nurse — anyone! — may be listening to this soap opera dialogue in the hall.

"Trust me, you'll feel much better when you visit me in Whistle Grove. Oh, I wish you could see the little cemetery in Whistle Grove, Eddie. You know what?" Her eyes grow wide, and she lifts her head off the pillow for the first time in days. "We should go see it together. We'll go today! Yes, Uncle Si will take us. Oh, it is so darling, Eddie. You will just love it there, I know it. Those big trees at the rim — they're like angels. No, like sentinels, guardians of generations past."

Trees are and always will be trees, but his English-teacher mother rarely speaks of anything she's passionate about without first dressing it up in a simile or metaphor. It's an endearing quality, really. At least, it is when she's not comparing a current of air to a molester. He rubs his weary eyes with his fists. He could use a shower.

"I want my ashes scattered at the feet of those giant guardians."

His head jerks away from his hands. "Your ashes?"

"Yes, when I'm cremated, pour my — "

"You will not be cremated, Mom. You will be buried. You've already picked out your casket. Oak, remember?"

"I've changed my mind."

Granted, he is sleepless from watching her breathe in the night, and so maybe his panic is an overreaction. But his mother appears to be losing her mind, not changing it. He reaches for her hands, grounding her thoughts with his touch.

"Mom, what are you talking about?"

"Ruby and I were talking — "

"Who's Ruby?"

"She's my neighbor. In Room 114. Anyway, she was telling me all about it, how much money it saves, how much better it is for the earth, how they collect your ashes in a beautiful urn, and how — "

"How they can't guarantee that all of the ashes are your own? Did Ruby tell you that?"

She looks up at him with a little pout, irritated at being interrupted.

"When they incinerate your body, Mom, they can't keep your remains from getting mixed up with whomever was burned before you. This beautiful urn you're talking about: How will I know there's not half of you and a third of Ruby in there?"

"Well, that doesn't add up to a whole person, now, does it?"

"That's not the point, Mom."

"Why does it matter so much if we all get mixed together a bit? Aren't we all one body in Christ, anyway?"

He had thought moving her into assisted living was the best option for her final years, given her limited mobility and unlimited desire for social interaction, but he is second-guessing the wisdom of that decision. He squeezes her hands firmly and tries another approach.

"Mom, there is no need to be cremated. You have a casket and a gravesite already picked out and ready to go for when the time comes. Besides, the Christian tradition is to be buried in a cemetery. The very word 'cemetery' comes from the Greek *κοιμητήριον*, which means 'bedroom' or 'place to rest.' Isn't that beautiful? Because that's what you'll be doing in the cemetery: sleeping in Jesus. And then He'll wake you up on the Last Day. He will raise your body from the grave, and you will live with Him forever."

"You say such beautiful things, Eddie. You're such a good pastor."

He knows that tone of voice. It's the placating one. She would also be patting his cheek, right now, if she were capable. She does this every time she's about to—

"But won't my body return to dust in the grave?"

"Yes."

"Ruby says, if Jesus can raise my dust, He can also raise my ashes."

He is forevermore convinced rubies to be the least of all gemstones. "Christians are buried, Mom, not cremated."

"But Ruby's a Christian, and she's being cremated."

He lets go of her hands and sits back in his chair. "I don't think you should worry about this anymore."

"Oh, I'm not worried."

"I mean, I'm going to take care of you, and so you don't need to think about it. It's my privilege to care for your remains. I love you. I'm your son."

"But you aren't my son."

He is so, so tired. It almost sounded as if she said—

"You are my son, of course. But you also aren't. Your father and I adopted you."

The earth brakes to a halt, and the violence of the sudden standstill pitches him forward in his chair.

"Oh, Eddie!" Her right hand fishes amongst the blankets for his head. His cheek is flush with the mattress, and upon finding it, she runs her fingers over and over his face like she used to do when he was a boy. "Eddie, my son! I'm so sorry! Of course, you are my son. A woman from the city birthed you, and then we adopted you. That is all. It's a simple edit, a small change to the first page of your story. But you are still my son. Our son. Nothing changes that. Nothing will ever change that."

Everything is sideways. He feels displaced, nauseated.

"We meant to tell you years ago, of course. So many times, we meant to tell you, but then the day would end with another sunset, and we'd say to each other, 'We'll tell him when the sun rises. This news is better in the light.' And then, one day, the sun rose on your father's death, and, well . . . How could I tell you without him?"

She is weeping, now, and he is letting her wipe the tears from his own cheeks.

"My son, my son!"

He is seven again, and he just opened his knee on the sidewalk after tripping in his new roller skates. He is lying in the grass, his cheek flush with the ground, and she is wiping his wet cheeks with her hand, soothing him, "My son, my son!"

+ + +

He buries her in the oak casket next to his father, but the very same day, he points his car west and south for a couple of hours, turning onto a series of corn-fenced, gravely roads, eventually pulling onto a dirt lane overgrown with black-eyed Susans.

There it is. The whitewashed church with the pinky-steeple.

He parks the car in the shade of a perfectly rounded maple and, pocketing both his keys and his clerical tab—it chokes him in this heat—wanders over to view some nearby headstones. *Inah and Perle Iken, 1882.* The next stone bears simply the name *Mary* with no surname. Here are some old graves with, he suspects, some sad stories.

"Is there a particular grave I can help you find?"

He is startled by the nearness of the voice. He looks to his right, and just ten feet away, sitting on the ground with his back against the trunk of an enormous cottonwood tree, is a middle-aged man reading a book.

"Forgive me, I scared you."

"No," Eddie assures, walking toward the tree, "though I've no idea how I missed you there."

"It's hard to see the trees for the forest here." The man closes his book and stands, brushing off the back of his pants and extending a welcoming hand. "Jacob Sterling."

"Edmund Oglethorpe. My friends call me Eddie."

"You're a pastor, I see." Jacob gestures toward Eddie's tab-less black shirt.

"Yes, as are you."

The quiet reader nods and pulls his own white tab out of his pocket. "They nearly choke a man toward the middle of the day, yes?"

"Sometimes long before that," and they both laugh.

"Where's your congregation?"

Eddie gestures in a southerly direction. "Northern suburb of Dallas."

"Texas?"

"Deep in the heart. Well, north and bit east of the heart."

"Big congregation?"

"Yes," but he hastily amends, "by Lutheran standards. By Texas standards, no."

Jacob chuckles, understanding. "You're not Missouri Synod, by any chance?"

"Born and bred. How about you? Is this your church?"

Jacob gestures grandly around the grove. "Behold, my Jerusalem. There's no Solomon's Portico, but it boasts a fine outdoor study. It's one of the perks of the country gig. You caught me prepping my sermon a bit ago."

"A brother pastor of a sister congregation," Eddie claps the younger man affectionately on the shoulder. "I must confess, I already know you're Missouri Synod. I looked up Bethlehem in the *Annual* before I came."

"Well, even if you hadn't, the big size of the church would give it away."

Eddie throws his head back and belly-laughs. He likes this self-effacing man. "Where'd you go to seminary?"

"St. Louis."

He immediately thinks of his birth mother from "the city." It's still so new to him, this mysterious feeling, this personal connection to a woman he's never met. Where is she, now? Is she still alive? What will she think when—

"How about you?"

"Hm?"

"Where'd you go to sem?"

"Oh, Springfield. Back in the day."

An emphatic, staccato trill interrupts their conversation, and they both look up for a view of the feisty, whistling warbler. There, sitting at the very peak of the cottonwood under which the local pastor had been reading, is a cardinal: the red-feathered pride of Illinois.

"Just think," Eddie propounds, "Jesus had the angels to minister to him in the wilderness, and you have the birds."

"I'll take all of the winged help I can get," Jacob nods soberly.

"How long have you been here?"

"Ten years, last year."

"First call?"

Jacob nods. "Fresh out of the sem. How about you?"

"I served six years in the Air Force before seminary, and then my first call was to the Minnesota North District. I've been in Texas for 15 years."

"You've been all over."

"I've seen enough of the north in winter to know what the wind can do to man's soul and enough of the south in summer to know that the sun's no kinder. But I hear this is paradise."

"I suppose every church brings a bit of heaven down to earth," a shadow passes over Jacob's face, "though this place'll make a man pine for eternal rest as much as any other. What brings you here?"

"My mother."

"She's buried here?"

"No."

He wants to say more. The secret is burning his mouth from the inside out, and he longs to spit it out. He has shared the news of his adoption with no one since his mother first stalled the earth with it two weeks before, and it would be such a relief to tell this stranger, this brother pastor. But all he says is, "My parents retired to Riverfield after my father left the Air Force, and they both fell in love with this grove, apparently. Simeon Reinking introduced them to it."

"Uncle Si!" Jacob's eyes light up for the first time. "Everyone loves Uncle Si."

"Well, my mother told me about this place just days before she died. The picture she painted of it made me want to see it for myself. I have to say, she wasn't far from the truth in her description. It really is lovely here. Peaceful."

"It can be."

Something in the other man's tone prompts Eddie to ask, "What's your congregation like?"

"Like every congregation, I suspect. Anchored in the Word, besieged by Satan."

Eddie nods, understanding.

"Honestly, it's been a bit rough the last few years. The economy, mostly. The head of a local family-owned factory died about six years back, and the son — Uncle Si's older brother, actually. Well, he mismanaged the business and had to declare bankruptcy and everything. When the factory finally closed three years ago, it put half the county out of work. Most of our families relocated to Riverfield for jobs, and we've never quite recovered from that. Financially, I mean."

"Do you have any family?"

"Me? No. Not anymore. That's good, I guess."

Eddie can't quite keep his eyebrows from lifting.

"I mean — you know what I mean," Jacob stumbles over his words, coloring a bit. "Benefits and all. Having no wife, no kids — it's not as costly for the congregation. Everyone's already so stressed financially. They can barely pay me as it is."

"No other businesses moving into the area?"

"Not for years."

"I'm sorry to hear that." He looks up at the beautiful church, a white ship built by the stewardship of generations past, but it is not past generations who will keep her afloat. "Do you have a school?"

"Had. One of the oldest in the synod." Jacob nods toward the square, squat building decaying just east of the lane. "They closed it mid-century."

"Why?"

"General disinterest among the community, from what I can tell. The local school district campaigned heavily for a full K through 12 program after the second world war, and Bramble — that's the town just east of here — it joined forces with a nearby village called Greyville. The two communities combined to build a new school, and that was the flame that drew all the moths."

"What a shame," Eddie shakes his head, for what flame was ever able to give any moth the thing most needful? "What do you use the building for, now?"

"It's basically a glorified tool shed."

"Now, there's a metaphor that would stun even my sainted mother!"

Jacob looks at him curiously.

"The school building now being a tool shed. To have the church trade in books for shovels and replace the liberal arts with science and technology. It's all sadly profound. My mother was an English teacher. She would appreciate the metaphor is all I'm saying."

"I was married."

Jacob's hurried confession takes Eddie by surprise, but he has been a pastor for too long to overreact in such a moment. He stands still. He waits and listens.

"She left me about five years ago."

"I'm sorry."

"Me, too." Jacob takes in a deep breath as if sighing in rewind. "I can be slow to act sometimes."

Another confession, this one too mysterious to be understood, and Jacob gives no further explanation.

"Are you married?"

"No," Eddie shakes his head, "the Lord has not seen fit to give me that gift."

"It is a gift," is all the local pastor says, and the two leave it at that.

+ + +

When Eddie drives back down the dirt lane, he glances in the rearview mirror and observes Jacob resettling himself against the cottonwood, though the man does not reopen his book. Instead, he stares out over the graves and then up into the trees and then back over the graves again.

Is this what a country parish is like, reliving the story of Eden? Looking upon all that God has made and seeing that it is good, all the while pondering the curse of Eve?

"'Then I heard the voice of the Lord saying,'" he quotes as he turns right onto the outer gravel road, "'Whom shall I send? And who will go for us?'"

It really is a beautiful grove.

"'And I said, Here am I. Send me!'"

The Cemetery

Chapter Nineteen

Saint Mary

+ 1939 +

Cherry is six months pregnant, and Ruthie offers to help her clean the church.

"I'll give you my pay."

"You'll do no such thing," Ruthie says, lifting an extra bucket out of the back of Papa Werth's Willys–Overland and shutting the trunk with a bang. "You cleaned my house for me three months straight after Miriam was born, and I didn't pay you a cent."

"Yes, you did. You read *Crime and Punishment* aloud to me while I scrubbed. It's been my favorite book ever since."

"How about you read to me while I clean, then? An even trade."

Cherry catches the toe of an Oxford on the first step of the front stoop.

"Careful, now," Ruthie warns, throwing out a hand to assist. "Yes, I think I'd like to hear *The Brothers Karamazov*. That'll be sufficient pay. Mother Renate's got a copy of it on her shelf, but I've never read it. I'll ask her if we can borrow it next week."

Cherry will not look at her friend. She is too close to being found out, and she risks, "That one's too long, don't you think?" She really doesn't know, but it's her best defense. "You'll have to clean the church for me clear through Christmas if you want me to get through that one."

"True," Ruthie laughs easily, and Cherry, relieved, breathes easier. "Pass me your key, will you? Oh, wait. Never mind, the door's unlocked."

Ruthie pushes through the front door and on into the vestibule, and the two busy themselves unloading the front closet of cleaning supplies.

"You know what," Cherry suggests, "how 'bout I pick out a book?"

"Okay. Surprise me."

Cherry most certainly will, as she has no plans of ever picking out a book to read to Ruthie. She'll just have to pretend that she keeps forgetting week after week and hope Ruthie moves on to a different idea.

"Sitting's easier than bending, right?"

Cherry nods.

"I'll mop, then, and you sit and polish the backs of the pews."

"Deal."

But Cherry and Ruthie never get to cleaning the church that day, for they discover a strange girl with large, frightened eyes huddled in the very back pew.

✛ ✛ ✛

"She can't be more than 11 or 12," Ruthie whispers in the front room of the old house. They decided to take the girl back to Cherry's place so as not to alert Papa or Mother Werth or anyone until they figure out what to do.

The girl is soaking in a copper tub in the middle of the kitchen. It took some convincing to get her to take off her dress, but Cherry finally won the day with the promise of bread with butter and plum preserves after bathing.

Cherry looks at the filthy frock in her hands. It is a thin, cotton day dress. The material appears to have been a bright blue floral print back in the day, but now it is faded, worn, and torn from use, even abuse. She probably should burn it, but something in her own proud nature warns her that this would be a mistake, a breach of whatever meager trust she's earned from the girl with the promise of food.

"You're going to wash it, aren't you?" Ruthie asks, her tone clearly communicating that burning is the better option.

"It's the only thing the girl owns. An' that book."

Ruthie picks up the hardbound volume with the curled pages sitting on the mantle of the fireplace. "*The Count of Monte Cristo*. Do you suppose that girl can even read? She hasn't spoken a word since we found her."

Cherry doesn't think it proper to speculate about such personal matters, and so she moves toward the front door. "If she does say anythin', let me know. I'm gonna see if I can't scrub the miles out o' these threads without breakin' 'em."

+ + +

Cherry gives the girl one of her own dresses to wear as the blue frock dries out on the line. It's too big for her, but an apron cinched tightly around her waist—the girl insists on doing this herself—keeps everything in place well enough.

Cherry pours her a third glass of milk and butters a fourth slice of bread. She has already eaten a fourth of this morning's loaf, and the littles are up from their naps and sitting at the table, doing their best to devour the rest of it.

"My name is Cherry Daniels, and these are my children. Matthew's four, and Flossie's two."

"I big girl," Flossie makes clear through a mouthful of bread.

"Chew an' swallow before you speak, big girl," Cherry smiles.

The girl is staring at Cherry's belly.

"Yes, another one. Flossie thinks it's a girl, but Mattie— "

"I askt Got for a baby brudder."

The girl is rather beautiful with the stain and stink washed from her skin, though willow-thin. Her hair is long and black and straight, hanging to her waist, and her blue-gray eyes are as faded as her dress. With pale-gray skin, she looks like moonlight sitting in their kitchen.

"I do think it's a boy," Cherry indulges in a knowing smile. "I had such terrible heartburn with Flossie, but I can eat anythin' with this baby. He's due in August."

But Cherry stops talking, for the girl begins to cry.

+ + +

The girl's day dress grows tight at the buttons, and Cherry assumes it is from the bread and butter, until she helps the girl into a borrowed sleeping gown one night.

"I think she's pregnant," she tells Ruthie the next morning.

"But she's practically a baby herself."

They ponder in silence the various, horrible scenarios that might result in such a plight.

"How far along, do you think?"

"Four months, at least." Cherry wipes at a tear.

They have asked her every question they think appropriate—"What is your name? Where are you from? Do you have any family?"—but the girl never says anything.

"What does Mark think?"

Cherry shrugs. "He doesn't know what to think. Neither of us do. Honestly, we thought she'd be on her way by now—people wand'rin' through these parts usually do, you know, pass through to wherever they're goin'. But this girl, she shows no purpose, no drive, no anythin'. What're we supposed to do with her? Don' get me wrong, she's no trouble. She's quite helpful around the house an' yard, even looks after the chickens an' ducks all on her own. I don' do any of the milkin' anymore. An' she's great with the kids. But she still doesn't talk. Only looks through her book or out the window."

"Do you suppose someone, some man . . . ?" but Ruthie won't say it.

"Yes. I do."

They decide to get Pastor Engel involved, and after consulting with the elders, the men decide to talk to the local authorities and pay for some ads to be run in local newspapers on the girl's behalf.

"Just to see if she has any family in the area," Pastor assures, but Cherry does not feel good about it. This girl came to her hungry, alone, and pregnant, and none of those conditions describe a child who comes from a family who loves its own.

+ + +

Cherry goes into labor in late July.

Mrs. Werth and Ruthie assist the doctor, but Cherry is certain afterward that she remembers the girl running hot water back and forth between the bedroom and the kitchen during the worst of it.

"Thank you," Cherry says, smiling at the girl as she brings her a glass of milk and some bread with butter and jam in bed. They are alone, the two of them with the baby, for Mark is out in the fields and Ruthie took the kids for the day so Cherry could rest. "Would you like to hold the baby?"

The girl's luminous eyes grow big and round and watery. It's like looking into two wells at the same time and seeing moonlight refracting on the rippling surfaces.

"You can hold 'im," Cherry assures, and though the girl looks frightened, she takes the swaddled boy in her arms and rests him cautiously on top of her own swollen belly. It will not be long before her own time will come.

"His name is Luke John," Cherry confides. "From the Bible. His daddy's Mark, of course, and then Mattie is Matthew. I guess we're gettin' a bit impatient to finish with the Gospels in our family."

The girl turns and steps out of the room then, and Cherry has a flash of panic. But in seconds, the girl returns to the bedroom and with the baby still in her arms. She is also holding her beloved book. She holds it out to Cherry.

"Oh. You want me to read it?"

The girl nods and lays the book on top of the sheets. An eye for an eye, a tooth for a tooth, and a book for a baby, it seems. Cherry is filled with compassion for the generous girl, and she tells her something she has never told anyone else, saving Mark. "I can't read."

The girl looks up from the baby, her mouth open in surprise. But her face does not project any judgment or pity or derision or any of the reactions Cherry fears. The girl is looking at her with what appears to be deference, even gratitude. In a moment, she closes her mouth and nods, handing Luke John back to Cherry with the greatest care.

"Oh, no, I didn't mean—"

But the girl has already retrieved the book and is moving toward a nearby chair.

"You may hold him longer if you want."

The girl shakes her head, opens the book to the first page, and then, offering the shyest of smiles to her hostess, stuns Cherry by reading aloud in a voice that sounds almost like home, "Chapter One: Marseilles—The Arrival. On the 24th of February, 1815, the look-out at Notre-Dame de la Garde signalled the three-master, the *Pharaon* from Smyrna, Triesta, and Naples . . ."

For the entire day, the girl reads aloud to Cherry, and the two of them laugh and cry along with Edmond Dantès, Mercédès, and Abbé Faria through a series of misadventures. Only when Ruthie knocks on the front door in the late afternoon does the girl close the book and her mouth for the rest of the night.

+ + +

There is no response to the local ads, and so Pastor Engel assumes the girl came in with the train.

"Most likely, she's from out of state—Arkansas, Missouri—though she could be from anywhere, really."

Cherry talks to Mark that night, and they agree.

"We'd like you to stay with us," she tells the girl that night before bed. It is late August, and the baby is coming soon. "You're safe here."

The girl says nothing, but she grips Cherry's hand on her way out the bedroom door. She is squeezing rather than saying thank you, and Cherry squeezes in return.

But the next morning, only the book is resting on the girl's pillow. The girl herself is gone.

✛ ✛ ✛

Cherry leads little Matthew and Flossie into the church and sits them on the floor of the vestibule with a basket of toys.

"Play here while Mama cleans the church."

She is carrying a swaddled, sleeping LJ, and she lays him next to his smitten sister—"No fingers in his mouth. Let him be."—before taking the mop and the bucket of cleaning supplies from the front closet and moving into the nave.

But from the start, something doesn't smell right.

"Hello?" she calls, flipping on the lights. She half expects a raccoon or a feral dog to run out from underneath a pew, but nothing stirs below or above. Still, she proceeds warily. Ever since discovering the girl in a back pew last spring, she never assumes she is alone in the church. "Anybody here?"

It is then that she hears it. A mewing kitten. Relieved, she expels the breath she is holding. Still, her milk lets down at the sound, and she leans the mop against a pew. "Mattie," she calls over her shoulder, "come 'ere. I think we've got ourselves a little, furry friend."

Matthew jumps up and runs ahead of her, talking to the cat before he can even see it. "Oh, kitty! Oh, kitty! Come here, kitty—" but the boy stops mute about halfway up the aisle.

"Mattie? What is it?"

The earthy smell reintroduces itself to Cherry's nose, and Matthew begins to whimper.

Flossie responds from behind with some fussing of her own, and Cherry's heart begins to pound. Something is terribly wrong, she can feel it, smell it. She strides toward her eldest son, pulling him behind her as fast as she can and blocking his body with her own. She sees the blood on the floor before she sees the bare feet curling toward her in a pew, and bile enters her mouth. Looking away, she gags and swallows and then pulls Matthew back to the narthex, shutting the doors to the nave behind her.

She is now feeling more than she is thinking, and she scoops LJ under one arm, swings Flossie onto her back with the other, and pushes Matthew with her knees out the church door and onto the front stoop.

"Race me, Mattie," she cries, trying her best to tame the fear out of her voice. Mattie is openly crying now, and so, balancing Flossie on her back, she risks a hand to half-drag her oldest son, aiming him for the trees. "Race me to the road, Mattie!"

Eventually, the sunshine and the wind and the appeal of a game distract the small boy from his emotions, and he begins to pick up his own feet. He even manages to outrun her when they cross the Fireling Road and the parsonage is in sight.

Theresa Engel answers the door, and Cherry pushes LJ into the unsuspecting pastor's wife's arms while sliding Flossie toward ground. She thrusts all three children through the doorway and pants, "We need a doctor at the church. And Pastor. Quick!"

And then she is running back to the grove, her lungs burning, her breasts weeping, and she stops in the lane to retch in the trees.

+ + +

Pastor Engel and Dr. Miller eventually come, but not right away. Cherry must walk back into the church alone, for the mewing haunts her memory and tugs at her conscience. She saw blood pooled on the floor, yes, and too much to translate into any hope, but that mewing had life in it.

She enters the vestibule, then the nave, and succeeds in putting one foot in front of the other. The church is silent but for the creaking of the floor under her own weight. There is no more crying of any kind, and the bile threatens to climb back up her throat.

There is the blood.

There is the body.

No, two bodies. It is the girl, just as she knew it would be, and she is lying on her side in the pew in her own mess. One arm is draped around a tiny, still baby tucked up under her chin.

Cherry cannot breathe or swallow or cry or think. All she can do is sink into the pew behind and look upon the mother and baby.

The pale girl is now a lifeless color, and when Cherry builds up enough nerve to reach for the baby, she cries out in distress to discover the girl's arm is already cold with death. But her cry succeeds in rousing the baby — "Thank you, Lord Jesus!" — and Cherry frantically pulls at the hoarse, shuddering thing, prying what little life is left from the young mother's death-grip.

It's a boy, and Cherry sinks back against the pew again and does the only thing she can.

She unbuttons the top of her dress and offers the starving baby her own breast.

+ + +

"What's goin' to happen to him?"

Cherry is sitting in a chair in the middle of the sacristy, utterly exhausted yet feeding LJ, and Ruthie is washing the birth off of the baby boy in the sink.

"I don't know. He'll be put up for adoption, most likely."

"Tell me that boy won't go to an orphanage."

"I'm not God, Cherry. I can't tell you what's going to happen."

They are both stressed and short of temper, but in a moment, the friends reach out one hand toward the other and grip each other fiercely. It is an apology and absolution all in one.

"We can't put him in an orphanage."

"There are worse things, Cherry. Much worse. And we don't know that he'll be put in an institution. There are couples out there who want a baby."

"With a depressed economy? And the war in Europe?" Cherry is all doom and gloom today. "Why don't you an' Orv take him?"

"We can't just take a baby!"

"That's not what I mean." Cherry watches as Ruthie bathes the child in the tub, methodically yet tenderly. "You could adopt him."

"Me?"

"Well, you an' Orv."

"Why not you and Mark?"

"Because," Cherry feels her face grow hot. The idea sits sound and upright in her own mind, but it tumbles out clumsily now that she's voicing it aloud. "I already have LJ on the breast. And Viola's due any day, and Drucilla's four months along— "

"Well, I can't."

"Why?"

Ruthie turns then, and the pink in her cheeks and the brightness in her eyes say it all.

"You're pregnant!"

She nods, her joy peeking through the grief of the day like sunlight through a corncrib wall.

"When?"

"Sometime in May."

And the two embrace over the babies, and the four of them cry for everything that is given and taken away.

+ + +

"We have some charitable plots reserved in the cemetery for Bethlehem's pastors and their wives. We can bury her there, I'm sure, if the elders agree. It's the least we can do for the girl."

They are sitting with the Engels in the parsonage kitchen, drinking coffee.

"Mark and I'll pay for the headstone," Cherry announces without even asking her husband.

"Headstone?" Ruthie challenges. "I want to honor the girl too, but seriously, Cherry. What's the point?"

"To mark her grave."

"No, I mean, we know nothing about her. What's the point of a headstone when we don't know her name or birthdate or anything else that goes on a headstone?"

These are things Cherry might be concerned with if she could read, but she can't. And she is adamant. "We know her death date."

"That, we do," Pastor Engel nods.

"And I think," Cherry starts, but emotion chokes her. She clears her throat. She feels a strong affection for the homeless girl, almost as much as for her own children. She blinks back tears and swallows. Something terrible and wonderful is becoming plain to her in this moment. Something profound is being made simple, and she gains strength from the epiphany: She is the girl's mother, now. "I think I do know her name."

"How?" Ruthie contests. "The girl couldn't even speak."

Cherry doesn't bother correcting her friend. She never told anyone how the girl read aloud to her that day after LJ's birth, just as she is certain the girl never told anyone that she can't read. Some experiences—some bonds—are too personal and private to be made public. "I just know."

Cherry may not be able to read words, but she can read people, and that humble girl came to the grove pregnant and without a husband, silent and pondering many things in her heart. The words "Let it be to me" permeated every mournful, resigned look on her submissive face.

"What is her name?" Pastor Engel asks, though Cherry suspects from the man's patient smile that he may already know, as well.

"Her name is Mary."

+ + +

"Where was the mother from?" the policeman asks.

"Well, sir," Mark answers measuredly, thoughtfully. "We don' rightly know. She wasn't from around here. That much we can tell you."

"Any documentation?"

"None."

"Just a book," Cherry offers. "Um, *The Count of Monte Cristo*."

"That's French, right?"

Cherry has no idea, but the names and places Mary read aloud sure didn't sound English.

"Was the girl French?" the policeman clarifies.

"No." Cherry is resolute.

"How do you know?" Mark challenges.

"I know."

"Could be from St. Louis, then," the officer muses. "Or Louisville, maybe."

"Why not France?" Mark asks, but Cherry elbows him in the ribs.

"Pastor Engel thought maybe she'd come in on the Greyville line. From out of state. Or some big city, at least."

"I'll make note of it in the boy's file, but we'll register the birth in Riverfield County." He moves his pen assertively across the certificate in broad, strong strokes. "And the boy's name?"

"We don' know — "

"Edmond," Cherry spurts.

"Really?" Mark turns and asks.

"Yes." She's not going to let a strange man name the child, that's for sure. And Edmond is the only male name she ever heard the girl speak aloud with a smile on her lips. Yes, Mary would like that name. "His name is Edmond."

"How do you spell that?" the officer asks, his pen poised and ready.

Cherry blinks, panicked, and elbows her husband in the ribs again. He looks at her like she's crazy, but she points wildly at the bent head of the officer, making the situation clear.

"Oh," Mark realizes, also looking a bit panicked. "Edmund?"

Cherry nods.

"Okay. Yes. Um, Edmund. E-D-M-U-N-D."

Chapter Twenty

Saint Edmund

✠ 2018 ✠

Gaudete Sunday in Advent, A.D. 2018

My dear Ms. Grisbone,

It is terribly awkward beginning any correspondence with an apology, but I will not write another word without first making right my wrong. Straight to it—

I beg you to forgive an old man, for I neglected to congratulate you on being the sole *legatee* of your Aunt Miriam's estate. We took such hasty leave of each other outside Berry's office the afternoon of the funeral, and, of course, we both were distracted and weighed down by heavy vocational responsibilities following the reading of the will. I confess, I was rather disarmed by your immediate refusal to serve on the cemetery board in your aunt's place. Your exact words have stuck with me these past weeks: "Christians persist in overpopulating the earth despite what is good for the rest of the world. I want no part in their campaign to overpopulate the ground as well." I am old and firm in my ways and needed time to ponder your assertion, and I am sorry that I let my broody nature get in the way of what I should have said in the moment.

So, I hope you will allow me now to assure you of my thankfulness that Werth hands—and capable ones at that!—still hold the deed to the finest acreage in the county. The two of us know what treasures that land holds both for this world and the next, and I wish you only the best, truly. Know that I have prayed for you every day since the reading of your Aunt Miriam's will, and I will continue to do so for as many days as the Lord gives me the mind and breath to do so.

And now for the reason this letter comes to you in a parcel rather than an envelope:

Before entering her eternal rest, your Aunt Miriam asked me to hunt down something of her mother's stowed in the old farmhouse attic and have it shipped to you. Now, I know what you are thinking, Ms. Grisbone: I am sorely belated in the execution of such a brief, and you are right to think so! Still, however overdue, I am a man of my word, and I braved a ladder yesterday morning in search of Miriam's buried treasure.

Now, table all passionate objections on my behalf, for my elderly ambition was closely monitored and even assisted by the benevolent Lila Daniels and her son Clark whose names you heretofore will recognize on the farmhouse's lease. They were the Lewis and Clark to my Manifest Destiny, for we discovered several new worlds in the layers of dust covering your aunt's attic stash. I do fear the native inhabitants of those worlds may have taken up residence in my lungs, but do not be alarmed. My cough is quickly abating in personality if not in frequency, and I do believe that my present sufferings are not worthy to be compared with the glory that was revealed in Box #3.

This is where I must confess that I made it through only three boxes total before being called down for a rather marvelous supper prepared by Lila. That dear woman fried me fish cakes. My mother used to make those for my father and me every Advent, and I must have told Lila as much at some point, though I cannot remember ever doing so. Still, my heart was warmed right along with my belly. I digress—

There remain at least ten or fifteen boxes in the attic to be sorted. If you would like them shipped to you unopened, I am certain Clark can figure out a way to get everything "over the river and through the woods" to Maine, though I can make no promise as to how soon. Lila and I are rather hopeful that you will choose to come home and visit us in the new year and spend some time prospecting in the attic yourself. In truth, you are much easier to ship than new worlds. Lila promises you free lodgings and hot suppers, and I cannot recommend either enough.

My main purpose for writing you today is that I could not wait to send you Miriam's treasure in Box #3 that is wrapped in tissue paper below this epistle: your Grandmother Werth's Catechism. I found it tucked amongst a dozen hand-embroidered table linens, some Christmas ornaments (too fragile to ship, I'm sorry), and an old package of cotton gloves. Don't let the worn binding fool you. The Catechism is overused, not neglected, I'm certain. And whatever you think of the words printed on the page by the publisher, you will most assuredly appreciate reading your grandmother's notes written in the margins. Now, do not be offended, Ms. Grisbone. Neither I nor your sainted aunt are proselytizing you. Not solely, anyway. We mean to ship you a bit of home and history for Christmas in addition to the proselytizing.

Before we take leave of each other again, I pray you will allow me to share one final thought. I have been considering your parting words to me regarding your concern that Whistle Grove is "littering" your family's land by perpetuating the cemetery. I have meditated on this matter and applied the best of my vocational prowess to it for the better part of the past few weeks, and I feel compelled to share with you something you may never have heard before. It is this: Every new day that dawns brings you and me closer to our deaths. And not only us, but also the death of this beautiful earth that you and I love so dearly. The land and sky and seas grow old right along with us, for they, too, exist in time, and time certainly passes. All of us who have a beginning also have an ending, and every scientist on this good, green earth knows it.

I feel a need to tell you this, for I suspect your concern is influenced by the fallacious spirit of our age that asserts the earth can and will keep on living forever and ever as long as we humans are good stewards of it. (I ask, when has good stewardship ever kept anything else that is living from dying?) But the environmentalist's line of thinking, however sincere, is backwards, for it is not the earth that is eternal, but Christ.

Jesus Christ, begotten of the Father, was not created. He exists outside of time, and even though He humbled Himself to be born of a virgin, in time, and to be sacrificed on a cross for our sin and shame, He is risen from the dead! He lives in the flesh—an historical fact—nevermore to die. He is eternal, and by His gracious benefaction He makes us humans, who were created in His image, eternal through Baptism into His own death and resurrection.

You, not the earth, are the pinnacle of God's creation. You, not the earth, are created in His image. It is you who are eternal and will live on, even though you die and though the earth passes away.

It is not cemeteries that are killing the earth. Time is killing the earth, and die it will.

In light of this reality, I think a cemetery is a beautiful, respectful way for a dying earth to serve God's eternal creation, and I believe that a woman as thoughtful and principled as you will make a worthy guardian and keeper of Whistle Grove.

When you do visit to prospect the attic, let's talk about what Christ promises to do when the earth dies.

Ever and sincerely yours,

Rev. Edmund G. Oglethorpe

Chapter Twenty-one

Saint Luke

+ 2015 +

Sally is pulled below the surface by the undertow of Mother's cancer diagnosis, but she clings tightly to the one life-preserver within reach: Aunt Miriam is flying to Maine.

Three times in her adult life Sally has flown by herself to meet Aunt Miriam in various exotic, literature-inspired destinations—London, Puducherry, then Cairo—but not once has Aunt Miriam made the journey east to visit the Grisbones, not when Mother debuted at Carnegie Hall and not even when Sally graduated from college *summa cum laude.* But today, Aunt Miriam is flying into Portland International and staying for three nights in Rockland, and Sally is both elated and terrified. For she adores her spirited aunt more than anyone else in the world and takes great comfort in her company, but the event of Aunt Miriam's finally coming and in her old age speaks to the seriousness of Mother's condition.

A vested attendant wheels Miriam to the car—"Is this really necessary?" Aunt Miriam entreats—but once they get her belted safely into the passenger seat, Sally expertly maneuvers her Subaru onto I-295 and toward home.

"You know," she begins, eager to talk about anything other than Mother, "Bangor is just 90 minutes north of Rockland."

"You've thrown me this bone before," Miriam returns, "but I've no interest in Stephen King and his broody hallucinations. Not one bit."

Sally grins. One always knows where Aunt Miriam stands on everything.

"Though you could talk me into driving to that donut place you always rave about. The one with the crunchy chocolate cake."

"The old-fashioned chocolate buttercrunch cake donut," Sally amends. "That's the Willow Bake Shoppe in Rockport. And, yes, I'm taking you there for breakfast tomorrow morning."

"You've always been a good girl," Miriam winks, and the two are at-home with each other as if never parted. "Now, what have you been reading?"

They share a love of books. Sometimes, they even read the same book simultaneously and discuss it over the phone, but of late, Sally has neglected their book club of two for more pressing deadlines at work. "I'm back in *Jane Eyre* for a quick visit."

Miriam reaches out a hand and pats her knee in quiet understanding. "I've been needing a comfort read this week, too."

Sally swallows hard against the ball that sneaks up the back of her throat.

"I picked up *Anne's House of Dreams* after you called me last week. That, and the Psalms. You know," she re-situates herself so that she can better watch Sally's profile, "we should try for Prince Edward Island next, don't you think?"

They chat about books and traveling and work and everything but cancer until they turn onto US Highway 1, and then Aunt Miriam dozes off and on, chin-to-chest, for the next hour.

+ + +

The Grisbone home is a large, manor-style house near Battery Point with a stunning view of the harbor.

"I told you we have a cook," Sally explains, when a woman with pleasant crinkles around her eyes and lips meets them in the front hall and carries Miriam's bags to her room.

"A cook who also bellhops?"

"And cleans. Gracie does a little bit of everything, really."

They attend to their necessary toilette, and then, hearing Brahms resonating from the grand piano in the front parlor, they follow their ears to Mother.

The sisters greet each other pleasantly enough. Mother stands straight and smiles and opens her arms for a hug, and Miriam laughs and chatters easily and leans into the embrace with her good left arm. They sit near each other but perpendicularly, Mother at the head of the coffee table in the Queen Anne chair, Miriam amidst a pile of pillows on the divan. Sally sits at the piano bench and touches her fingers to the keys, sometimes playing a light tune and sometimes not, but mostly watching and listening and monitoring the mutual, cautious reassessment being performed across the room.

The Werth women resemble each other, both of them small and lean with firm chins and loose, accordion-like skin hanging around their necks. But Miriam's white curls toss and turn freely as she talks, and Mother's silver bun sits exactly where it has been confined; Miriam's eyes sparkle with the fire of starlight, and Mother's eyes glow soft and steady, like two moons; Miriam's left hand fiddles with the nearest textile, and Mother's hands remain clasped in her lap.

"Miriam, please, don't do that."

"What?"

"The pillow. Please, don't unravel the trim like that."

Miriam releases the pillow and murmurs, "I'm sorry."

"It's just that they're custom-made. I can't replace them, you see? Not easily, anyway."

"Of course."

The first frost enters the room, and Sally shivers at the piano.

"How are you feeling?" Miriam tries, keeping her hand still, her elbows pulled in close to her body.

"Fine. Really, I do."

"No pain?"

"None at all."

"That's a blessing."

"Not having cancer would be a blessing."

Sally watches Aunt Miriam out of the corner of her eye. Her aunt wisely doesn't take the dangled bait but simply answers, "It would."

Mother releases a hand to ring the silver bell on the side table, then refolds her hands in her lap, waiting in silence. They all do. When Gracie appears in the doorway, instructions are given for lobster rolls and iced tea to be served in the dining room.

"Or would soup be easier for you to eat?" Mother turns and asks her sister.

"Than what, a lobster roll?"

"Your hand, I mean. Is a spoon easier for you to hold than a hoagie? It's been so long since we've shared a meal together."

Sally is mortified. She must look away to hide the heat in her cheeks, but Aunt Miriam fields the question with a smile in her voice.

"How about we have both? Especially if it's chowder." Miriam turns toward the doorway and practically sings, "Is it possible to have chowder with the lobster rolls, Gracie? It's been so long since I've had fresh clams."

Gracie eyes her mistress first, then smiles and nods at the guest—"Yes, ma'am"—and disappears.

Mother recrosses her ankles the other direction and dresses her voice up with cheer. "So, tell me all the news from the grove."

"Well," Miriam relaxes her back against the couch, but her elbows remain tightly pressed against her sides, "we have a new pastor."

Mother brushes a piece of lint off of the knee of her pants.

"Actually, he's not that new. He's been there 11 years, now," Miriam realizes, her curls nodding in agreement, "but he's serving our vacancy part-time, and, well . . . you know how it goes in a country church. A pastor can preach in a pulpit for 20 years straight, but if he comes to that pulpit even a day later than you've been sitting in the pew, he'll always feel new."

"What's his name?"

"Edmund Oglethorpe."

"An Englishman in the grove? What a scandal."

"Well, he's no German, I can tell you that. But he eats and sings like one. And he's smart as a whip and sharp as a tack and all of those other idioms. And he's the kindest spiritual father I've ever known."

"Kinder than Pastor Engel?"

"Good point," Miriam allows, even her curls assenting. "Pastor Oglethorpe's the second kindest spiritual father I've ever known. A close second. Anyway, we love him."

"How many people attend Bethlehem these days?"

"Two. No, that's not fair. On a good day, we have three."

Sally chuckles at the piano, but Mother turns to look at her, confused. Humor has never been easy for Mother. It's part of why she doesn't enjoy reading.

"LJ Daniels died last month."

Mother looks back at Miriam. "Little Luke John?"

"Well, he wasn't so little in the end. He and Marcy had five sons, did you know? Yes, and the sons went on to give them 16 granddaughters and two grandsons."

"Good gracious," Marta blinks. "That's excessive."

Always with the appraisals! Sally lands her fingers a little too aggressively on the keys—"Sorry"—but Miriam smoothly covers with, "Wasn't LJ in your grade?"

"No, a year ahead of me."

"That's right."

"How did he die?"

Miriam struggles to answer right away, and Sally immediately knows it was cancer. Mother does, too.

"You know how those boys smoked," is all Miriam can say.

"Whatever happened to the youngest Daniels girl? Lila?"

"She's still renting the old house. She lives there with her son Clark."

"Loose Lila's renting our house?"

Miriam flinches at Mother's choice of modifier.

"I thought the older brother was running the farm. Roman."

"No. Roman retired years ago. It's Lila's boy who farms for us, now."

"The bastard son?"

Miriam now looks as if she's been shot. "Really, Marta. That's ugly."

"It's the truth."

"Clark is decent and hardworking and . . . more than his parentage. Every child is. And Lila cleaned up years ago."

"Did she, though?"

"Yes, she did. She's fully reformed from the sins of her youth. It's remarkable, really. She does quite a bit at the church — cleans just as Cherry used to do, and serves as secretary of the congregation. I know she's a big help to Pastor Oglethorpe in his study."

"I would imagine so."

"Marta!"

"No, I mean it. People like that don't reform, Miriam."

"The Bible is full of people who reform with the help of the Spirit. And the world today is full of people who reform with the same help."

Mother doesn't roll her eyes, but she does tilt her head. It is powerful when she compromises her perfect posture with a head tilt.

"Lila is perfectly lovely. I really like her, and her son is a straight shooter. He does good work for us."

"Well, you know what I think about the matter. I've told you for years that we should turn the Daniels family out of that house."

"I see no good reason to do such a thing."

Marta silently points her eyebrows toward Miriam's lame arm. "You know better than anyone the harm that family has done to us."

Miriam's sadness comes on so suddenly that her lips begin to quake, and Sally is just about sick from the sight of her aunt's grief. But Mother sees her standing and redirects her before she can even make it to the couch.

"Baby, would you please get me and your aunt some water? My throat is tired with all of this talk."

✢ ✢ ✢

Aunt Miriam broaches the subject again over the clam chowder.

"I'm thinking of leaving Lila the old house in my will."

Mother sets her spoon down next to her bowl and gives a resolute shake of her tight, unyielding bun. "Absolutely not."

"Why?"

"And turn our family homestead into a house of fornication?"

"Really, Marta," Miriam also sets down her spoon. "I must ask you to stop saying that about Lila. She is repentant, and she is forgiven."

"She's a Daniels, and I will not consent to a Daniels owning our family home."

"When you allow yourself to talk that way, Marta, it says much more about your character than Lila's."

Sally stares into her bowl. No one ever speaks to Mother this way and gets away with it. Father tried a few times, but he never held out for long. And his heart gave way in the end.

"Mother never wanted this," Marta argues. "She was clear about her wishes. She always wanted Sally to have the house, and so do I."

"Says the Werth who wants nothing to do with the farm."

"Says the Werth who can't do anything but farm."

Sally opens her mouth to stay the next attack, but her mother will not be bested.

"Baby, would you please tell Gracie we need more mayonnaise on these rolls?"

+ + +

Sally drives Miriam back to the airport one day early at Mother's suggestion.

"I'm almost 40, and she still calls me Baby."

Aunt Miriam is quiet, but her eyes burn with their usual star-fire. "Oh, let her. It's what our mother always called her."

Sally knows that if she waits long enough, Miriam will dig deeper into the same thought.

"She's just doing what she knows."

And if she waits even longer—

"She's trying to be affectionate. It's her way. Go easy on her, Sal."

"Why does she pick on you like that?"

"She's . . . frustrated."

Miriam is always defending Mother, while Mother is always criticizing Miriam. It is a dynamic Sally has never understood, and it irritates her. No, it disgusts her.

"Does this have something to do with Oskar?"

This is met with silence.

"Mother doesn't speak about him much anymore, but she used to. And then, for the first time in years, she mentioned him last week. You know, after the diagnosis."

"What did she say?"

"That she took him from you."

Miriam turns her head to stare out the passenger side window, and Sally can't help but dig.

"What is it, Aunt Miriam? I know something happened between you two. I can pick up on subtext my first time through a story let alone in a years-long saga in my own family. What happened?"

"It's your mother's story to tell," is all Miriam says.

"Yeah, and my mother's dying! We're running out of time!"

Miriam breaks for a moment, hanging her head and touching her fingers to her temples, but then she lifts her face again to stare back out the window. "I love my sister."

"Then what's the problem?"

Miriam sighs, facing forward but not quite looking at Sally. "Your mother is trapped. She wants to forgive me, but she can't."

"Forgive you? For what?"

"For, well, everything. For pushing her down the porch stairs when we were kids. For knocking over her stick fortress playing croquet. For getting out of mopping the kitchen floor by pretending to be sick. For borrowing her hairbrush and never returning it. For winning at Yahtzee. For," and her voice catches, "loving Oskar."

"But that's," Sally lowers her voice, suddenly concerned that they just turned a page in the story that she will not be able to understand, subtext or no, "all normal family stuff."

"Not to your mother."

"Then she's being fussy."

"Maybe. But she's doing the only thing she knows to do to survive."

Sally is thrown by this. "What does that mean?"

"It means, she has trouble forgiving me in small things, because she refuses to believe that I can forgive her in big things. It's her way of keeping things even between us, of controlling the situation."

Sally risks asking the question she's not supposed to ask. "What big thing did you forgive her for?"

"It's her story to tell," Miriam repeats.

Sally feels desperate. "But Mother doesn't tell her story. Ever."

"And we'll respect her privacy," though Miriam's face ages years in a single moment. "It won't do any good to push the matter, anyway, not when she's on the defensive. Besides, it doesn't matter. I forgave her years ago."

They ride in a solemn silence for a couple of minutes before Sally tries lightening the mood. "So, what'll we read next?"

"How about the Book of Genesis?"

"How about not?"

"It would be good for you."

Sally tries not to roll her eyes out of respect for Miriam's culture. "Let's read something neither of us have read before. Something frivolous and girly and set on a beach."

"Genesis has a beach in it."

She can't quite keep her eyes from rolling this time.

"Oh, come on, Sal! Read Genesis with me. It's exciting. There's a murder and a flood and some hospital drama — "

"Hospital drama?"

"Yes," Miriam's voice reclaims some of its natural tone of delight. "There's a circumcision. Several, actually."

Sally throws back her head and laughs, and Miriam joins her. It feels so good to laugh together again, but Miriam cuts the party short.

"Please, read the Bible with me, Sal. It's important. It's part of your history. It's who you are."

"No, it's who *you* are, Aunt Miriam."

This quiets her aunt for a time longer than Sally is comfortable enduring, and she fills the silence with stories and comments and observations that don't matter to either of them. Only when she veers the Subaru toward the curb of the terminal and pulls at the parking brake does Miriam grab her free hand with her own and cling to it with a strength that belies her age.

"Oskar changed things."

"What?" Sally blinks.

"Oskar. He changed things between your mother and me."

"How?"

"He," that horrible sadness is pulling at Miriam's face again, "didn't marry me."

Sally is afraid of the answer, but she asks the question anyway. "Because of Mother?"

Stars fall from Miriam's eyes, taking away her light. "Yes."

Chapter Twenty-two

Saint Oskar

+ 1958 +

Marta finds Oskar swinging an ax near Dandy Creek.

"Hello, Marty," he nods, hearing her coming through the brush. His blade lands at the base of a sycamore with a strong whack.

She sets the jug of lemonade on a nearby stump and takes an empty tin cup out of her satchel. Oskar pulls the ax loose and rests the handle against the injured sycamore, wipes his brow on a towel hung over a nearby limb, and takes the extended refreshment.

"How do you always know where to find me?"

She looks anywhere but at his flushed face. She has been tracking his daily progress felling Lindel trees along Dandy Creek for weeks, but he doesn't need to know that. She only shrugs.

Oskar lowers his sweaty frame onto a patch of cleared ground and pats a seat next to him. She bends at the knees and sits on her feet beside him, refilling his cup every time he empties it. Neither of them speak for a while, but even his silence is musical, for an occasional hum punctuates his thoughts.

"She's so stubborn, Marty," he finally offers.

She knows he is talking about Miriam.

"And her temper is hotter than my ax. I can't always tell what's going to set her off, you know?"

"I know."

He nods. "I bet you do, Marty."

He turns toward her then, a burst of laughter trumpeting from his open mouth at their shared experience. This is what she loves most about him. His generosity. He is always sharing his music with her, inviting her to join in and make life's song a duet.

"Aw, Marty," he sighs. "What am I gonna do?"

"About what?" She already knows. It's always the same thing—Miriam is mad about something stupid, and Oskar is pining for her, anyway—but she harbors a desperate hope that it will be about something else this time.

"About making things right with Miri."

Her love is an ax, and for Oskar, she wields it. She swings high, aiming at the root of that one, desperate hope. "Apologize. Even though it's not your fault."

"How are you so sure it's not my fault?"

She purses her lips knowingly and raises her eyebrows.

He laughs again.

"She'll never apologize first, no matter whose fault it is. You have to make the first move."

He thinks on this a moment and nods. "She's embarrassed."

Marta would have said proud. "She has trouble waiting."

"For what?"

She closes her eyes and brings the ax down hard for the felling. "For you to marry her."

When she opens her eyes, the light in his own burns more fiercely than the midday sun, and her last standing hope crashes into the creek bed.

+ + +

She is sitting at the kitchen table with Mother that night when they hear the strange scraping sound.

"What in the—?" Mother asks, looking up, then pauses and listens. There it is again. Outside.

Mother purses her lips and rises, setting a pair of pinking shears on top of the cherry-printed calico spread out over the table. She walks toward the back door, pushing aside the lace curtain with an index finger, peering out into the dark.

"For heaven's sake!"

"What?"

Mother is craning her neck, still peeking behind the curtain, now shaking her head.

This time the scraping sound is accompanied by a male grunt.

"Of all the ridiculous things," Mother mutters, letting the curtain fall back in place and turning around, her head still shaking, but her lips are no longer pursed.

"What is it?"

"It's Oskar."

Marta lowers her own pair of scissors. "Oskar?"

"Yes." Mother is maddeningly succinct, sitting and resuming her pinking as if everything is just as it should be.

"What is he doing?"

Mother's voice betrays a hint of delight. "I presume he's climbing Rapunzel's tower."

"What?"

Marta drops the belt she is trimming on the table and moves toward the door. She can't see clearly out into the night, so she turns off the kitchen light. Mother makes a sound of disapproval, but Marta dismisses all noise behind her with a wave of her hand.

There he is. Just above and to the right of the door. In his work boots, Oskar is climbing the stonework at the back of the house toward the golden glow of Miriam's bedroom light.

"Your father once tried something similar," Mother confides in the dark, her voice soft with a secret, happy knowing.

Another scrape and a grunt.

"Though he climbed a rope."

Marta's eyes are fixed on those boots, though she turns an ear toward the table. She would like to hear more about this happy knowing of Mother's.

But Oskar's form is suddenly shadowed from the light above by a wash of dark hair cascading from the open window. Miriam's cry of surprise is quickly shushed by Oskar who, pulling himself up by his hands to the windowsill, balances against the stones with the toe of his boots. She hears his muffled, musical baritone. He is apologizing, she is certain, for everything and for nothing. Then he leans into Miriam's hair, and Marta closes her eyes against the torturous sight. It should be her window. It should be her kiss.

That is when she hears it, the same soft tone of Mother's, only this time coming out as a sigh from the lips of her sister.

Miriam has beat her to the happy knowing.

"Baby?" Mother stands in the dark, bewildered. "What's wrong?"

But Marta can only sob her song of lament into Mother's shoulder.

+ + +

It is the morning of Miriam's birthday when Mr. Lindel knocks on the front door.

Marta closes the lid on the piano to answer the door just as Miriam hollers from upstairs, "I'll get it!"

Down the stairs her sister flies, her cheeks glowing and her dark hair flowing. She pauses to smooth out the front of her new cotton dress with her left hand. Even Marta admires how the tiny leaves atop each of the red cherries dotting the fabric are brought out by the green belt trimming her waist.

"Well, don't you look pretty!" Mr. Lindel exclaims as the door opens.

Miriam's smile throws sunbeams on the man. "Thank you. It's my birthday. Mother made my dress."

Marta made the belt, but Miriam remains silent on the matter.

"It's your birthday, is it? Well, Happy Birthday, Miss Miriam, and many happy returns." He squeezes the hat in his hand distractedly, peeking around the birthday girl into the house. "I don't expect your mother's in?"

"For heaven's sake, Miriam!" Mother cries, entering the living room from the kitchen doorway. "Invite Mr. Lindel inside the house. Do come in and have a seat, Art."

"Thank you, Ruthie, but I'd better stay right where I am. I've been tromping 'round the creek, and my boots'll track mud onto your nice, clean floors."

The three of them glance spontaneously at his telltale boots and then toward the raindrops streaming from the eaves of the front porch.

"Rain's been coming down all night." The worry in Mr. Lindel's voice is obvious, and Marta thinks the man might ruin his hat with his nervous twisting.

"Is there anything we can do for you, Art?"

"The rain's swelling the creek faster than the Lord can drain it, and if I wait too much longer to drag those logs Oskar felled this week, they'll form a dam against the chaff in the runoff from the fields."

A dam in Dandy Creek will flood the cemetery.

"And my tractor chose this morning of all mornings not to start up."

"I'll put a call in to Cherry right away." Mother moves toward the kitchen. "She'll send Mark or one of the boys down with our tractor."

"They're out of town." Another twist of the hat. "I already checked."

"I see." Mother stalls and purses her lips.

"But I'd still like to use your tractor, if you don't mind someone else driving it."

"Oskar knows how," Marta chimes in.

Miriam shoots her a look as pointed and as hot as an iron in a fire.

"Well, Miss Marty, I won't lie and pretend as if that's not exactly what I was hoping for."

"But Oskar's not here." Miriam shrugs nonchalantly, but the deep flush of her cheeks reveals her true concern. "But here you are, Mr. Lindel. Surely you can drive the tractor yourself."

"Miriam!" Mother looks appalled.

"What I mean is, time's not for wasting in such a matter." Miriam tries adding a smile to sweeten her explanation, but it has no warmth.

"A job like this takes two, Miss Miriam. One to drive the tractor and one to chain the logs. Driving the tractor is the better job, believe me."

Miriam's cheeks now match the color of the cherries on her dress. "But Oskar and I have plans to drive into Riverfield today." She is looking only at Mother, and her pleading eyes add a silent, *It's my birthday!*

"It won't take all day, will it Mr. Lindel?" Marta asks.

"Surely not. A couple of hours at the most. Maybe three."

She turns toward her sister, a genuine smile playing at her lips. "Then, why can't Oskar do both? If he starts now, he can be done by lunchtime, and that'll give him plenty of time to wash up and take you into town for supper." This little side job, however long it takes, will cut nicely into Miriam's happy plans, and it serves her sister right for selfishly making everyone else's life revolve around her own.

Mother nods. "Oskar'll be happy to help, I'm sure. I'll put a call out to the Blumes straight away. Art, head on over to the old farmhouse. The Ford's in the main shed. I'll tell Oskar to meet you at the creek."

Marta, pleased with herself and with the percussive sound of Miriam's aggravated stomping up the stairs, sits back down at the piano and plays a cheerful chorus of "Happy Birthday."

+ + +

It is late in the afternoon when they receive the call. Mother says little before hanging up the phone and grabbing her purse.

"In the car. Please."

"What is it?" Miriam asks, but her voice betrays a fearful understanding beyond their present knowing. Her sister has been edgy all day, barely eating a bite at lunch, and her irritability had grown to a wild, wide-eyed silence the hour before the call came through. Once, she had even put on her jacket with the intent of walking to the creek herself, but Mother had stayed her with a reminder of how easily her dress would wilt in the rain. Not once the entire afternoon did Miriam look at or speak to Marta.

The drive to the creek is sick with silence, for Mother says nothing other than, "Viola said to come right away. There's been an accident. I know nothing more. Pray, girls."

There are four other vehicles parked along the edge of the Lindel field when they pull up to the wooded creek. One of them is Pastor Engel's. Miriam jumps out of the car before Mother brakes to a complete stop. Marta is paralyzed in the backseat. She cannot move her elbows, and her lungs won't take in any air. Surely her heart has stopped. Something is terribly wrong, she knows it, for all of the world's music has ceased.

"Help!"

Miriam's scream cuts through the rain.

Mother jumps out of the car, forgetting to close the door.

"Mother! Mother!" Her sister's screams are agonized gurgles, and Marta closes her eyes against them. "Help him! Someone, help him! He can't breathe down there!"

Marta cannot move her frozen limbs to cover her ears. She knows, and the knowing steals her sight. She chokes on a whimper and, reflexively, sucks in a searing knife of air. In a burst of panic, she leans against the car door, fumbles to unlatch it, and vomits into the mud.

"Why are you all standing around? Someone, help! Move the stupid tractor!"

There must be no need to move the tractor, or someone would try. Art Lindel would surely try.

Marta retches once more out the car door.

With limbs shaking, she stands and moves toward the trees.

Miriam's shrieks are now the yelps of a wild animal. It is the most primal, terrifying song Marta has ever heard.

One glance is all she can suffer before turning back to the car.

Mother is sitting in the mud, holding Miriam to her lap with both arms. Men are standing along the bank, soaked to the skin, their heads down. The tractor is overturned in the creek, a log underneath it, still chained to the rig. Oskar is lying just beneath the surface of the water, pinned beneath the steering wheel.

Miriam will never forgive her.

She will never forgive herself.

Chapter Twenty-three

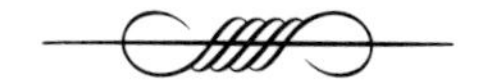

Saint Simeon

✢ 1997 ✢

He is old enough to be her father, but love is ageless. Even more so after blowing out 86 candles, for a good bride is hard to find let alone see once trifocals frame the world. And what are a few measly decades between friends when one day is as a thousand years with the Lord? Certainly, the number of birthdays matters less looking backward than forward, especially when fewer heartbeats remain ahead than are logged behind. And he has loved her for almost 40 years and with a fidelity that trumps most of the marriage vows in the county. If only she knew it.

"A flower for a flowering beauty," he says.

He ushers every third Sunday of the month and makes certain to tuck a flower in her bulletin every time. She loves all flowers but especially zinnias and marigolds. He knows this, because she plants them every May on the graves of her family and friends. He sometimes helps her if she is in the mood for company. This Sunday, a delicate stem from the patch of pinks blooming just outside the church door peeks its head above the folded paper.

"Thank you, Uncle Si." She smiles fondly, taking the flowering bulletin from his hand and tucking it in the front pocket of her purse.

He wishes she wouldn't call him that, but she always does. Every child born this side of the Depression calls him that and has done so for as long as they, and he, can remember. It started with Art and Viola's children and stuck in the congregation when he never got around to marrying and having children of his own. He doesn't mind, really. Only when she says it.

"If I had known you would be picking me a pink this morning, I wouldn't have worn red."

"But the best of valentines wear both colors."

She is pleased, he can tell, and he hums with satisfaction as he watches her make her way to her usual seat between Vivian and Lila.

She is walking more slowly these days. She fell a few years back, out on the icy lane leading up to the church doors, and ever since, her gait has grown cautious and deliberate. He misses her former exuberance, but everyone's hair silvers if they stand long enough. Doesn't he know it!

He found a way to take her out for supper several years back: a celebration of the arrival of her AARP card in the mail. He paid for the meal, assuring her it was because she was now such a cheap date. Ten years later, they still go out for monthly suppers in Riverfield, and on his dime. He tips the waitress extra to make sure the bill is always laid on his side of the table, and she resigns herself to his generosity, though she always manages to buy his ice cream at the DQ afterward.

"Uncle Si," she asks him one summer afternoon while pulling weeds from the church flower beds, "do you know anything about that wagon wheel sticking out of the ground at the edge of the lawn?"

He is seated on a stool at her side, steadying the compost bucket between his feet. "Only that my great-great-grandpa had something to do with it. You can tell by the signature on the rim. Reinkings were known for having their wagon wheels made in St. Louis. I always assumed this one was buried to serve as a hitch for tying up horses, but my mother once told me that she and her brothers used it for base when playing tag after church." He smiles at a happy notion. "I would like to have seen my mother running. I only ever saw the woman sitting with those broad shoulders fixed as if painted in a portrait. Or standing with her boots planted in front of the kitchen stove with that terrifying wooden spoon sticking out of her apron pocket. I always felt it in my bones that she indulged in a sprint or two whenever I wasn't looking." He winks at her. "All great women have some fire in their feet."

She doesn't notice that he is complimenting her.

"It seems we should plant some flowers around it, the wagon wheel. If it's important to your family history."

He nods. "Marigolds or zinnias? I've got extra seeds from what we saved last year."

"I was thinking a couple of lilacs might be nice. One on either side. The blooms each spring would be nice for cutting and beautifying the altar around Easter."

Flowers are their connection, and so he orders two old-fashioned lilacs from the nursery in Riverfield before she can say "perennial." They plant them in the fall.

He thinks she begins to suspect his singular affection when they stand at the church kitchen counter to arrange bouquets for the

Leesmann wedding. Late summer roses, asters, and Queen Anne's lace stand ready in five-gallon buckets on the linoleum floor. One by one, she pulls a choice stem, he trims a quarter-inch off its end, and she places it—with the exacting care of an artist making tangible a vision—in one of the plastic liners for the brass altar vases.

He manages to sneak a tiny pink rose from the bucket behind her back, the bud still unopened, and snapping the stem just below the bloom, tucks it behind her right ear among her mop of silver curls. She blushes, and his old heart nearly jumps out of his chest.

"Uncle Si—"

"You may call me just Simeon. If you like."

Her cheeks deepen in shade to that of the rose. She focuses on finding the perfect spot for the aster in hand, but he is certain that neither of them are breathing. Finally, sticking the aster in the center of one of the arrangements, she pulls the bud from her hair and manages, "We need these flowers for the bouquets."

He does not push the matter, but he notices that she tucks the bloom in her left jacket pocket instead of in the trash.

It is after the Leesmann baptism the following year that the world stops spinning for an entire minute. They are standing over the graves of her father and mother, cottonwood seeds blowing in the wind, when she tucks her hand in the bend of his elbow and says, "Simeon—"

But he hears nothing of what comes next.

The scene before him stalls in a motionless, golden-green landscape of sunshine and joy. The trees stop their waving, the birds hold their trills on the leafy limbs, and the fluffy cottonwood seeds hang suspended in the air before him.

She called him by his name. Not as an uncle, but as a man.

When the world regains its motion, he finds himself walking with her, arm in arm, between gravestones. He bends at the waist to pluck a bright orange zinnia bloom, and when he places it behind her ear, this time, she lets it remain.

By Advent, only the red berries on the evergreen holly bushes offer some reprieve to the brown, barren grounds of the church.

"I wonder, Simeon," she ponders, lifting a string of colored lights to Honey Lindel on a nearby ladder, "if we would still hang lights in the winter if we weren't missing all of the colorful flowers from the spring."

He is about to answer when a stab of pain shoots down his left arm, knocking the wind right out of his lungs. He leans against the church wall for support, but he cannot keep himself from falling to his knees, and then to his face, on the cold ground.

When he awakes, she is seated beside the hospital bed, holding his left hand in hers, and Gene and Drucilla are standing at his feet. He tries to speak, to assure her that he has more heartbeats left in him, but an oxygen mask covering his face makes it impossible to form a single word.

"It's your ticker, Si!" Gene barks from the foot of the bed. His older brother always shouts. It's from all of those years walking the noisy factory floors unprotected, but his brother refuses ever to wear hearing aids. "It gave out on you again."

She squeezes his hand, and he would suffer a heart attack all over again if she would keep her hand tucked in his like this. He tries his best to squeeze those precious fingers in return before closing his eyes for a quick rest.

When he reawakens in the middle of the night, she is still there. The mask is no longer silencing him, and he rasps, "My flower."

She shushes him and scoots her chair forward, using a damp cloth to cool his forehead. She then takes a wet Q-tip and touches it, ever so gently, around his lips. He did the same thing for his father ten years before, and that is when he knows. He is dying.

"Pastor was here a couple of hours ago. He said he would return in the morning. Shall I call for the nurse?"

He shakes his head.

"Would you like me to read to you?"

"Just sit," he wheezes, "with me."

She takes his feverish hand in hers again.

His heartbeats are few, so he wastes no time. "Will you marry me?"

Her eyes widen for a long moment, but then her face relaxes into a knowing smile. "You dear man."

She thinks he is teasing.

"I mean it."

Her smile falters, but she holds his gaze.

"I love you."

She blushes, then, lowering her gaze, "I know."

"More than you know."

He watches as her downcast eyes close tight, and then she crumbles before him, crying into her lap.

He has said too much. Asked too much.

He tries to squeeze her hand, still in his. "It's okay."

She shakes her head. "I'm so sorry."

He is spent and cannot take in enough air to say all that is in his heart. He simply watches and waits for all of her tears to empty. He understands. He has always understood. He was standing on the bank that rainy day when her tender heart was broken beyond repair, and he has watched and waited and loved her ever since.

His tongue is dryer than a stick, but he forces out, "Promise me one thing."

She eyes him warily.

"When you plant flowers on Oskar's grave this spring," he wheezes, "toss a few seeds on mine, as well."

She smiles at him then, and holding his hand close to her heart, she rises and kisses him firmly on the forehead.

"Yours will be the loveliest in the grove. I promise."

He can die a happy man.

Chapter Twenty-four

Saint Sparrow

✠ 2004 ✠

It is his first funeral in the grove since serving Bethlehem's vacancy, and he is burying Sparrow Finch. *Prettiest bird in Whistle Grove*, her headstone reads, which is a bit in the face of Sparrow's two older sisters, Robin and Dove. But no one gathered around the open grave seems terribly offended by the superlative, and he will never be able to judge the matter for himself. Sparrow's car was tragically side-rammed by a train racing northeast on the Greyville line, and hers is a closed casket funeral.

It was no suicide, everyone is certain. In fact, the local paper goes so far as to ascribe Sparrow's death to a mysterious "carrier curse," and her obituary characterizes the accident as "a sacrifice of service." For Sparrow was the mail carrier for two of Bramble's rural routes, and apparently, fatal train accidents such as hers are not so uncommon as one would expect.

"It's the overfamiliarity with the route that does it," Miriam Werth explains to him just ahead of the wake. "Our rural carriers drive back and forth on these country roads day in and day out, year after year, and they cross those tracks a hundred times a month. And most of the time, there's never any train, you see? It gets easier and easier to grow sloppy, to just slow down and coast over the tracks rather than stop and check properly."

"Especially if there's a Johnny Cash song blarin' on the radio," Honey Lindel adds over Miriam's shoulder. "Johnny might hear the train a-comin', but you sure won't."

Miriam shakes her head, continuing, "And that Fireling intersection doesn't have a light, so be careful on those roads, Pastor Oglethorpe. Don't let Johnny or Dolly or anyone get the better of you. Light or no, you stop at the tracks. Every time."

He does stop every time, but more from a spirit of reverence than of caution. The track is old in this part of the county, and so are the trees that line it. He likes to roll down his window and listen to the ballads the birds sing back and forth to each other from the oak and ash boughs. Sometimes, he ventures out of the car and walks on the ballast for a bit, especially at the Fireling intersection. He never could indulge in such luxurious, solitary meditations in Dallas. Not out-of-doors, anyway.

He really loves exploring these backcountry roads. They change in personality with every season. His sainted mother loved them, too, and he often recalls with a smile her melodramatic similes and metaphors applied to them whenever driving to and from the church:

"In the summer sun, the backroads grow soft and oily, sticking to your shoes like a clingy lover. But during harvest, they gnarl and crack like an angry, avenging woman, baiting you with potholes and rocks loosened by the frequent abuse of heavy farm equipment. When winter hits, they turn introspective, hiding their battered faces from you under layers of sleet, ice, and snow. But in the melt of spring—Oh, Eddie, what a sight!—they forget their troubles and throw off every facade, adorning themselves with crocus, hyacinth, and narcissus blooms, the prettiest of Easter bonnets."

Yes, he loves living where the very roads cry out with resurrection joy!

In truth, he has never been so content as in this little grove. It was an easy move back to his parents' property in Riverside after retiring from the big church in Dallas, and Bethlehem sat here waiting for him on her little hill, vacant and demure, as if saving her pulpit just for him. All it took was one visit to the grove, one call to the district president's office, one voters' meeting, and his clericals were back out of the closet. He was never going to travel or play in his retirement, anyway. What are golf courses and bridge clubs compared to this little Eden?

Though he did make one short side trip on his way to Illinois. He stayed a month with his old friend Jacob Sterling, now serving a congregation in southeast Missouri, and visited every hospital in St. Louis County that was birthing babies in the late 1930s. But he found no record of any baby boy, named or otherwise, that matched him to anyone who could be his birth mother, nor did he find a birth certificate in the county archives for anyone named "Edmund" born in 1939. It was a pipe dream from the start, finding his birth mother, since all he ever had to go on was a passing mention of "the city" from his late mother. That could be anywhere, really, though he had hoped she was alluding to the city nearest Riverfield. Someday, when he has more time, he'll try looking through the archives of Sangamon or Cook County next.

But he does not need every question answered in life to enjoy the peace that surpasses all understanding, and he is happy serving Bethlehem. So much so, that one of the first things he does upon moving to Riverfield is seek to purchase a burial plot in Whistle Grove, fulfilling his mother's dying wish of sorts. Though it is he, rather than she, who will be buried there.

"Oh, you don't need to buy a plot, Pastor," Lila Daniels, the acting sexton of the church's cemetery, had to explain to him at the time. "You're granted a plot here for free."

"For free?"

"Yes, we have a pastor's circle, a section reserved near the church for ministers who serve Bethlehem. We have three pastors buried there, already, along with their wives. Oh, and Mary."

Mary. Yes, he remembers the very grave. He saw it the first time he visited Whistle Grove.

"Is she a pastor's widow?"

"We don't really know who she is other than that she came through Whistle Grove sometime before the war—lots of people did in those days—and she died without any money. At least, that's what my mama told me. The pastor at the time charitably had her buried in the circle."

"Well, I'm most grateful to the church for this gift, Lila. Thank you. To rise on the Last Day next to my fellow servants in Christ—I can think of little else that would bring me so much joy."

But today is not his burial. It is Sparrow's, and he stands with the family as Clark Daniels lowers the casket into the vault. Only when Robin, Dove, and everyone else depart in their respective vehicles does Lila step out from behind a tree to assist her son with the clean-up.

"You were hiding all this time, Lila. Why?"

She steps under the tent and begins picking up abandoned bulletins. "No one wants me around at times like these, Pastor."

"How do you know?"

"I know."

He is new to the grove, but he has heard the gossip. And in his experience, gossip is a cheap wine. It looks good when poured and can even taste sweet on the tongue, but swallowing it yields a headache and storing it yields vinegar. No matter what anyone else says about it, he learned years ago always to read the label himself before opening a bottle. Now appears to be the right moment to read Lila's label. "What do you mean?"

"People don't like me."

"Is there a good reason for that?" It is a risk, pushing this way, especially in these early days. But Lila is under his spiritual care now, and it is sad seeing her resort to hiding out in the open. And at an interment, when she is the cemetery's sexton.

She folds and stuffs the bulletins up her sweater sleeve and then busies herself with the folding chairs. Only when her son finishes loading his rig onto his truck and drives away does she turn toward him and ask, "Haven't you heard?"

"Heard what?"

She stares silently at him, measuring him, even daring him with her eyes. "I'm a whore."

Well, there's no going back, now. He offers up a silent prayer before admitting, "I have heard something of that nature, yes, but I'm wondering if it's true."

She continues in her silent staring, so he prods, "Are you?" He can't bring himself to say the actual word.

"I'm not married, if that's what you're asking."

"No, that's not what I'm asking. I'm asking if you sleep with men for money."

She barks out an acerbic laugh. "No man's ever been kind enough to offer me any money."

His heart sinks to his soles. It is even sadder than he expected, but as usual, the gossip is off the mark. "You have a son."

"Yes."

"Where is his father?" He does not mean to wound her, only to understand her, and he suspects she has gone too long without the mercy of being understood in this grove.

"In jail."

"That is difficult."

Her shoulders relax a bit at his sympathy, but she watches him, chin down, like a dog accustomed to cowering before the raised hand of an owner. Compassion for this wounded woman rises in his stomach and tastes like sickness in his throat. He swallows.

"Was the man in jail your husband?"

She lifts her shoulders toward her ears and turns away, busying herself with the chairs. Her habit of self-distancing will cause only more pain and isolation if he does not intervene.

"Lila, you do not appear to be married to any man, but you have a son. Do you share your bed with men as if married to them?"

She stops fussing with the chairs and crosses her arms. "I'm not perfect, but neither is anyone else."

"This is most certainly true," he nods. "But the thing is, my sins don't cancel out your sins. It's not an eye for an eye when it comes to righteousness. That's not how we are justified before God. Sin needs atoned for, not avenged."

"I don't even know what that means."

"It means," he sighs, "that I'm getting ahead of myself."

He walks over to one of the remaining chairs and sits down. She is still standing with her arms crossed like a shield in front of her heart, but she does not run away. She remains where she is, silent and standing, and so he tries another way. "Lila, why did you hide from everyone at the funeral if you've done nothing wrong?"

"I'm tired of playing the part of Mary Magdalene at every church gathering. These people stone me every chance they get, though they're in no position to be casting stones."

"Are you Mary Magdalene?"

She turns and looks at him. "I'm not a whore like everyone says. I've only ever been with Clark's father and one other man. Well, two other men, but that last one—I was drunk and . . . just two men that counted."

"Two is enough. If neither of them are your husband."

"But I loved them both. And not at the same time. And it was such a long time ago. I may not have married either of them, but I loved them. What's so terrible about that? Why am I condemned for loving when everyone else should be condemned for hating?"

"You aren't condemned for loving, Lila. You're condemned for being 'wise in your own eyes.'"

"What does that even mean?"

"It means, you like your way of looking at the world better than God's."

She shakes her head. "That's not true."

"Isn't it? When you slept with those men, what did your parents have to say about it?"

She does not answer, which is her answer.

"'Honor your father and your mother,' is God's clear command, but you've dishonored your parents. Not with your loving—though let's be clear, Lila. Fornication is not love. It's pollution. It pollutes your body to be one flesh with a man who is not your husband, and it defiles the Lord's body at the same time. For is He not joined to you in baptism? Would you then join your Savior's body to 'a prostitute?'"

She is head-bent, silent.

"You dishonored your parents when you despised their wisdom, the wisdom given to them from God: 'a man will leave his father and mother and be united to his wife, and they will become one flesh.' God's Word is clear. A man holds fast to 'his wife,' Lila, not his lady-friend."

She must have faith at least the size of a mustard seed, for he sees pain and torment in the clenching of her jaw. The law hit its mark, and Lila's heart appears to be bleeding repentance.

"I didn't mean to dishonor them. I don't mean to dishonor anyone."

"Don't you? Come, Lila. You're too smart not to know how your fornication hurts your family, your church, your Lord. Yet you do it."

"Not anymore."

"But you did it. And today, you defend it as loving. That is being wise in your own eyes."

Tears pour down her face with a force and at a rate as if she is flushing her eyes of all self-wisdom. She covers her face with her hands. She bends at the waist and sobs, "But what can I do about it, now? It's all over and done, Pastor. It's been over and done for a long time."

"Then, you be done with it, too. Give it to the Lord. Let Him bear your burden, and stop hiding from your own church family."

"I—I don't know how to do that."

He loves her like a daughter, and so he speaks to her like a father. "'Fear the Lord and shun evil.'"

"I do. I have."

"Then, hear this, and believe it." He stands and raises his hand of blessing, lest she think he does not believe the Lord's blood-bought atonement worthy of the greatest respect. "'There is now no condemnation for those who are in Christ Jesus,' and you are baptized, Lila. You are in Christ Jesus."

She is still bent low, hushed and listening, and he stands over her, ready to bless.

"Do you believe that what I say is from Christ himself?"

"Yes."

"Then, 'receive the forgiveness of Christ won for you by his Passion, death, and resurrection. By the command of our Lord Jesus Christ I, a called and ordained servant of the Word, forgive you your sins,'" he releases the blessing of peace from his hand like a dove, making the sign of the cross, "'in the name of the Father and of the Son and of the Holy Spirit.'"

She openly weeps within the sanctuary of her hair, and he is moved with compassion. He leans down, and resting both hands upon her crown, speaks directly into her right ear, "'Trust in the LORD with all your heart,' Lila, 'and lean not on your own understanding.' Not when it comes to love, especially. For you are confused on this matter, and your misunderstanding is leading you to hide from God in this grove, like Adam and Eve in the garden. It would be good to study afresh what God says in His Word about love, for He Himself is love and 'from His mouth come knowledge and understanding.' I will write out some passages from 1 Corinthians and 1 Thessalonians for you to meditate on tonight. 'This will bring health to your body and nourishment to your bones.'"

She coughs a sob into her hands and nods.

He writes those passages out for her and then sees her safely to her car. He stands in the middle of the dirt lane and watches her drive away. He does not know it now, but this is a litany the two of them will perform over and over again during his tenure at Bethlehem: Lila will pour repentance from her eyes, and he will pour comfort into her ears; she will come to him in fear, and he will watch her leave in peace.

It is in this moment that he begins another ritual he will repeat over and over again in the years to come. He looks out over the graves and up into the trees and out over the graves again and sings unto the Lord a new-old song,

The earth is the LORD's, and everything in it,
the world, and all who live in it;
for he founded it upon the seas
and established it upon the waters.
Who may ascend the hill of the LORD?
Who may stand in his holy place?
He who has clean hands and a pure heart,
who does not lift up his soul to an idol
or swear by what is false.
He will receive blessing from the LORD
and vindication from God his Savior.
Such is the generation of those who seek him,
who seek your face, O God of Jacob.

Chapter Twenty-five

Saint Alma

+ 2019 +

Twenty-two boxes are delivered via certified mail to Sally Grisbone's home address with an introductory letter that reads:

GLENN BERRY & ASSOCIATES
200 S. Main Street
Riverfield, Illinois

<u>In the Matter of the Estate of Edmund G. Oglethorpe</u>

To Sally A. Grisbone:

This is formal Notice that Edmund G. Oglethorpe died on January 23, 2019.

The following assets of the Estate of Edmund G. Oglethorpe are bequeathed to you by the decedent:

```
    one theological library
    one sealed letter

Executed by the administrator of the Estate of
Edmund G. Oglethorpe on January 27, 2019.

Glenn F. Berry, Administrator of the Estate
```

And then, handwritten in a sprawling script at the very bottom:

Eddie was the best of men. My sincere condolences. GFB.

"One theological library," Sally mutters. "Good God."

Her living room could be the Badlands for all of the buttes and ravines the reverend's boxes form across the floor. She shakes her head, stupefied by the seismic power of the little man's resolve, even in death. And he will have the last word, of course. She looks down at the "one sealed letter" in her hand, her name written on the back in his own, shaky cursive. She recognizes it from his last letter.

Well, she might as well get this over with. She pushes at a short stack of boxes to clear a path to Mother's favorite walnut parlor chair and, taking a seat, she opens the envelope and reads:

The Epiphany of Our Lord, A.D. 2019

My dear Ms. Grisbone,

If you are receiving this letter, then I have reached my eternal rest and am waiting in the grove for the Lord's blessed reawakening.

Yes, I am giving you my library. I have no children of my own, no nieces or nephews on which to unload my worldly goods, and my brother pastors already own much of what I bothered keeping on my shelves. I have few friends still alive who will appreciate reading my comments and various markings in the margins of the books themselves. In truth, I am hoping you will find my observations interesting. Think of it as a continuation of our conversation of sorts, and I hope you will make observations of your own above, under, and next to mine. I like to think of this as an act of chivalry, my giving you the final word—the final mark—in our discourse.

The matter is simple, Ms. Grisbone. I want you to have these books, and I want you to read them. Start with C. S. Lewis' *Mere Christianity* and follow it up with Bo Giertz's *Hammer of God*. And when you get to Alvin Schmidt's *Cremation, Embalmment, or Neither?* smile and remember an old, insignificant man who found you significantly important in this big, small world.

You may be pleased to learn that I was prospecting in the Werth attic again. Read: Clark Daniels carried three more boxes down to the kitchen where Lila and I sorted through them while indulging in a light supper of smoked salmon crostini and scalloped potato soup followed by iced sugar cookies with molasses punch. Have you ever tasted molasses punch? It's an old family recipe of Cherry's, Lila's mother. She brought it north with her from Arkansas, and it's like drinking Christmas. I digress—

I found several items of note and of varying degree of interest and import in those boxes—all of them waiting for you in the guest room of the old house: When are you visiting, my dear?—but the treasure that can suffer neither the wait nor the risk of your not visiting the old homestead is a little brass dish, picture enclosed. I will not have it shipped, as it appears to be a family heirloom that is uninsurable. Its value, as you will soon understand, is beyond that of any monetary measure. Simply, it is irreplaceable.

As you can see from the picture, the dish looks more like a tiny time capsule than anything else. Clark thinks it looks like a coffee carafe that has been shrunk to pocket-size, but it is not intended for food, I think, and most definitely not for drink. It is quite heavy, yet it has the most delicate filigree along the edges, as if decorated to match a wedding cake. Most curious of all, it has a screw-top lid. Lila thinks it is a jewelry or cosmetic box of some kind.

What I cannot wait to share with you is that this dish belonged to your Great-great-great-great-grandmother Alma Auguste Wilhelmine Saxon. If Lila and I are reading the German correctly, Alma was born and raised in a castle before she married a young, ambitious Friedrich Werth and left her family and wealth in Germany to settle and farm what is now Werth Farms, Inc. You see, it is Friedrich and Alma who donated the land for the church and cemetery which we now fondly call Whistle Grove.

It would seem, my dear Ms. Grisbone, that you are the daughter of nobility. You are also the child of a world-class pianist, a World War II martyr, a World War I survivor, a farmer, and a shepherd. I have been reading through the diary of the daughter of the shepherd, your Great-great-grandmother Sarah Lindel Werth. Page after page is covered with prayers and pleas to the Lord for the gift of a child—a daughter specifically—and we know that the Lord granted her only one son, your Great-grandfather Ernst Werth. Yet, here you are today, Ms. Grisbone, the daughter of her great-granddaughter's womb. You are the blessed answer to her prayer. I marvel to think of it.

Think on it yourself. You are not so alone in this life nor in the next. You are one in a line of many, and your people are here. Do not stay away too long.

And do not grieve my death too much, my dear. "Heaven and earth will pass away," but I am alive in Christ. We will meet again, in the flesh, and you shall behold me with your own eyes.

Resting from my labors,

Rev. Edmund G. Oglethorpe

P.S. Forgive me! One final word, but not from me: Before she died, your Aunt Miriam begged me to encourage you to look beyond her own experiences and consider marriage for the gift that it is in this life, though she advises that you marry not just anyone. She suggests you marry a super man.

Chapter Twenty-six

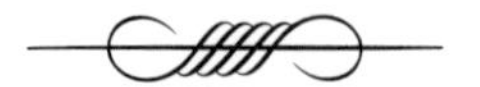

Saint Cherry

✢ 2019 ✢

Sally exits the stuffy, old clapboard church, locking the door and leaving the key atop the doorframe per specific instruction. That indefatigable, little man left more than just financial bequests in his will. He also left — and to her alone — dozens of sealed, handwritten letters explaining the who, what, where, why, and how of every detail regarding the ongoing care of the cemetery. She shakes her head. Even in death, the old reverend persists in playing the part of the voice of her conscience.

She steps down onto the grass — That last concrete step is crumbling on the corner and needs re-pouring. She makes a mental note. — and wanders over to the Werth section of the cemetery. Her first quarterly meeting of the cemetery board is in the books, and she is the last to leave the building, having asked to stay behind to poke around in the old filing cabinets. No one dared deny her peculiar request, most likely because she had just handed them a check for $350,000 from Aunt Miriam's estate. From what she understands, that amount of money is enough to cover the maintenance expenses of Whistle Grove for the next 50 years. Again, she shakes her head, baffled by these besotted people. What is it about this tiny piece of land that inspires Aunt Miriam and the reverend to care so much about what is buried and gone?

She is not looking for him, but she is warmed to find him all the same. The granite headstone is a deep gray and shinier than the others, and it reads:

Edmund Garret Oglethorpe
1939 - 2019
"Jesus, remember me when
you come into your kingdom."

"Well, Father, you got your way in just about everything, didn't you? Except one thing."

She leans down and places a grimy, silver key atop his stone. "I had the locks changed on the church doors."

She indulges in a tiny, victorious grin.

"There's no use arguing. I checked the invoices myself. It's been 25 years since the locks have been updated, and it makes absolutely no sense to maintain a lock whose key has been copied enough times to occupy most of the pockets in the county. That's not even counting the pockets already buried here. But don't worry. I honored your liberal policy on hospitality. I left a copy of the new key in the usual spot. Your beloved, wandering vagrants will never suffer sleeping under the stars in this grove, not under my watch."

An old limestone gravestone just to the left of Pastor Oglethorpe's plot catches her eye. It is labeled simply:

Mary
d. 1939

but with no surname. And no birthdate. There's a story under that headstone, Sally is certain, and she makes a mental note to look for the girl's name in the filing cabinet tomorrow. She continues on toward the Werths in the southeast end of the grove and finds Alma by finding Miriam. Near them is Grandma Werth and Grandpa Werth, who she never met.

"Someday," she can hear the old man saying over her shoulder as if they are looking down into a six-foot hole and arguing again. "You'll meet him someday, when we all shall rise . . ."

There is a Wilhelm and Sarah Werth further to the north, as well as an Alwin. She leans in closer to read, *1850*. That's an old one. She hopes there's a file on him, too. Or a baptismal record or something.

She stands up and takes in a deep breath of the country air—it smells like the dandelion tea her mother used to drink—and expels it slowly. So many names, so many graves, so many stories lying underneath these headstones.

"Not stories, Ms. Grisbone. Saints," she hears him correct.

That is when she notices it, the whispering. She looks up into the golden-green sunlight, admiring the waving and bending of so many branches overhead and the whispering of the wind brushing up against the broad leaves of the deciduous trees. Though, this is not called Whispering Grove, and she knows why. She remembers clearly the shrill whistle of the wind blowing through these same, naked trees last November. But there is no shrill reproach in the wind today, only kind regards. The wind seems happy to meet the verdant trees.

She pulls a small notepad and pencil out of her canvas handbag and hastily scribbles down these impressions, then she moves toward the car. The day is already thick with hours, and she has a whole list of tasks to accomplish before nightfall. First on the list is visiting the old Werth farmhouse.

✢ ✢ ✢

She knows she has seen this house before. It is too familiar to be strange, but she has no memory of the interior of the house or the barn or the shed. Though at the sight of the smokehouse out back — How does she know to call it a smokehouse? — her nose remembers sage sausages and apple butter. Did Mother take her here when she was little? Or Aunt Miriam?

She exits the car, bending to brush a dried burr of some kind from her left Converse and taking a manilla envelope out of her handbag before looping the straps over her shoulder. She walks up the front steps of the covered porch and knocks on the red front door. This shouldn't take long, but there is no answer. She can see no doorbell, so she knocks again — even knocks directly on the leaded pane of glass of a nearby window — before walking around to the back of the house.

"Hello?"

There is no one. Not a dog or cat or horse or cow, not a human, not any other creature she can recognize. She sees only a lone sparrow perched on the rim of a large copper pot hanging above a fire pit from the apex of an old iron tripod. Back here, she does hear the cooing and pecking of chickens, and she follows the babble to a populated coop built along the back of the smokehouse. From here, she spies a tribe of curious goats staring at her from a pen behind the metal shed, but there is still no human to be found. She wipes at her forehead with the back of her hand and sears her sinuses again and again breathing in the hot, stuffy air. The atmosphere feels as thick and heavy as a fog from home, but no misty droplets and absolutely no romance adorns this kind of humidity.

She puts the envelope back in her shouldered bag and shields her eyes with both hands, looking out over what appears to be acres of pastureland. There are the cows! She grins in spite of herself—here's a bit of romance—and bends and twists and limbos and hops over and under and around the electric fence bordering the pasture. Once she is safely on the side where the grass is leaner, her Converses, of their own volition, hunt out a trail of packed dirt and pull her toward the beautiful cattle with the excitement and anticipation of school children let out for recess. But she is not a hundred paces into the foxtail when she runs into a tall, tan farmer bent over a shovel.

She is startled, then mortified, then a little angry. Unfortunately, her tendency to grow arrogant when vulnerable overtakes her better qualities, and she pushes a haughty hand toward the dusty stranger and barks, "Sally Augusta Grisbone."

The man stares at her, unmoving, as she fries like an egg in this pan of a pasture, sizzling in the oil of humiliation. For like an idiot, she just offered this stranger her full name as if submitting a résumé, not a greeting, in her extended hand. She might fry to a crisp in the man's silent contempt, but he begins to chuckle. A row of white teeth flash out at her from underneath the seed corn cap, and she is reminded of her favorite lighthouse at Owl's Head back home.

"You're Miriam's niece. I saw you at the interment."

The man with the hydraulic rig!

He pulls off a worn pair of leather gloves and stuffs them in a back pocket of his jeans. Leaning one arm on top of his shovel handle, he reaches out and enfolds her own hand in a big, rough paw, emphasizing every word in what sounds like open mockery, "Clark. Kent. Daniels."

She pulls her hand away and wrinkles her nose at him. "Clark Kent? Your parents named you after Superman?"

His smile could break any wave. "Why not? Word is, I'm a super guy."

She opens her mouth with a smart retort, but her throat closes swiftly in remembering—a super man!—and she turns away, coughing and sputtering into her hand. Aunt Miriam, that sly, old matchmaker and—she shakes her head, resisting him to the end—Rev. Oglethorpe, the eternal interferer!

"What is it?"

She waves a dismissing hand at the farmer and tries to recover a sense of dignity amidst the piles of manure and buzzing flies.

"My mom tells me it was between Clark Kent or Rhett Butler Daniels, so I'll take what I've got, thank you very much." He keeps confronting her pride with powerful ease. "It was your Aunt Miriam who taught my Grams to read, or so I've been told. Apparently, she used my uncle's comic books to do it, and Superman was the first thing Grams read aloud to my mom. Mom is very sentimental."

"So was Aunt Miriam." And the Rev. Oglethorpe. She wrinkles her nose again, more in defense than from any disappointment. She will choose her own path in life—thank you very much—but she can never quite get around that quirky little cleric and his graveside sermons and epistles.

"You in town for long?"

Her mind catches on the irony of that phrase. Everyone uses it, of course, but the two of them are miles from any town. "For a couple of months, at least. Maybe three."

He crosses him arms and leans them both on the shovel handle, nodding his head toward the old homestead across the pasture. "I suppose, you'll be wanting to stay at the house?"

"What? Oh. No." She shakes her head and hugs her bag close to her ribs, thinking of the undelivered envelope. "I'm already set up at Aunt Miriam's place. My place, I mean. Though, I'll be wanting to go through the stuff in your attic while I'm here. Maybe take it back with me to Aunt Miri—my house—to sort it. If that's convenient?"

"Convenient?" Clark lifts and resettles his hat on his head. "Hell, it's your house. You can do whatever you want, Sally Augusta Werth."

"Grisbone," but she doesn't press the matter. She is beginning to feel the heat and gestures toward the old house. "I came here to talk to your mother about all of this, but she's not home."

"It's Wednesday," he nods. "She attends a blue hair Bible study over at old Trinity in Covenant. That's a couple of townships over, but she won't be long for home. I pulled four flats of tomatoes off the vine for her this morning, and she'll want to start juicing them by midday, or she won't get them canned before dark. Here, walk with me. We'll wait for her on the porch. The sun's high and hot, and you're sweating."

"I'm fine."

But he steps closer and touches her elbow to usher her toward the house.

She grows defensive at his chivalry and barks, "I'll race you."

"You'll what?"

She will be an idiot today, it seems. "I'll race you to the porch."

"You want to race me?" His nostrils flare to match the arch of his eyebrows. "Aren't we a bit past third grade?"

She might die right here in this very pasture, but not without a fight. She squints up into his appraising face. His eyes are dark under the bill of his hat. They are as dark as the drenched bark of the pines clinging to Rockland Harbor. "I'm going to beat you. I'm going to beat Superman."

He returns her stare, her dare. "Loser buys supper tonight."

But she is already running.

+ + +

"Why don't you have a dog?"

"I'm allergic."

How strange. She assumes every farmer has a dog.

He returns with, "What're you doing in Whistle Grove for months at a time, anyway? Don't you work?"

They are sitting on the porch swing sipping iced tea, and she holds the sweating glass against her neck, then her cheek, then her temple. Her pores, incensed by the long sprint through the Midwest sauna, are now openly weeping, and the cold glass countervails the salty tears.

"Yes, I work."

"Doing what?"

"I'm a writer. A journalist, mainly."

"And so, what? You can work remotely?"

"Sometimes." She likes his straightforward manner. It's easy, refreshing, slightly bitter, like the cold tea. "My magazine is commissioning a series of stories from me. Ten stories for ten issues, maybe more if they're well-received." She thrills to say the next part out loud. "They're considering publishing them as a book."

It will be her first, this book, and the idea for it came to her after reading Pastor Oglethorpe's last letter. She proposed the idea to her editor — What about a series of stories on a cemetery? One story per headstone? Historical pieces about the lives and circumstances of real people buried in a little grove of trees in the middle of America? — and surprisingly, he went for it.

"Mom's late." He is eyeing the scant shadow of a nearby maple tree, reading some ancient clock known only to farmers.

She stands then, setting her sweating glass down onto a little iron side table and shouldering her bag. "Thank you for the tea, but I should be going. I've got a list of things to get done in Riverfield this afternoon before tonight."

"What time shall I pick you up?"

She looks down at him. He is still seated in the swing, lazily pushing at the floor with the heel of one boot. She knows he let her win.

"Seven."

"Miriam's place?"

"My place."

He smiles and nods. "That's right. I wasn't thinking."

She reaches into her bag and pulls out the envelope. "I came to give your mother this. Will you do me the honors?"

He stands and sets his empty glass next to hers. Wiping his hands on his jeans, he takes the envelope and folds it longways, stuffing it in his back pocket. He answers her look of horror with, "It's just so I won't forget it. Nothing ever gets lost in my back pocket."

He walks her to her car.

"So, this book you're writing. What's it about?"

"A bunch of dead people."

"That sounds . . . depressing."

"You think so?" She shrugs, trying out his easy confidence on her shoulders like a letterman's jacket. "I think it'll be good."

"People dying is good?"

She wrinkles her Werth nose at him. "You haven't heard, then."

"Heard what?"

She gets in the car, and just before shutting the door, "The dead. I've heard they're going to rise in the end."

+ + +

Lila is bringing a pot of tomato juice to a boil on the stove when she remembers the envelope from Sally. She wipes her hands on a dishtowel, and leaning against the counter, uses a paring knife to break the seal. She pulls out a rather official looking document that is unnecessarily crumpled—Oh, Clark.—with a handwritten note paper-clipped to the top. She reaches out a hand to stir the pot, simultaneously reading the note, but she drops the spoon back into the pot with a clang.

"Clark?"

"What?"

"Come in here!"

"What?" He is on the back stoop shucking corn, and the alarm in his voice rises to match her own pitch for pitch. She hears all four legs of a metal chair being returned to the stoop, a bucket being kicked aside, and corn spilling—followed by a hissed word she chooses not to repeat—and then her son comes banging through the back screen door of the kitchen. "What is it? What's wrong?"

She hands him the handwritten note. "Read it. Aloud."

He complies, but only because she has him scared.

"'Aunt Miriam left it to me because Mother insisted, but I know that she always wanted you to have it. I signed the paperwork this morning. It's yours. Sally A. Grisbone.'" He looks up. "What's yours?"

Lila holds up the deed to the old house.

+ + +

Sally wishes she could be present when Lila Daniels opens the envelope, but it is better this way. Some matters are private, and she is a Werth, not a Daniels. Let the Daniels family have their moment. Though, now that she has met Clark, she would like having a memory of his reaction. Already, she wishes the man joy, and she usually does not bother with wishing.

"Did you see that one coming, Reverend?"

She is driving, but a sudden, familiar sting burns her eyes, and she passes the back of a hand across her wet lashes.

That peculiar, *dear* old man.

Most likely, he did see it coming, and she finds that notion terribly comforting.

Family Trees

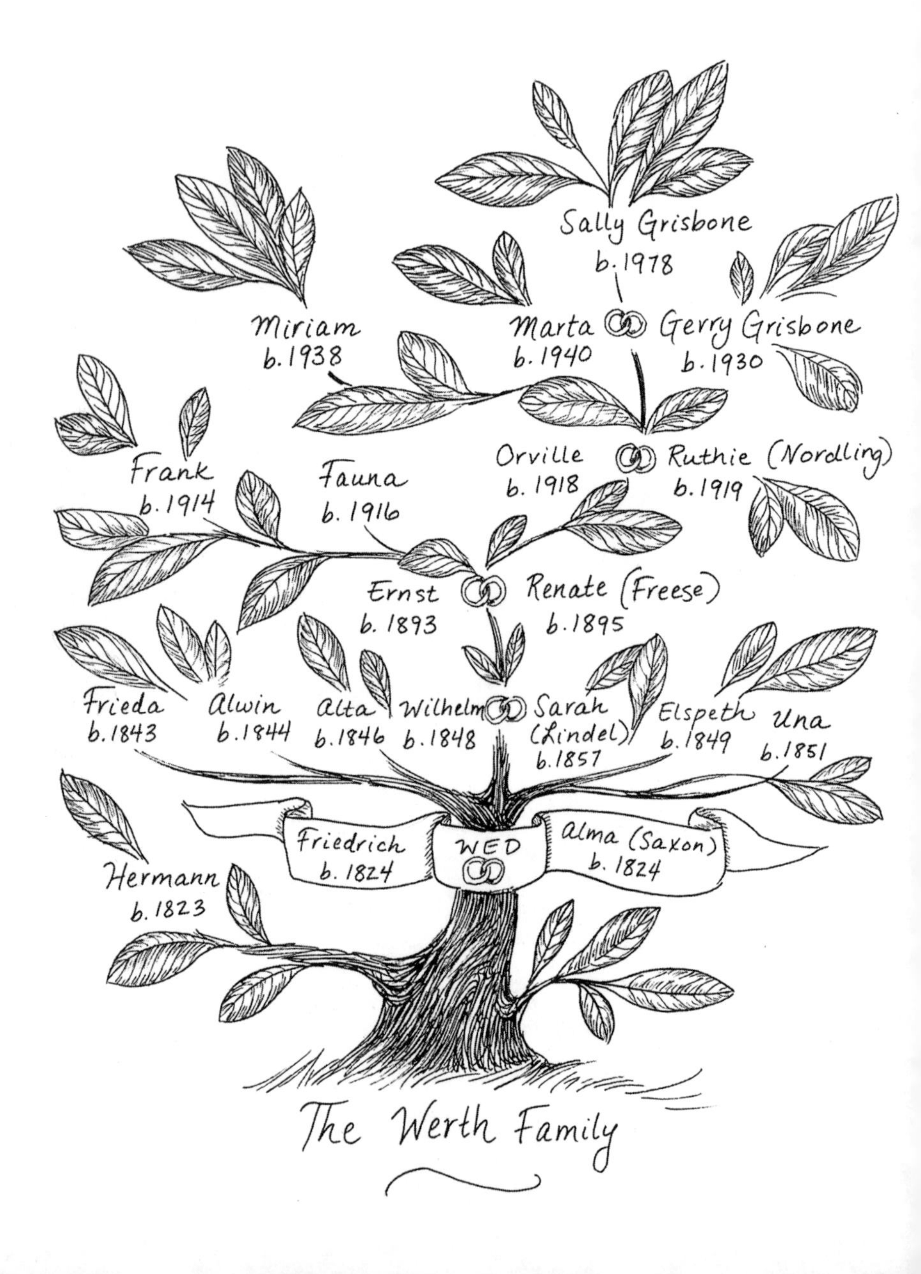

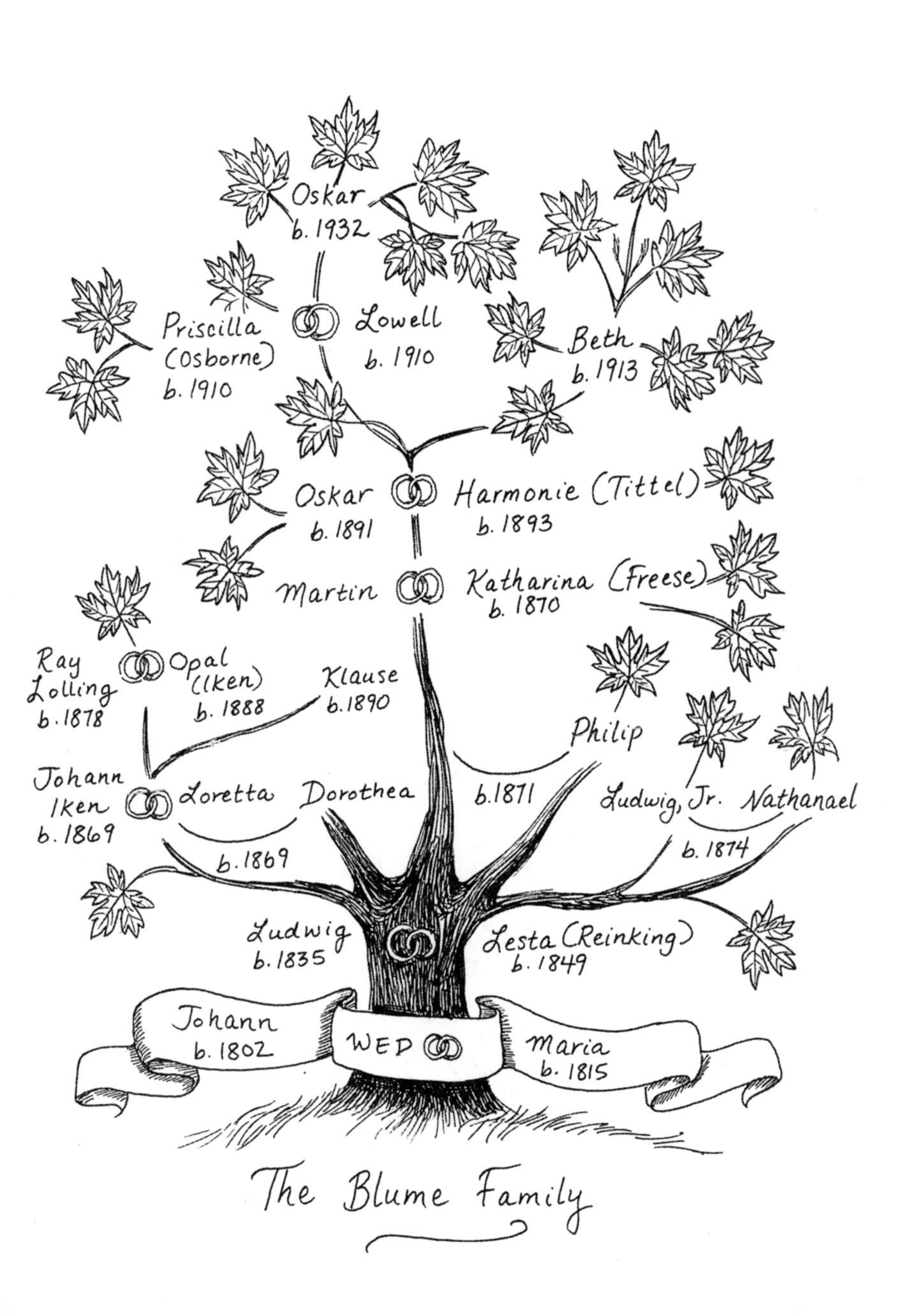
Oskar
b. 1932
Priscilla
(Osborne)
b. 1910
Lowell
b. 1910
Beth
b. 1913
Oskar
b. 1891
Harmonie (Tittel)
b. 1893
Martin
Katharina (Freese)
b. 1870
Ray
Lolling
b. 1878
Opal
(Iken)
b. 1888
Klause
b. 1890
Philip
b. 1871
Johann
Iken
b. 1869
Loretta
b. 1869
Dorothea
Ludwig, Jr.
Nathanael
b. 1874
Ludwig
b. 1835
Lesta (Reinking)
b. 1849
Johann
b. 1802
WED
Maria
b. 1815
The Blume Family

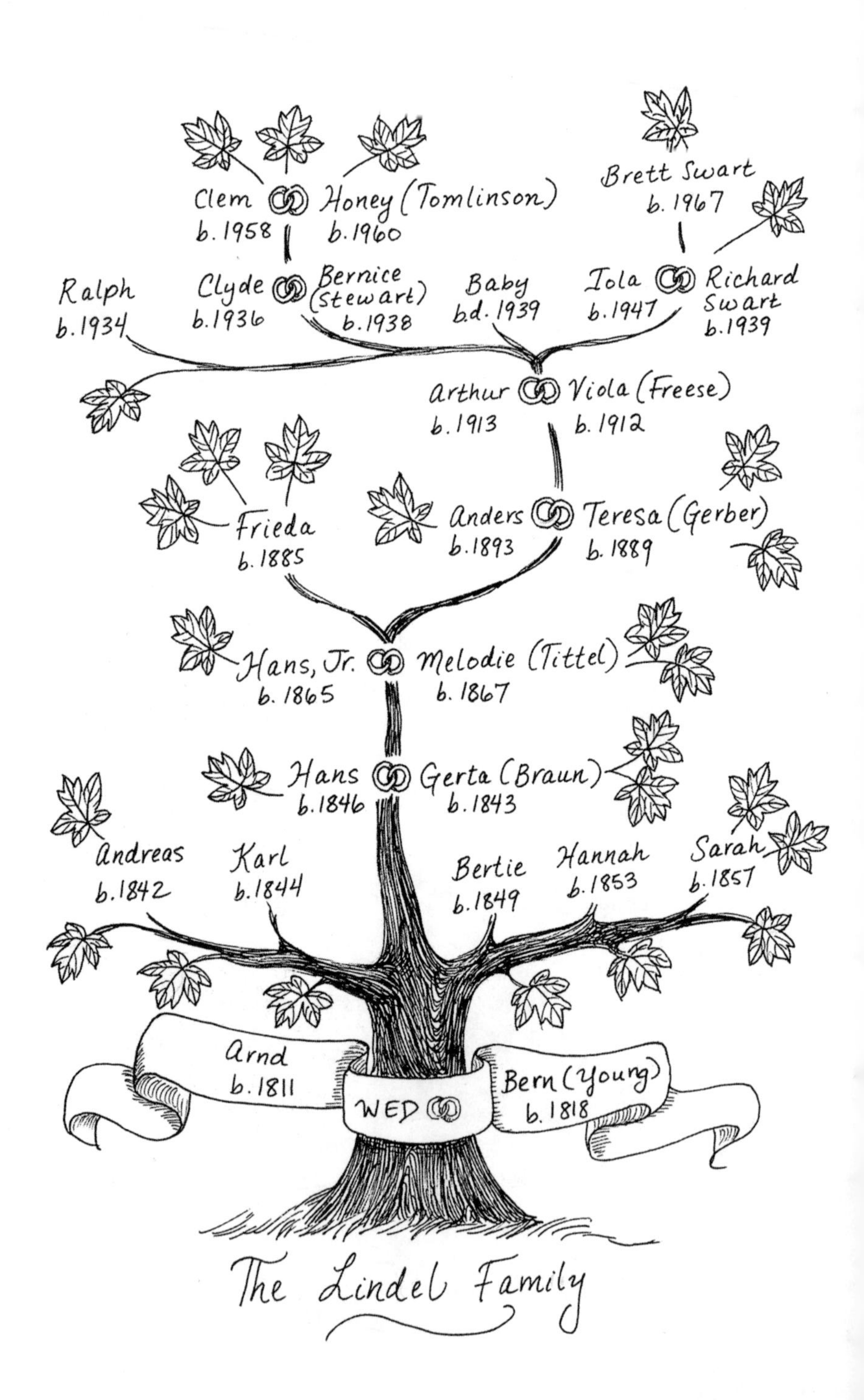
Clem b. 1958
Honey (Tomlinson) b. 1960
Brett Swart b. 1967
Ralph b. 1934
Clyde b. 1936
Bernice (Stewart) b. 1938
Baby b.d. 1939
Iola b. 1947
Richard Swart b. 1939
Arthur b. 1913
Viola (Freese) b. 1912
Frieda b. 1885
Anders b. 1893
Teresa (Gerber) b. 1889
Hans, Jr. b. 1865
Melodie (Tittel) b. 1867
Hans b. 1846
Gerta (Braun) b. 1843
Andreas b. 1842
Karl b. 1844
Bertie b. 1849
Hannah b. 1853
Sarah b. 1857
Arnd b. 1811
WED
Bern (Young) b. 1818
The Lindel Family

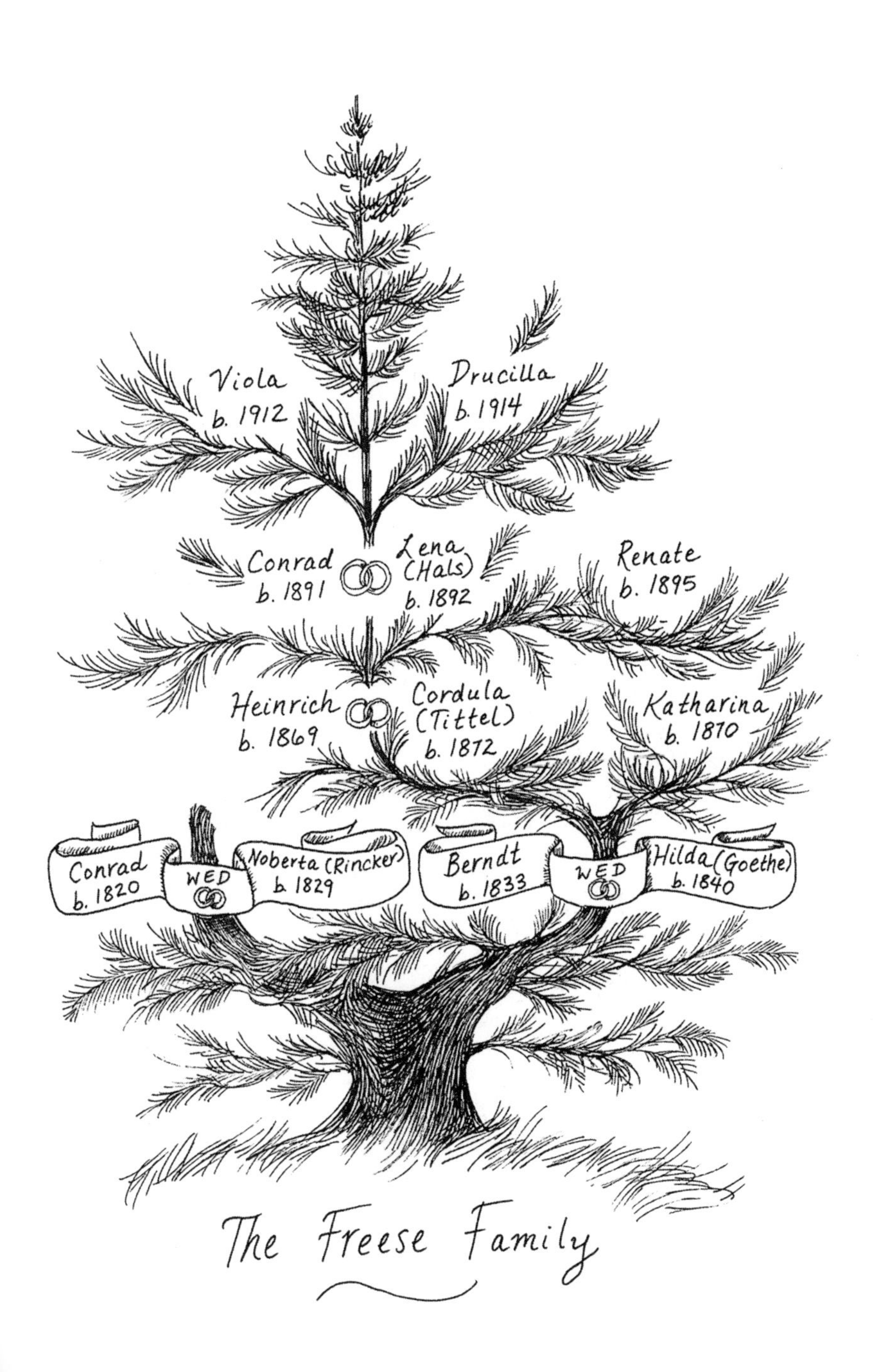
Viola
b. 1912
Drucilla
b. 1914
Conrad
b. 1891
Lena
(Hals)
b. 1892
Renate
b. 1895
Heinrich
b. 1869
Cordula
(Tittel)
b. 1872
Katharina
b. 1870
Conrad
b. 1820
WED
Noberta (Rincker)
b. 1829
Berndt
b. 1833
WED
Hilda (Goethe)
b. 1840
The Freese Family

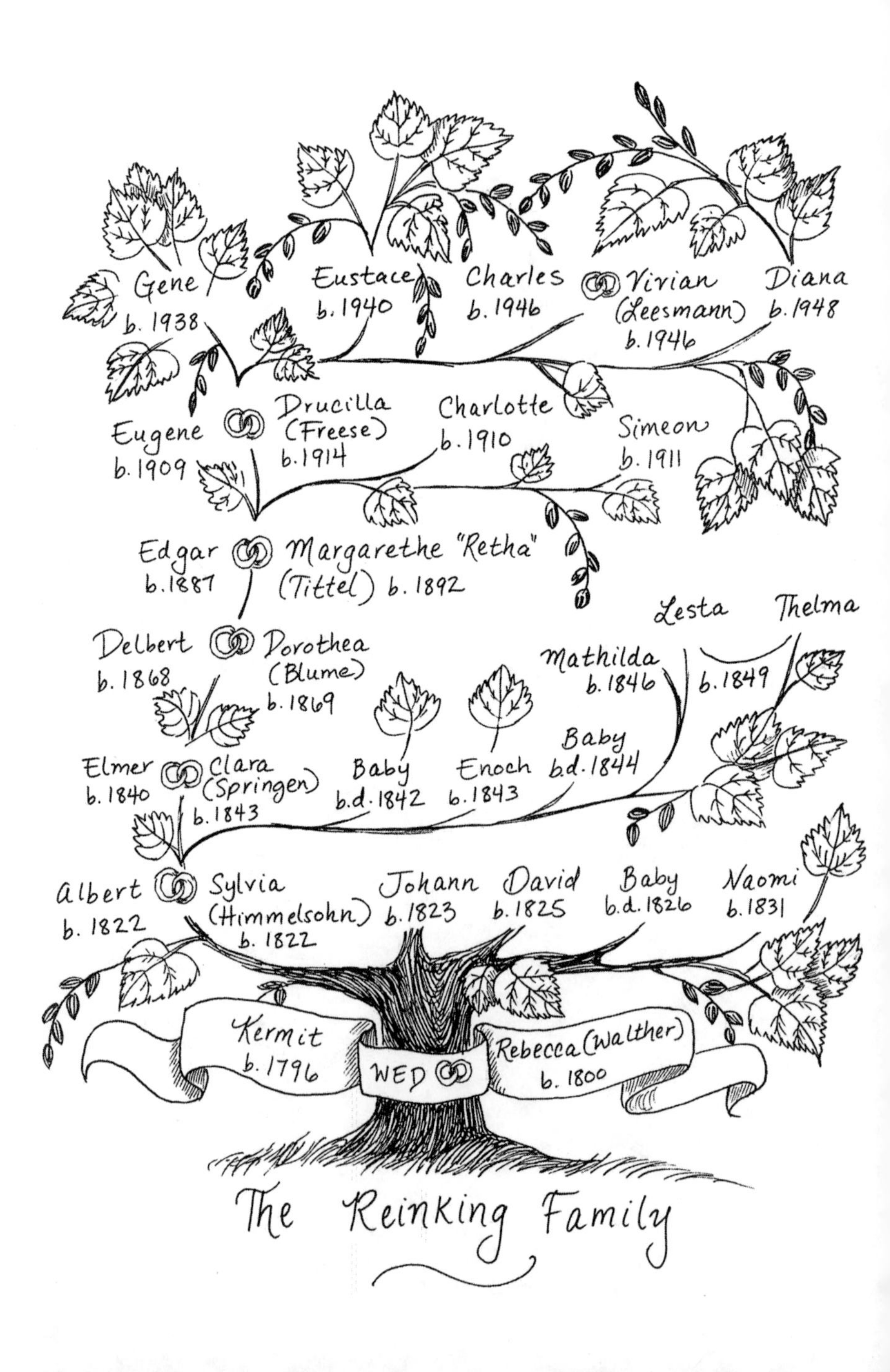
Gene
b. 1938
Eustace
b. 1940
Charles
b. 1946
Vivian
(Leesmann)
b. 1946
Diana
b. 1948
Eugene
b. 1909
Drucilla
(Freese)
b. 1914
Charlotte
b. 1910
Simeon
b. 1911
Edgar
b. 1887
Margarethe "Retha"
(Tittel) b. 1892
Lesta
Thelma
b. 1849
Delbert
b. 1868
Dorothea
(Blume)
b. 1869
Mathilda
b. 1846
Baby
b.d. 1844
Elmer
b. 1840
Clara
(Springen)
b. 1843
Baby
b.d. 1842
Enoch
b. 1843
Albert
b. 1822
Sylvia
(Himmelsohn)
b. 1822
Johann
b. 1823
David
b. 1825
Baby
b.d. 1826
Naomi
b. 1831
Kermit
b. 1796
WED
Rebecca (Walther)
b. 1800
The Reinking Family

German Lexicon

auf Englisch
: in English

Butterkuchen
: a yeasted butter cake sprinkled with sugar

Christenlehre
: post-confirmation instruction of the youth specifically given by the pastor; functioning as a type of Sunday school, it was often performed in drill fashion after the Sunday sermon with the adults listening in

die Heilige Schrift
: The Holy Bible

Doktor
: doctor

Frau
: missus, addressing a married woman

Fräulein
: miss, addressing an unmarried woman

Germania
: Latin for Germany, also the name of a statue personifying Germany usually depicted as a woman wearing armor and wielding the *Reichsschwert* (imperial sword) and wearing or holding the imperial crown of the German Empire

Grossonkel
: great uncle

Grosstante

great aunt

Gulden

German currency

Herr, erbarme dich!

Lord, have mercy!

Heil

salvation

Herr

mister, addressing a grown man

Hochzeitsbitter

usually a male relative of a bridegroom who wears a hat and rides on horseback door to door in a community inviting families to an upcoming wedding; each invitee pins a ribbon to his hat, and on the day of the wedding, he wears the ribboned hat and rides ahead of the wedding procession, whooping and hollering

Kirche

church; church service

Kirche auf Deutsch

have church in German

Meine Brüder

my brothers

Meine Frau

my wife

meine Lieben

my dear ones

Mein Gott

my God

mein Kind

my child

mein Liebchen
    my darling
mein Sohn
    my son
Mutter / Mutti
    mother / mommy
Nehmen sie den Leib,
Gut, Ehr, Kind und Weib:
lass fahren dahin,
sie haben's kein' Gewinn
das Reich muss uns doch bleiben.
    And take they our life,
    Goods, fame, child, and wife,
    Let these all be gone,
    They yet have nothing won;
    The Kingdom ours remaineth.
Oma
    grandma
Opa
    grandpa
O Welt, ich muss dich lassen
    O world, I must leave thee
O wie selig seid ihr doch, ihr Frommen
    O how blessed are ye, ye pious
Pfarrer
    pastor
Pickert
    potato pancake
Rauschenhain
    Whistle Grove

reine Lehre
pure doctrine

Rosenstrasse
Rose Street

Sauerkraut
fermented cabbage

Schottische
literally Scottish, but also a partnered country dance originating in Bohemia

Schulhaus
schoolhouse

Seelsorger
pastor

Stille Nacht
silent night

Strudel
layered pastry with a filling, usually fruit or cheese

Tante
aunt

Vater / Vati
father / daddy

verboten
forbidden

Discussion Questions

1. People die, but do churches ever die?

2. Pastor Oglethorpe chooses to stay in Whistle Grove past Bethlehem's closing. Why?

3. This story explores various ways people deal with loss in life, both individually and corporately. Which characters in this book bring you comfort amidst scenes of loss, and why? Which characters bring you discomfort, and why?

4. Are cemeteries beneficial or harmful to life on this earth?

5. Whose fault is it when a church closes?

6. What makes for a faithful, pious man in the church? for a faithful, pious woman?

7. Compare the strengths and weaknesses of Pastor Seefeldt and Pastor Sterling.

8. How are Frieda Lindel and Georgia Sterling similar? How are they different?

9. Why do Miriam and Marta struggle to agree on most things?

10. Does Sally believe in the resurrection of the dead?

11. What good may come from Sally's researching and writing about the lives and deaths of her people?

12. What sets Christian burial practices apart from those of other major world religions?

13. What hope is there for the individual who outlives a congregation?

14. Who are your people, and where are they laid to rest to await the Last Day?

Acknowledgments

THANK YOU TO MY BELOVED HEAD, Michael, for tirelessly reading my chapters aloud to me at the end of a long day, for never giving an affirmative to my regular questioning of him over the past five years—"Do you think I should stop writing this book?"—but patiently and persistently affirming, "Keep writing," and for joyfully being my husband and pastor; Kirk and Lawanda Meyer, whose friendship and collaboration over the past ten years have borne fruit even greater than books—Thank you for partnering with me to turn beneficial stories into beautiful books and all for the good of our beautiful people; the Rev. Tony Oliphant for noticing, celebrating, preserving, and fortifying every bit of layering and echoing written into Whistle Grove, for helping me lay Mary to rest at exactly the right time, and for editing my book in the most excellent fashion—You are a fiction writer's dream editor; Dr. Cameron MacKenzie, godfather of the grove, for so kindly and graciously and repeatedly corresponding with me about people and places that are not real, all the while helping me achieve greater verisimilitude in our shared little "frayed back-pocket of the earth"—Thank you for understanding the what and why of this book and for so beautifully explaining both in your foreword; Mrs. Kelly Schumacher Uffenbeck for taking my pitiful sketches, maps, family trees, and authorial imaginations and turning them into stunning, vibrant works of art that invite us into a deeper understanding of the written work; the Rev. Dr. Jon Vieker for encouraging me in all creative undertakings, for tying my historical loose threads into artful, believable bows, and for facilitating the Church's song in Whistle Grove, especially *O wie selig*; Dr. Roland Ziegler for shepherding my German into the correct century; Herr Daniel Flora for advising me in historical accuracy, for researching my own people for my own edification, and for giving me permission to quote his grandfather's own *Pfarrer*; Herr Jan Nottmeier for helping me choose which *lecker Kuchen* should be pocketed and consumed in the grove; Dr. Joseph Herl for applying his keen eye to my every sentence and for seeing what even authors and editors fail to see; Dr. Mackenzie Wells for advising me on the greatness of dogs as well as for tending to the details of Fritz's internal injuries with the utmost professional respect; Mariya Vandivort, my realtor and friend, for teaching Sally how to record a deed; Gloria Wells for always taking the time to advise me on best copyright practices; Beth Resner, Mel Bower, and Shriners Children's St. Louis for fielding and granting my request to use historical documents published in the 1930s to create fictional correspondence between hospital staff and the Blume family; Sally Krueger for residing in my head and in my heart in the most influential, motherly of ways; Matthew Braun, Julia Habrecht, Cheryl Swope, Rebekah Curtis, Rebecca Mayes, Jeff Schwartz, Mollie Hemingway, and Drew Witte for kindly, wisely, cheerfully advising me in all matters personal and professional; my generous and supportive parents for moving my sisters and me back to the country where we could be raised amidst our extended families, those related by birth, by adoption, and by baptism; my father for all horticultural and burial advisements; my mother and sainted grandmother for their insight into polio as well as for sharing with me the letters and pictures of my grandfather's stay with the Shriners; Mrs. Lucy Brown, godmother of the grove, for her steadfast support of my family of two, for birthing more than just her own children, and for bearing my burdens, fictional and non-; Deaconess Frances Szeto for beautifying Whistle Grove as well as my life with her soulful wit, astute observations, compassionate understanding, and bosom friendship; Dr. Lindsay Kelpinski for being my writing companion and assuring me that Oskar is best spelled with a "k"; Eve and also a generous gentleman in Iowa for introducing me to the beauty of jewelry boxes; Michael, Becky, Lucy, Frances, Jon, Tony, Drew, Becca, Lindsay, Janet, Julia, Heidi, Kirk, Lawanda, Aly, Stephanie, Mollie, and Joe for reading my chapters before anyone else; the sainted Rev. Bo Giertz, Lutheranism's greatest storyteller, and his teachings on creation, the resurrection, and eternity; the sainted Rev. Alvin Schmidt for his writings and lectures on Christian burial; the saints at Good Shepherd Lutheran Church in Sherman, Illinois and University Lutheran Church in Champaign, Illinois for singing God's promises into my ears Sunday upon Sunday during the writing of this book; all the saints who have come before, whose days walking this earth have shaped my life and this story, especially: Robert and Cynthia Roley, Bobby and Loraine Bridges, Roy and Josie Bridges, Orville and Flora Engel, Dean and June Roley, Leverett Compton, Philipp Heinrich Rincker, Heinrich Rincker, and Friedrich and Wilhelmina Stremming; and finally, our Lord Jesus Christ, the Giver of all good gifts, on Whose promise to raise the dead to life eternal my own pitiful life completely depends. Come quickly, Lord Jesus.

+ SDG +

About the Artist

KELLY SCHUMACHER UFFENBECK dreamed of being a book illustrator since she was a child. Kelly collected Caldecott illustrated books and would pore over the beautiful pictures for hours on end. Many of the books Kelly loved were inspired by medieval religious artwork.

Upon graduation from the Pennsylvania Academy of the Fine Arts with her MFA degree, Kelly created Agnus Dei Liturgical Arts. Through Agnus Dei, Kelly uses painting to make churches beautiful and to aid in catechesis for families. She paints and draws religious artwork illustrating biblical narratives and has illustrated several children's picture books. Additionally, Kelly paints religious artwork and realistic portraits for private commissions.

Kelly is married to David Uffenbeck, and they reside in St. Louis, Missouri. To view more of Kelly's artwork, visit agnusdeiarts.com.

About the Author

Katie Schuermann grew up in rural Illinois within one mile of a grove such as the one featured in this book. She saw it every day in passing through the dusty window of her school bus, but she never set foot in the grove as a child. It was not until she was an adult, when she and her husband were home visiting her parents, that the two of them drove the family mule (motored, not mammal) to the grove and poked around the abandoned church and cemetery tucked behind the trees, only to discover that some of her own people are buried there. It was then, while gazing upon forgotten tombstones and the vandalized shell of a church that once housed the prayers of an entire community, that her sympathies were stirred and a story was born.

It would be many years before the words "Whistle Grove" ever found their way onto any page, but Schuermann spent those years steeping in the stories of her family and the history of her beloved Lutheran Church–Missouri Synod, imagining what it would be like to witness the birth and death of such a country church.

While the people of Whistle Grove do not exist, they are alive in the author's heart and mind and, hopefully now, in yours. Nothing would make her happier than if, in getting to know the people of Whistle Grove, you are inspired to get to know your own people and visit the cemeteries that cradle and protect their remains until the blessed Last Day.

To learn more about Katie Schuermann and her books, visit katieschuermann.com.

+ *Soli Deo Gloria* +